FATAL MOON

By L. E. Perry

Fatal Moon

The characters in this book are entirely fictional. Any resemblance to actual persons living or dead is entirely coincidental.

ISBN 978-1980800750
Second Edition
Edited by Tiffany Galleski
Published electronically and in print in the United States of America

uberlark@google.com
https://www.facebook.com/ LEPerryAuthor/
Visit www.moonphasebooks.com for further information on the Moonphase world and upcoming books by this author.

ACKNOWLEDGE-MENTS

I am ever so grateful to Carl Flamm, Chad at the Daytona Beach Dunkin' Donuts, my mom Carol Summers, my writer's groups in Daytona Beach and at Portland CSL, the librarians at Brighton's Anythink Library, Robert W. Walker, NaNoWriMo.org, BeTheMatch.org, and the Oxford comma.

Other works by L. E. Perry
Moonphase series:
Fatal Moon
Kindred Moon
Foul Moon
Letters Across Time:
Nikola Tesla: Coming to America

CHAPTER 1 –
THE OFFER

"Is that a real fire?" a fleshy lady in hot pink shorts asked the man next to her.

"Of course it's real. All that metal's hiding the gas pipes that feed it," he huffed, sweating in the heat.

Jordan tightened his lips, resisting the urge to correct the tourists with a few choice words as he hammered the glowing red steel of the sword blade. A dark-skinned, remarkably muscular young man who, at twenty-four, appeared to be in his thirties, he bore little evidence of his red-headed Scottish mother's influence. He wore a sleeveless, homespun cotton shirt to cover his back and chest, over which he had a leather apron to protect his body from the scorching hot metal he maneuvered as he shaped the claymore he was tasked with constructing. Acting as a living museum piece for the tourists who paid for the privilege to see what life was like in medieval times wasn't the ideal position for Jordan. As a "master," he was given the contracts from the weapons guild which sold authentically crafted blades to medieval enthusiasts, which he enjoyed, but it came with the meaningless tedium of answering questions about the blacksmithing process from the daily crowds.

Jordan swung the sword around to thrust it back onto the anvil. The blade flew a little too close to the polycarbonate shield and the crowd gasped as they moved back. He wasn't allowed to voice his displeasure with the crowd's inane chatter, which came to him through a speaker system so he could respond to their ridiculous inquiries. *At least this crowd isn't accusing me of being an audio-animatronic figure*, he thought. There were those who couldn't believe anyone as big and as steady as Jordan could be real. Why they believed a European medieval theme village in Los Angeles would order a blacksmith robot with Mediterranean features was beyond him. He resumed striking the blade with the hammer, then turned it over with the tongs and inspected the length, width, thickness, and alignment. He loved claymores. They were big, solid blades, for fighting men.

The metal was still hot enough that it didn't need more forge time yet. He swung the hammer to shape it, the rhythm mesmerizing... short swings followed by sharp clangs. The bright red color faded gradually as he shaped it. The adult portion of the crowd, having seen enough, moved on to the next exhibit. To his chagrin, several giggling teenage girls remained. They collected around his display like flies. It wasn't so much his looks as the way his muscles on his five-foot-ten-inch frame rolled under his shirt, especially in the firelight.

He'd begun weightlifting seriously when he was twelve in the hopes of being able to defend himself from his father, and athletic authorities had accused him of being on steroids since he was fifteen. He'd been forced to take drug tests on a frequent basis for the wrestling he'd competed in all through high school, hoping to earn a college scholarship. Jordan was a fortress of a man, physically and mentally. Few people understood him when it came down to it, and he saw no reason to change that since he would have to reveal things about his youth that he felt were better left untold.

Jordan continued muscling the sword into its proper shape as the teens giggled. "Jordan," murmured a deep voice that came through the speaker and jarred his rhythm. He lost his grip on the tongs and the steel dropped to the floor. Small flames shot up from the ground where it fell, igniting lint and other flammable detritus, and the girls squealed in alarm. It surprised him the first time he learned that steel hot enough to shape was also hot enough to ignite what looked like mere dirt on concrete, and apparently it surprised them as well. He focused on the task at hand, grasping the almost-formed blade with the tongs, but fumbled. It slipped from the pin-cer grip, but his next grab whisked and thunked the sword on the anvil. The voice that caused the combustion was one he hadn't expected to hear again. The face attached to that voice was pale gold and a touch red from the Southern Califor-nia sun, burnt with the slightest exposure, un-like Jordan who was a natural copper color over every inch of his body. The visitor's curly, dark-blond hair supported a pair of Tom Ford sun-glasses and his pale blue eyes regarded Jordan in-tently. It was Carl Sanders. Jordan didn't answer.

Jordan had been bodyguard and, as a cover, personal trainer to Carl for a much needed twenty dollars an hour back when they both went to the same magnet high school. Carl was a privileged, British-born addition to Jor-dan's class, and seemed out of place in a public school. The school was in Jordan's rough area of town and Carl's family had enough money to make him a target for kidnapping; a private school would have been safer. But his Labour party father earned his money fighting for-profit healthcare in the U.S., and his parents had a de-sire to keep the boy humble and to teach him about the pitfalls of classism, even if it made the daily experience a bit risky for their son. So they'd discreetly hired Jordan to watch over him during the day, while the young heir travelled to and from school by chauffeur and professional bodyguard, who always nodded at Jordan as he made sure Carl didn't miss his ride.

But that was six years ago. The question was, what was Carl doing here now?

Jordan opened the tongs and grabbed the blade more securely this time, putting it back in the forge, when the door behind him leading into the exhibit opened. His coworker, who was also his apprentice and lunchtime replacement, had arrived. Jordan pulled the blade out of the forge and set it aside instead. He thought briefly about the competing theme park farther north where the blacksmith position was almost entirely blade work. There he could just focus on the craft, which left him alone with his thoughts. The blacksmith demo area at this other place had no polycarbonate shields, but also no speakers, and the distance between blacksmith and crowd made questions difficult to hear. It seemed blissful compared to this human interaction crap.

Jordan stood up and stretched his tired shoulders to the sound of coos from the gallery. Disdaining to glance their direction, or toward Carl, he left through the same back door his replacement had come in. Stopping at the message board down the hall, Jordan tore off the note asking him to meet Carl at the pub across the street. Still no clue as to why he was here. From what Jordan could see, Carl looked quite a bit slimmer than he had been in high school, but some of the weight loss could be attributed to the fact that Carl was a medical student now. He and Carl had discussed their college options back when Jordan had them, but his mother's injury by his father when he was seventeen precluded Jordan from accepting offers, despite all the hours he'd spent studying calculus, chemistry and college-level English. He'd reluctantly turned down athletic scholarships to work full-time instead, to support his mother and younger sister after his mother was injured.

Jordan showered briefly and changed to loose-cut jeans and a huge short-sleeved shirt, oversized so that it hung loosely over his forty-eight-inch chest. He preferred even looser cut jeans, but few men had his measurements. It was hard enough to find jeans that fit him at all at a price he could afford, especially ones that could be belted in without having to fold the waistband over several times; big men were usually unfit men. He left the building and walked toward the pub wishing he could avoid the inevitable, but Carl could be a persistent fool. Jordan needed to find out what Carl wanted then nip it in the bud. Carl was part of his past, and Jordan wasn't interested in changing that.

Carl's car, a yellow Jaguar, was parked outside. After six years Jordan was surprised that Carl had held onto the long-nosed coupe. Entering the pub, Jordan took a swift look around the dimly lit room to find Carl sitting at a small table in the corner, laughing with the waitress. Still a charismatic son-of-a-bitch.

Carl smiled, rose to his feet and offered his hand when he saw Jordan, who strode over, pulled out a chair and sat down abruptly.

"How did you find me?" Jordan asked before Carl could say anything. Taken aback, Carl paused for a moment, his hand still in the air. The waitress left swiftly.

"I... need to talk with you," he responded with less of a British accent than Jordan recalled. Carl slowly dropped his hand and sank into his chair.

"That's not an answer, Sanders. I can't even get my magazines delivered when I move. I haven't been in touch with anyone from high school since we graduated. If you can find me I want to know how," Jordan growled.

Carl paused, almost frowned, but grinned instead. "I had to try pretty hard, actually. I hired a man to find you. He followed your work files. He started with the most recent W-2 we had for you. Fortunately, your last name is Fontana rather than Smith."

There was silence. "So, I suppose you know my whole friggin' work history, then?"

Carl pursed his lips. "I didn't want to inquire about your work history. . . though I must admit that your income was of interest. You're worth a lot more than you bring in, Jordan."

More silence.

"I can make you a rather lucrative offer," Carl ventured. "I'd appreciate it if you'd listen. You know, of course, that you're under no obligation to accept."

Jordan sat back warily. He wasn't listed in the phone book and lived in a secure apartment building, having rented the space under the stairs cheap from a young woman who liked having him around as visual security, though she hoped for more. Not even all of his "friends" had his number, and he had left strict orders with the people at work not to release any of his contact information to anyone at all. It was no surprise that Carl had been unable to locate him except through his record of employment, but Jordan disapproved of personal business of any sort crossing over with his job, even remotely. The thought that Carl had discovered things Jordan considered private, like his income, was infuriating. On the other hand, he was in a position of damage control now.

"I'm listening," Jordan said finally.

Carl relaxed slightly. "I . . . would like to take you on again as a . . . trainer."

Jordan watched Carl's eyes as he spoke. He saw the slightest trace of something: guilt? Fear? "As a personal trainer?" he said slowly, gauging Carl's response carefully.

"At a minimum, actually. I'm ill– not contagious," Carl added quickly as Jordan immediately leaned away from him. "I'm indisposed several times a month. I'm also losing weight. I don't want it publicized. You know how the gossip rags like to follow our family. I just want to retire to the mountains, to the old cabin, and I need some-one to assist me until I've recovered fully."

Jordan shook his head and moved to stand up. "Wasting your time –" he stopped abruptly as Carl put out a hand to grip his wrist. He looked down at Carl's hand balefully: Carl didn't let go and Jordan finally met his eyes.

"Jordan, I need your help. I've known many people throughout my life, but not many that are absolutely trustworthy. Not many who are as intelligent, as widely skilled, and as health-con-scious . . ." he paused in consideration. "I admit, I'm aware of your work history–"

Jordan stood, flexed his muscles and threw off Carl's hand explosively, his lips thinning even past their normal grimness and his eyes narrow-ing to black slits in his dark face.

Carl stood up and faced him directly. "Just lis-ten for once, damn it," he whispered fiercely. "I came 1500 miles to talk to you. Look, you owe me nothing, but I'd appreciate it if you'd hear me out."

He was serious, then. Jordan realized people were staring at them and slid back into the chair just to avoid being a spectacle.

Carl sat down slowly as the waitress quickly came over to take their order, as if she had been at fault for the tension between the men. Carl kept his eyes on Jordan as he dropped a silver credit card on the table to signal that lunch was on him, to which Jordan nodded briefly. Jordan suggested the pub's specialty, a thick roast beef sandwich with house fries and a soft drink in a pewter mug. For Jordan they made it cider. He took water on the side as well and drained it immediately for the waitress to come back and refill at once. Since he started blacksmithing he was going through more than two hundred ounces a day.

"So this is about that training I did for you in high school," Jordan said finally.

"You did well. I gained twenty-five pounds of pure muscle in a single year," Carl reminded him.

"And fell twenty percent short of your potential," Jordan replied, refusing to be flattered.

Carl rolled his eyes expressively. "It's just a game, Jordan. One I never intended to play past high school. I had to concern myself with chemistry and biology."

Jordan took another swallow of water before asking, "So why did you play at all?" His eyes were narrow as always, and calculating.

Carl gave Jordan a self-deprecating smile. "You know my father. He always wanted a strapping boy to play American football, and all he got was me, a tall and relatively slim one. But as long as I was on the team he had something to boast about to the relatives."

"You were pretty damned good for a long-legged blond."

Carl pressed the palms of his hands together and put them against his chin. "I need you to do it again. I've been losing a great deal of weight and I can't seem to get my diet and workout routine quite right. At best I can maintain, but overall it's still a gradual loss."

Jordan frowned. "Eat more."

Carl shook his head. "It's not that simple. I don't need more fat, I need muscle. I can explain more –" Carl looked around the restaurant, "somewhere else."

Jordan paused, then nodded. Carl's face looked too thin. Jordan had learned that face quite well in the three years he'd spent as Carl's trainer and bodyguard. What Carl didn't know was that Jordan did feel indebted to Carl for hiring Jordan in high school. Jordan had been strong even before he started weightlifting when he was a kid, but he had unintentionally run his father out of the house three years later. It had been hard to hide his bulk in huge sweatshirts when his father was still throwing him around periodically, and Jordan's added mass finally became too obvious when his father ripped Jordan's shirt off his back to whip him one evening. Jordan simply grabbed the man and threw him into a wall, reversing their roles for once. After that, his father left abruptly, but not before he beat Jordan's mother so badly she would never walk again. Out of guilt and need, Jordan started taking heavy labor jobs to help support his mother and sister while his mother endured years of surgery and physical rehabilitation. If it weren't for Carl he would have been working ships in Alaska every summer just to survive, leaving his mom and his sister alone and vulnerable.

Carl and Jordan studied each other intently for a while before Carl began to speak again. "I'm willing to work with you on this. I know you have a life here, a steady job and all. I know you aren't the kind of man to throw that away. I'm willing to make it worth your while."

Jordan's ears perked up. "How worth it?"

"Eighty thousand a year."

After a shocked moment, Jordan snorted.

"Plus room and board," Carl added with a hint of desperation.

"Mmm?"

"At the summer house in The Cascades where I'll be living."

Jordan tilted his head at that. He'd never been to the "cabin" Carl's parents had built up on Stevens Pass, but he remembered a few times when he'd gone hiking up in the clean air of The Cascades, following steep forest trails until they broke through the treelines and exposed sapphire blue mountain lakes. It was country a person could lose themselves in, could forget the grit of the city, become one with the scent of pine, the trail of bird tracks across snowfields. "And when you're feeling better, I'm jobless, with no unemployment benefits," Jordan answered with contempt.

"I can guarantee you a year of pay."

"A year!" Jordan responded incredulously, then leaned away. "What've you got, anyway?"

A line of tension formed on the bridge of Carl's nose. "Nothing you're going to catch just by being near me. I can guarantee you a year because whatever I have hasn't been documented. I need to research it, and I need you to help me. Even if we get my weight leveled out, I want to have you there for a while, just in case, while I continue my research."

Jordan saw the intensity in Carl's eyes and paused. He needed to know more. "Okay, then; put it all in a PDF. Email it to me by five tonight, I'll write my new email down for you. I'll look at it and we can talk this weekend. Where are you staying?"

"I'll be at the Beverly Hilton."

Jordan nodded, chewing slowly. He rolled his fries in a napkin to degrease them and looked out the window as he spoke. "Write it all down. Everything you want me to do, and the most you're willing to pay me for it. I'll reply with my counter-offer tomorrow, and we can talk Saturday morning. I won't turn you down outright, but I'll tell you what it would take to hire me." He looked back at Carl. "Accept it or reject it, that'll be your choice. But I warn you, if I agree and later on you want me to do anything that you don't write down, you might regret it when I refuse to do it. Get it in now or don't plan on me doing it." Jordan hadn't heard anything about being a bodyguard yet; if he had, he'd have left already. He'd looked out for Carl during school hours, then come home to watch over his own mom and sister, and it had made him exhaustingly paranoid, looking over his shoulder and fearing an attack every moment of the day. He never wanted to spend another hour of his life protecting anyone but himself. Never again.

During the rest of the hour, they discussed what they'd done since high school, sticking to safe topics such as exercise and weather. Aside from Jordan's email address no personal information was exchanged, particularly on Jordan's part. Jordan had no intention of making his terms acceptable to Carl. Every time he looked at the guy he remembered his life when he was younger, and with it everything he'd lost in one afternoon. He compared his current meager existence working in an outdated theme park and living in a closet to the college degree and professional career he could have had. Should have had. It wasn't Carl's fault; still, he didn't want to be reminded of that.

*   *   *

Jordan finished his morning workout and was just stepping out of the shower Saturday morning when his cell phone rang. The email from Carl had been simple enough: Carl had raised his offer to $100,000 a year plus benefits, as well as room and board, which was quite substantial. In return, Jordan would be round-the-clock squire and maid and cook and personal trainer, with a few other titles to boot, but mostly physical trainer and assistant dietician. To all appearances Carl wanted a single servant to cater to all his needs, on-call twenty-four hours a day. Jordan was sure there was more to it, but the letter hadn't said anything about bodyguard duties. What was Jordan missing?

He briskly toweled himself dry and threw on a short, thick robe his mother had made for him, then redialed the last number that had called him while he was showering.

"I thought you'd run out on me!" Carl's voice sounded panicky.

"If I hadn't planned to talk to you I wouldn't have given you the number," Jordan replied, logically. "Did you get my email?"

"Yes, I'm looking at it now," Carl replied.

Jordan paused. He had raised his counteroffer to $140,000 to force Carl into turning it down. "And you're still willing to talk?"

"I don't think you understand; I haven't got a choice. Have you eaten?"

"Not a full meal. I was working out," Jordan responded.

"Why don't I come by then and we can talk? If you give me an address I'll pick you up in, say, half an hour?" Carl's voice sounded strained.

"Right." Puzzled, Jordan reluctantly decided

to give him the address and hung up the phone.

Carl's father was a self-made man, and Carl had always been careful with money after a few indulgences like the car. If Carl accepted the terms Jordan had counter-offered he would be throwing a lot of that money away, wouldn't he? Jordan began to wonder whether it was still billions or into the trillions that the Sanders were worth by now, and how many more hospitals they'd bought or built to get there. More than that, he wondered what could make Carl so insistent. He didn't want to make this decision between the money he could use to take care of his mom, and the fear that he'd lose what little control he had over his own life. *Shit*, he thought, *now what do I do*?

CHAPTER 2
– CRAZY

Carl's car was waiting in the loading zone when Jordan walked out of the apartment building carrying a notebook with a copy of the terms inside. Jordan checked his watch. He was early. So much for being fashionable. He opened the car door and slid down into the leather bucket seat.

"Which way?" Carl asked, looking at the traffic in the rearview mirror.

"Breakfast or lunch?" Jordan asked.

"Lunch, I suppose," Carl replied slowly.

Jordan thought for a moment. "Take a left at the next light," he said.

Carl looked at him and shook his head, pulling out onto the one-way. "Not likely. Changing four lanes in less than half a block is a bit much. I can go a block past and circle right, can't I?"

Jordan grinned. "So, you do have limits."

"Bloody bastard," Carl said, only half joking, then stopped at the light. Carl put his head down on the steering wheel.

"Tired?" Jordan asked.

Carl nodded, not lifting his head. "I couldn't sleep. You're driving a hard bargain."

"Didn't think 'no' would be such a hard answer."

"'No' would be the easy one. It's 'yes' that I find difficult to swallow."

In a minute the light turned green and several people blew their horns at them. Jordan glanced irritably at Carl, who jumped at the cacophony. "Want me to drive?" Jordan asked impatiently.

Carl surprised him by pulling the car around the corner and nodding, stopping in another loading zone. Jordan walked around to the driver's side and lowered himself into the seat while Carl wearily circled the opposite direction. It was like sinking into a cloud. The stick-shift was right where his hand wanted it to be after he adjusted the seat forward several inches. The clutch was high. Carl's head lolled back against the neck-rest as Jordan pulled out and nearly had to slam on the breaks, not prepared for the surge of power. Carl crooked an eyebrow at him for a moment then closed his eyes. It didn't take Jordan long to get used to how responsive car was. It was like an addiction. He began to think he'd been had, that access to the high-performance car was a ploy to get him hired, but looking at Carl he could see Carl was beyond the point of plots. He was asleep.

After an extended jaunt on the freeways and a winding path through several back streets

Jordan saw the forest of bamboo that cloaked the parking lot, as he'd expected, and pulled in slowly then parked in the back corner. Carl finally rolled over and mumbled, "Sorry."

"For what?"

"Falling asleep," Carl answered, yawning.

Jordan grabbed the notebook and stepped out. Carl yawned again, stepped out, stretched languorously, then followed Jordan into the restaurant.

Foreign music filled their ears as they looked at lacquered screens and gold cloisonné baubles. A six-armed gold statue of a woman sat cross-legged in front of the hostess station. The windows were curtained so heavily it was impossible to tell whether it was day or night outside. The essence of garlic, ginger, lemongrass, and chili wafted through the air and Jordan heard Carl's stomach growl. He'd heard this little Thai restaurant had great food, and the smell was intoxicating.

Jordan asked for a table in the back, and the dark-eyed hostess nodded, motioning them to follow. There was a dancer on a stage they passed, swaying to the music. Jordan had to assume it was Thai dancing, to Thai music. He'd only heard of this place; that it was expensive, served excellent food, and that "business" deals could be cemented in privacy. It was the type of place Jordan avoided, but today the ability to talk without being seen or heard was his highest priority. Something was off about this whole interaction with Carl and he wanted to get to the bottom of it.

The hostess guided them to a small table next to a huge mural of a tropical rainforest. The lights were low, and the small lamps at every table burned, glowing with both light and a hint of jasmine fragrance as well.

They sat down as the girl left and a waitress arrived immediately. "Anything to drink?" she asked with a mild accent.

"Tea, no caffeine," Jordan answered.

"Is mint okay?" She asked, and Jordan nodded in assent.

"I'd like a coffee," Carl said. "Black, please."

She nodded and walked away. Carl and Jordan were left staring at each other in the dim lamp-glow. Carl's face still looked harsh, even in this light. It had been six years since they'd graduated and Carl had been accepted to college. Jordan was grudgingly jealous of Carl for that. For having to work hard, himself, full-time in summers and part-time during the school year, still studying several hours a day as he attended community college. And for all that work, he had nothing after making payments on his mother's hospital bills, while Carl had breezed into college without a single worry.

The coffee and tea came as the two young men continued to study each other, sifting through memories for some essence of camaraderie. Jordan perused the menu quickly, canceling out the curries, the beefs, the porks, the high-fat sauces. After checking with the waitress to assure it wasn't prepared with a sauce, he ordered a chicken, mint, and lime dish with red onions and cashews, and went for four out of five stars on the spiciness scale. Carl's eyebrows lifted, surprised that Jordan cared for food that fiery.

"I suggest it, if you can take it," Jordan said. "Would wake you up."

Carl grimaced and ordered a three-star green curry. As the waitress left with their orders, Carl said, "I wouldn't be falling asleep if you were being a tad more reasonable."

"You're bitchy when you're tired," Jordan replied.

Carl gave him a disgusted look. "Well, where do we start?" he asked. "Your terms are fairly broad in scope."

Jordan grunted. "I'm still not sure I know why you want me."

Carl put his head in his hands. "I don't cook, I've never shopped for groceries, I don't know a dust-mop from a dishrag, and I need to put on weight. I'm going into isolation where I can't pick up take-out on the way home every evening. If I were to hire one person for each task, there would be too many sources of leaks. I need one man, one that I can trust. Aside from needing someone to help me get my muscle mass back, I've known you long enough and well enough to know you keep other people's business to yourself. You keep everything to yourself."

Jordan could just hear Carl's voice over the music. The restaurant was sparsely populated, but even someone at the next booth would be hard put to realize they were speaking at all. He leaned over. "That's what gets me. Why do you need someone who can keep secrets? What's your secret? What's the real story?"

"I . . . lose my memory, three nights in a row, once a month." Carl's brows drew together in apparent discomfort.

"What does that mean?" Jordan asked. It still didn't sound like an illness.

Carl looked at the draped the window before answering. "It's nothing I understand, by any means. A couple nights a month I feel excruciating pain in the evening, then I wake up the next morning... in the nearest forest or field, stark naked, with no memory of how I got that way."

Jordan's eyes widened slightly, then narrowed down to their usual slitted awareness again. "A couple nights a month?"

Carl nodded.

"Predictably?"

The waitress filled their mugs again, giving Carl time to look down and gather himself. After the waitress left, he looked up. "Three evenings in a row, then nothing at all for twenty-five days. Aside from the weight problem, of course; I lose too much those three days to regain it before the next . . . whatever."

Jordan looked out the window. Crazy story. Collecting himself, he promised himself he would keep a straight face through the rest of the conversation. It was still a good offer, though he didn't want it. He'd learned not to burn his bridges, whether forward or backward.

"Jordan, please don't mention this to anyone," Carl said anxiously. "I've already had to deal with questions from a crazed journalist over checking into a hospital recently. I can't afford to have them find me up at the cabin. So far, we've kept the place's existence a secret. According to the books it's owned by someone else."

Jordan was hardly paying attention to his words. "Are you eating right?"

"Better than ever, and more protein than before," Carl's blue eyes concentrated steadily on Jordan's face.

"Tired?" Jordan asked.

"Not really. I suppose I had more energy than usual at the beginning."

Jordan started chewing a fingernail. "Anything else?"

"I'm losing weight."

Jordan looked at him and frowned. "You said that."

"But that's the key reason I need you, and no one else. I need to start a weight-gaining program. I know that I can do it with your help. Nothing I've tried myself works."

Jordan chewed on the edge of his thumbnail. "Just a matter of balancing input and outgo. Shouldn't be a problem."

"Is that a yes?" Carl asked, hopefully.

"No," Jordan growled, then, "I don't know enough yet."

Carl began to tap his fingers against the salt-shaker in his right hand.

Jordan took a sip of tea. "Isn't there anyone in your life? No friends? No family?" He paused. "No …woman?"

Carl turned away, then looked back. "I'd rather not drag my friends into this – no offense. My family is back in England. My mother wanted to be near my grandmother when grandfather died. And as for a woman. . ." Carl stopped and his eyes creased with pain. "She's gone."

"Gone?" Jordan prodded.

"We were engaged to get married." He looked up at Jordan. "If you were a woman, what would you think if your future husband started calling you a couple of mornings in a row, asking to be picked up miles from home? And naked, with no reasonable explanation?"

Jordan's eyes narrowed. "She thinks you were fooling around."

"She probably thinks I'm insane! For all I know, I may very well be."

"If so, I expect severance pay when you go into the asylum."

Carl gave him a disapproving frown.

"Hey, buddy, you said yourself you're not trying to hire a friend."

"It could also be a plot," Carl said, after taking a sip of coffee. "That's another reason I'd like to hire you. People don't mess with you."

Jordan nodded matter-of-factly. "That wasn't on the list."

Carl looked up from his coffee. "Certainly it was!"

"Where?"

"Do you have the list with you?"

Jordan picked the notebook up from the seat next to him and pulled a piece of paper out of it. Carl scanned it quickly. "I'm terribly sorry! I thought I had worded that in a different manner. Here," he took the paper, crossed off a few words and wrote above them, then handed it back.

Jordan looked at the corrected line then looked up. "No," he said, and handed the paper back.

Carl looked up from the paper in alarm. "Jordan, you have to . . . what will it take?"

"More than that. I was a bodyguard, once." Jordan stared coolly. "I didn't care for it."

Carl drummed his fingers on the table. "Equipment?"

Jordan frowned questioningly.

"Any piece – every piece of exercise equipment you ask for, and you can take it with you when the job is over."

Jordan gripped his chin in his hand. The food

came, steaming. The waitress left.

"That was a mighty shallow offer," Jordan finally responded. Actually, it sounded quite good. Jordan had frequently considered formally starting his own personal training service, with his own equipment, but he couldn't afford the equipment.

Carl released the breath he'd been holding in a huff of air, then asked, "What ... do... I... have... to... do?"

Jordan smiled slowly. "Up the offer by fifty thousand. Give me a lock on my bedroom and stay out of it ... The kitchen will be mine. I want an hour and a half a day to myself, no interruptions under any circumstances except death or dismemberment. Before I'm disturbed. Music – any that I request. And that equipment, as a matter of fact, and a room big enough to set it up in. A masseuse, as needed. Five weeks per year vacation. Retirement plan, same terms I have now but better rates. Use of your vehicle. Friday evenings and the following Saturday up to three times a month, as needed. Any other items that I consider necessary to do my job." As an afterthought, he added, "And a hot tub, if you don't have one."

Carl sat for a moment, then got up and went to the restroom. Knowing Carl, Jordan was quite sure he'd be pacing the floor. Carl never could sit still when dealing with a problem. He had even paced in class during particularly hard tests in high school. The teachers weren't about to tell him not to; his parents funded the new stadium. Jordan preferred to eat alone in any case, and the food was excellent. Jordan was nearly done with the bowl of jasmine-steamed rice he'd ordered on the side when Carl returned.

"All right, you've got it."

Jordan fumbled and dropped his fork. "What?"

"The deal. I'll pay you one-hundred ninety thousand a year, plus all the fringe benefits in your email, and the items you just added at present," Carl answered irritably, sitting down.

Jordan stared in consternation. "The hot tub?"

"I have one, of course."

"The masseuse?"

"From one to four times a month. Give me veto power on the items you consider necessary to do your job."

Jordan eyed Carl warily. "No."

Carl rested his forehead in his hands. "Jordan, that gives you quite a lot of latitude. How can I know you won't take advantage of me?"

Jordan's voice was taut. "You have to trust me."

Carl considered, poking at his food, then spooned the curry over his rice and pushed it around a little. Grimacing, he answered. "I have to put my life in your hands then."

"No more than I put mine in yours. And when

I tell you what weights to lift and what to eat, you do it, not like in high school. You fell a good twenty percent short of your potential. I'm not throwing my job, my students – yes," he said when he saw Carl's surprise, "I've also been training guys at the club in my spare time, which was not in your income assessment, as it's all under the table. I'm not tossing it all aside for nothing. And you'll guarantee me employment for two years minimum, or severance pay equal to it." Jordan was sure, now, that he'd gone beyond Carl's limits.

He was wrong. As Jordan ate the last piece of chicken, Carl answered, "yes."

Jordan stopped chewing and swallowed. "And the kitchen?"

"It's yours," Carl answered, scrubbing his eyes with his fist.

"You'll stay out of it?"

"Yes," came the reluctant reply.

"No munching, no crumbs on the counter?"

"Yes! I said," Carl paused and looked over at Jordan, "yes."

Jordan was floored. "And if you're lying to me, I'm released with severance pay."

Carl closed his eyes and put his head in his hands. "How many times must I accept your terms? When does it end?"

"When I'm convinced," Jordan answered tersely. This was crazy.

Jordan had purposely made his demands unacceptable, having promised to take the job if Carl accepted them. Jordan could make good use of that money, but to commit to nearly round-the-clock work, and live in someone else's house to do it, was giving up more control than he could stand. He'd tried to force Carl to make the decision he wanted so he'd be guaranteed to give up on this crazy idea. But it had gone the wrong way. With that much money, he could buy his mom a house she'd be willing to move into, and get her out of that God-forsaken slum. That was it. That was what he wanted more than anything. At $190,000 a year for two years, he could do it. Especially if he didn't even have to pay for a place to live for those two years. Everything he needed was covered, the income was free and clear.

The waitress came to remove the plates and Carl dropped his card on the edge of the table. She lifted it deftly with Jordan's dishes and disappeared.

"I'll need two weeks to give my boss time to find a replacement," Jordan said finally, pulling a notebook out to look at a calendar in the front of it.

Carl rubbed his face. There was blond stubble on the pale gold skin. "I need you in three weeks at the outside, Jordan. Twenty-two days from now, on the evening of the twenty-first."

"You'll have me, but no sooner. I haven't seen my family for a year, and I'll be working overtime for the next few weeks, training their journey-man to reach a master level. I won't have time to call . . . Huh . . ." Jordan was staring at the calendar.

"What is it?" Carl asked.

Jordan pointed at the day he'd marked on the calendar. "Full moon. Apparently you're freakin' loony."

Carl shook his head, but Jordan saw a wariness in his eyes. He'd probably hit it on the nose. Carl thought he was transforming into some kind of monster when the moon was full. So Jordan could take the job, get the pay, and when Carl was institutionalized after he talked to Carl's father about everything, Jordan could walk away with enough money to finally take care of his mom, and to start a business.

They cemented the deal with signatures, not handshakes. Jordan still felt like he was being bought, and he didn't like it, but he'd put up with it for just long enough to get what he wanted out of the deal.

CHAPTER 3 – THE NEW JOB

Three weeks later Jordan sat on a city bus, staring out the window at the freeway as it rushed past. There was sun over the water of the Puget Sound, but a damp mist fell on the buildings, in they typical contradiction of a Seattle summer. After taking two days to get from Los Angeles to Seattle he was getting tired of buses, whether greyhound or city transit. Carl's deadline had left him four days at home with his mother and sister, who was thirteen and growing fast, but he had been exhausted during their time together, considering work and personal arrangements. He should have taken Carl's offer of a plane ticket, but there was less leg room on a plane than a bus, and he knew bus stations, not airports. Travelling by bus also gave him transition time. The thought of stepping on a plane in one part of his life and stepping off it a few hours later in another part was unnerving. He still wasn't sure he'd made the right choice about accepting the position, but he'd given his word and he couldn't go back now.

Aside from the few clothes he had in his pack and his two handguns, including a semi-automatic pistol he had in a shoulder holster under his windbreaker, his belongings had been shipped ahead of him. They consisted of a dozen or so large pillows he slept on when he had kinks in his muscles, (the mattress he'd been using was borrowed,) some clothes, some weights, and a guitar and amplifier given him by the family of a friend. He'd rather have kept the friend, but death was a cruel negotiator.

The bus pulled off the freeway in downtown Seattle. He'd watched the misty skyline as they came in, but he couldn't see the Space Needle from here. Someone had told him once that if Seattle had a major earthquake, that iconic structure would be the last thing to fall. He found that hard to believe, it looked so spindly compared with the rock-solid obsidian face of the Columbia Tower or any of the other familiar buildings of the Seattle skyline.

He pulled his bag out from under the seat and got ready to be elbowed. It only happened when people didn't see him. When they turned around to apologize, their jaws would drop in dismay at his size. They cowered away from him as if he would crush their skulls for putting an elbow in his ribs by accident.

He thought of his mother and sister again, in the same house he'd grown up in. It sat in a subdivision called Rainier, a dismal namesake of the beautiful mountain visible from the bustling city on the rare days the sky was clear. The neighborhood was still going steadily downhill. The assistant he'd hired for his mother recently was apparently doing a good job at helping her get around. Maybe, with the extra money he'd have when he started getting paid by Carl, he'd be able to hire an RN. Even after nine years his mother still had a lot of pain and spent too much time at her doctor's office. He'd told her it would be better if she simply moved to a wheelchair-efficient home, but she refused. It would cost too much. He wanted her out of there, along with his little sister Kira. He didn't care to visit that house; too many memories, and too easy for his violent father to find.

He saw Carl's car from the window as the bus pulled into the slot reserved for it at the corner. Amazing. Parking downtown was a major undertaking. Jordan wondered how much Carl paid the previous occupant for the metered parking spot. Stepping through the automatic door, Jordan alighted, stood aside, and stretched in the lightly falling mist. Carl jogged over, slightly damp.

"Come on, mate, we've got to hustle," Carl said in his soft British accent. "I've only got three months of data, shows me losing it in less than two hours. I'd rather be at home well before this happens. This it? You travel light. Quickly now, you'll have to drive. If I lose it on the highway we'll become a traffic jam, and the ticket for that is horrific. Over there," Carl was directing him the whole time he spoke, though it was obvious to Jordan where he was going. Carl was wearing a stylish pair of sun-sensitive, wire-rimmed glasses.

Jordan made a point of standing solidly at the corner and waiting for the light to change. Carl looked like he was going to jaywalk and dodge the cars, and Jordan didn't want his new job to start in the emergency room. When the light changed they crossed to the car, Carl opened the trunk and quickly took Jordan's bag from him.

"Good thing I travel light," Jordan stated, looking at the tiny compartment.

"It's got a bit of room behind the seats as well," Carl answered, handing him the keys. Jordan unlocked the doors, slid down into the seat and started the car. As the systems in the vehicle powered on, he found the stereo tuned to a classical station and a blare of violins assaulted his ears. He turned the noise off and heard the car purring as if it had missed him. Checking his rearview, he pulled out into traffic and up to the light, remembering how the car had responded before. His memory hadn't done it justice. It handled like a dream.

Stopping at a red light, Jordan looked down one of Seattle's many commercialized alleyways. A memory of new age, ethnic restaurants fronted on neon-gothic alleys flooded over him.

"Is I-5 the best way?" Jordan asked, turning to Carl.

"You could cross the lake and take 405, but at this hour you wouldn't gain anything. Traffic is surprisingly light right now. We'll be taking Highway 2, which begins after the two converge up north."

Jordan checked his controls briefly, then shifted into first again as the light turned green. He'd need to turn left within two blocks. Driving with a manual transmission downtown was usually a hassle because of the steep hills, but the well-adjusted clutch on the Jaguar made it seem nearly as smooth as a highway. Turning onto the entrance ramp, Jordan considered taking it to its limit on a familiar freeway, but thought better of it with a glance at Carl, who was engrossed in his phone. He was charting his temperature with a temporal thermometer every few minutes, alternating with a blood pressure cuff, recording all of it in the notes app on his phone. Leave it to Carl to have exactly the right equipment everywhere he went.

"Anything?" Jordan asked a short while later, looking across the bridge toward the University of Washington campus and thinking about the cherry blossoms that lined a pathway between the old brick buildings called "The Quad." All through high school he had dreamed of walking through them on his way to class, books under his arm. He still dreamed of it.

He realized Carl had answered his question. What was it he'd said? *Slow rise?*

"Temperature or blood pressure?" They were past the Huskies stadium. He had missed seeing the Space Needle again while transferring lanes repeatedly through the downtown area.

"Temperature is increasing slightly. That's likely to be nerves. Blood pressure just lowers on following mornings, but I thought I'd check."

"What's your resting pulse rate now?" he checked the rearview and shifted lanes.

"Seventy," Carl answered, jotting more notes on the page.

Jordan mouthed 'seventy' before saying anything. "What happened to you?"

"Classes, books... this infernal illness."

"Whatever happened to walking between classes?"

"Classes all in the same place," came the terse reply.

Jordan made a mental note to himself to take a wide variety of classes each semester if he ever got the chance. Then he shook his head. "You had a resting pulse rate of forty-five in high school."

"I was running every day in high school, and I drank a great deal less coffee."

"How much has this . . . this condition affected your resting pulse rate?"

"Eh ..." Carl answered, then looked up at the windshield, thinking. "My resting pulse rate was lower early on, but it's back up now. A little higher, actually."

Carl appeared more interested in his measurements than their conversation so Jordan left him alone for the rest of the trip, except to get directions every half hour or so. They began to climb steadily up into the mountains as the mist gave way to sunshine, and Jordan looked up at the deep blue peaks, the emerald fir trees, and the rivers, so clear you could see the rocks at the bottom as if through warped glass. He could almost taste the ice-cold water, and he rolled the window down to smell the evergreen trees. It was quite a bit cooler up here than downtown.

Carl directed him to a winding road on the left, and they followed the river higher still. Jordan could see the timberline far above them, where the trees just dwindled to shrubs, then to grass, and finally to bare gray rock with patches of snow on the shaded north slopes. He had to pay too much attention to the road to see if there were any goats visible. If they were up there it would take a great deal of patience to spot them. They would look like pale rocks, or small patches of snow, until one moved. He watched the river dance along beside him, rushing in the other direction. Once Carl was hospitalized for his delusions, Jordan would take his severance and spend a few weeks up here (thank God he had that in ink, and with bodyguard duty removed, too.) The beauty of the place always took his breath away.

And scaling the peaks was a hell of a good work-out if you did it right.

Twenty minutes later, after passing a quaint combination café, lounge and tiny grocery store, Carl motioned him to turn off onto an oiled dirt road. He slowed down rapidly to deal with the ruts and the washboard marks made by logging trucks coming down with heavy loads.

Carl barely spoke, only gesturing instructions for the route with a loose wave here or there. After several turns the road took them to a huge grassy field, the top of which was adorned by a castle of a house Carl had referred to as the "cabin." The huge structure was made of gray stone on the lower half, with enormous wood timbers holding up a slate roof with sharp, steep lines, and a vast triangle of windows between diagonal roof braces. It was set against a backdrop of granite peaks that jutted skyward like fists raised in defiance of gravity. Jordan half expected to see a moat below the wide basalt steps that led up to solid mahogany doors. There was also an entrance on the side, covered, where a car could pull up and dispense passengers beneath a rain canopy. The driveway led past the canopy and around back. *Roughing it,* Jordan thought sardonically.

Carl had the thermometer in his mouth again and was thumbing the data into his phone furiously. Jordan pulled up to the garage in the back. A short, covered walkway bridged the short distance to the house, which was nestled against a rise of stone at the northern edge of the clearing. Carl jumped out of the car, motioning for Jordan to do the same. Jordan looked at his watch. It was 8:45 p.m. The sun was well behind the tall peaks, though the sky was still clear blue. The valley where the house was situated would have given a view of the sunrise, if it weren't for the tall peaks beyond. Carl shoved the notebook into Jordan's hands, having taken the last reading.

"I'll need to have you watch me closely and record everything that occurs."

"Reinforcing?"

"Steel reinforcement. I'll be locking myself in. There are bars on the windows, all that, so I don't crash through and tear my skin like I've done before. I'm tired of having to find my way home every morning, and then having to bandage myself."

Jordan looked for scars on Carl's hands and arms, but there weren't any. He was angry that Carl hadn't mentioned this sooner, but he followed him in after plucking his bag out of the trunk, not sure yet whether he would be sleeping tonight. Carl was jogging into the covered walkway that led between the garage and through one of two back doors, the only doors Jordan had seen without stairs. It looked like a servant's entrance.

Carl stopped in the doorway and waved at the bright, airy kitchen with a series of brushed-nickel appliances. "Kitchen with stocked pantry.

It's all yours; restock it as you need. I have accounts with the companies listed on the inside of the cupboard by the telephone, and I've already added you to several, including Rosie's down in Baring." He jogged down a short hallway toward the front of the house, then up a broad curved mahogany staircase that led up from the opulent wooden doors of the front entrance.

Jordan studied the astounding architecture and huge slate floor tiles while following Carl up the curved staircase. Once he'd left the brightly lit kitchen area, it was like some European "Tara," only darker. Carl turned left, then showed him a door that led to a bedroom. "Your boxes are in there, or at least three of them are. If you own any more, they haven't arrived. There are intercoms hooked up to the sound system in the living room downstairs, where there's also a library of music on the computer and tablet, mostly retro-pop. The bath is down the hall."

Jordan stopped him. "Have you ever used a gun?"

Carl looked at him quizzically. "No. Why would I?"

Jordan dropped his bag and reached into the vest of the light jacket he wore, pulling out his pistol. "Smith and Wesson nine-millimeter. I keep it by the front door wherever I live so I can get to it quickly." He didn't mention the one he'd be keeping at his bedside. "You got a closet by the front door?"

Carl was staring at the gun. "Ah, no... why don't you keep it in your own room?"

"Not much good there if I'm downstairs when someone comes up to the door," Jordan didn't mention the one he'd keep upstairs.

"Are you expecting someone?" Carl asked quietly.

Jordan stared at him for several seconds. "How about the back door?"

"There's a closet there, but–"

"The gun goes in the closet. Don't touch the gun until I've shown you how to use it. This thing'll blow your hand off with the type of bullets I have in it."

"I'd rather not have it in the house."

"You get me, you get the gun. Live with it." Jordan put the gun back in its holster.

Carl frowned. "You work for me."

"And you live with me," Jordan repeated, meeting Carl's eyes.

Carl nodded warily. "I'd like to complete the tour, but I'm a bit pressed for time–" he halted abruptly, and Jordan heard the hiss of breath that was all a person ever heard of pain from Carl. He might be pampered but he was never a coward. Carl dropped into a crouch, holding his rib cage. He finally crumpled to the floor. His flesh went pale, then he stumbled back up into a wide-legged stance, pulling his glasses off and tossing them onto a rug. "Mark the time, Jordan, and stay on my heels here. Your assignment has just begun."

Carl ran down the hallway, talking over his shoulder. "Keep a record of everything you see and check the time at which you see it. Every move I make, every sound, the way I breathe—" Carl stopped to clutch his arms and hunch over. Jordan checked his watch, then ran to catch Carl, supporting him as he slowed. Carl stepped down the staircase gingerly with Jordan's aid.

They went swiftly through a hallway and down another set of stairs. Carl seemed to be losing control of himself rapidly. He dodged into a room just off the base of the stairs and slammed a steel-barred door shut between himself and Jordan. Jordan heard the solid clink of an automatic locking mechanism, then watched through the bars as Carl dropped to the floor and immediately pulled his clothes off. Jordan was about ready to walk out when he saw Carl convulse, then stretch taut like a wire. Jordan started recording a video on his phone to capture what was happening, since he didn't trust his senses.

Carl's arms began to shorten slowly and he shook his head, curly blond locks of hair flying away in large clumps. The palms of his hands sprouted thick pads as the fingers shrank to short stubs. The fingernails fell off and heavy claws gradually emerged. Carl's legs transformed more rapidly, shrinking in toward his body and seeming almost to bend backwards as his feet elongated to become part of his legs. His chest became deeper and narrower. His face twisted in a grimace of agony and his ears rose tall and triangular as they migrated like living creatures up to the top of his skull, which became narrow and flat. His jaw, upper and lower, stretched outward, and his nose turned flat and wet as it was carried forward on his lips, which spread wide and black as if splitting his face in two.

Jordan felt his stomach turn, then something at the other end of the creature caught his attention and he watched in horror as the monster's spine extended like a telescope. Throughout the process, Carl's skin appeared to be slowly turning gray as thick fur grew from every follicle. The tail was the last to be covered with fur, which shot out to several inches in length. Once the scene played out, it took several moments for Jordan to realize that there was nothing left of Carl. In his place lay a large gray wolf, panting as if exhausted.

CHAPTER 4 – NOW WHAT

Unable to think of an appropriate response to the situation, Jordan went with his last orders as he tried to catch his breath. It seemed like all the oxygen had been sucked out of the air. He breathed hard for several minutes, trying to get enough air, then checked the time and wrote it down, trying to hold the phone's camera steady as he jotted down the pertinent details in a notebook, always returning his gaze to the wolf. What the hell had just happened? Carl was gone. There was a wolf in his place. Jordan had watched the change occur and he didn't trust his senses, but he had it on video. He'd have to review what the camera captured to see if it matched what he thought he just saw.

They stared at each other until the wolf pulled its lips back to growl, then leapt abruptly at the barred metal door. The notebook flew as Jordan jumped back in fear for his life, or his soul. The wolf shoved its paw between the bars, reaching out for him as it tried to chew on the metal. It wasn't long before the gnawing stopped.

The wolf stared again at Jordan, then appeared to dismiss him. It pulled its leg back in and rose to inspect its prison, pacing along the walls and sniffing carefully. The walls were covered with vertical bars of steel, and there was a cage around the light in the ceiling as well as the small window in the top of the far wall. It proceeded to sniff the floor and walls, stopping in several places to test the metal with teeth and claws. It stood up on its hind legs to place its front paws on the wall, checking the high, short window, then paced back and forth a few times and stood up on its hindquarters to scratch higher on the door before turning around to sit, staring at Jordan with eerily human blue eyes. Jordan hadn't moved or blinked since he had marked the time, and he wasn't inclined to, aside from blinking to quell the stinging in his eyes. He sat down, motionless. It was more than an hour later when he finally moved, his muscles protesting the tense inactivity. He pulled his pistol from the holster. He flicked the safety off, pulled the slide back to load it, and set it down next to him, still eyeing the wolf.

"Carl?" Jordan whispered. The wolf's ears swiveled to the front. "Carl," Jordan said, more loudly. The wolf showed no sign of comprehension. "Carl, if that's you, give me a sign." The wolf remained still, watching him. Jordan shuddered as he considered what he might do if the wolf attacked him. His fear of the supernatural creature before him warred with his need to protect Carl from this thing that had taken over his body. His mind shifted erratically from the belief that this was Carl who sat before him to the idea that this was a monster superficially resembling a wild animal and that Carl wasn't any part of the shaggy grey form behind the bars.

Through the rest of the night he and the wolf stared at each other, the beast moving just once to drop to its belly and rest its head on its paws.

After what seemed like days to Jordan, one of the wolf's hind legs twitched. Jordan's eyes were stinging again, so he blinked, then quickly glanced at his watch. The sun should be rising soon, if not already. He stared at the wolf, wishing he could press his eyes closed for a few moments, but he'd let them burn forever if the wolf would become Carl – or any human at all – again. Less than a minute later there was another twitch, more violent in the forequarters, and the wolf twisted to bite at its flanks. It was completely still for another minute or two before it arched its back suddenly and began to drool. Expecting something just as shocking as before, Jordan took out his phone to document the incident with the camera on his phone. The melting, shifting process began again, in reverse, but the fur and claws remained behind, falling out in patches all over the body of the transforming creature. The tail telescoped back in as the face flattened inward, the arms and legs lengthened, feet shortened, and paws resolved themselves into fingers while claws fell out and nails grew into place. The wolf became Carl, and Jordan was desperately gasping for air again. His vision began to fade and he blacked out.

When Jordan came around he saw Carl lying motionless, curled in on himself and naked in the incandescent light. Bits of fur still clung to his damp skin. Jordan was half inclined to go in and cover him; Carl had to be cold in the chilled air of the basement. Carl whimpered, then was still. His head was tucked in, so Jordan couldn't tell if he was conscious or not. Ten minutes later, nothing had changed.

"Carl," Jordan whispered desperately. Carl's flesh was covered with goosebumps, but he didn't shiver. What if he was dead? The loss of air had to have affected him as well. What had happened to the air? Had the transformation somehow sucked all the oxygen out of the room? "Carl!" Jordan nearly shouted. Carl finally shuddered, then uncurled slowly. His skin was pale, almost translucent. Carl sighed, hardly looking at Jordan. His eyes were unfocused. He shivered again.

"Carl ... You okay?" Jordan asked, not really wanting to open the door and check, but not willing to see Carl die, if that was what was happening. Carl watched Jordan's form as Jordan walked up to the bars.

"I'm conscious," Carl breathed, his drive to submit scientific observations taking over.

Jordan looked at his motionless body. What would a butler do? "Can I get you a blanket, a robe, something?"

Carl was still for a moment, then answered, "A blanket."

"Where?"

It took Carl a while to answer. He was staring at the wall. "Hall closet, top of the stairs, by your room."

Jordan yawned. He hadn't slept in twenty-four hours, and he was beyond exhausted. He jogged up to get the blanket, came back downstairs with a down comforter, found the release on the metal door and pressed it, watching the door open. Carl was still staring at the wall when Jordan moved forward to kneel and drape the comforter over him.

Jordan sat back on the heels of his black biker boots. "How do you feel?" he asked. After quite some time, Jordan decided Carl wasn't going to answer, then a wispy voice filtered through the quilt.

"Fine."

Jordan swore. "The hell you do! You're tired... lethargic . . . apathetic or . . . something ..." Calling Carl out made the situation hit home for Jordan and he felt as if the entire world tilted under his feet for a moment. Looking at Carl, who was currently human, Jordan managed, "Are you hungry?"

Carl paused before nodding.

Jordan could see he wasn't going to get much out of Carl, so he went up to the kitchen to get some food. He found bread and a leftover Cornish game hen, still prepackaged the way the gourmet stores sold them; pre-stuffed, precooked, just heat and serve. What Carl meant when he said the kitchen was stocked Jordan didn't know, but right now he didn't want to take time to find out. He took both the bread and the hen down. If Carl was anywhere near as hungry as Jordan was, he'd eat both.

But Carl wasn't in the room when Jordan returned, only the comforter was. Carl's clothes were still strewn across the floor.

Jordan heard a click down the hall and strode down the corridor with the food. He found a laboratory of sorts and Carl, stark naked, was pulling a scalpel out of a drawer. Jordan watched in silence until Carl placed the scalpel against his wrist. Jordan dropped the food and lunged at him, grabbing his arms from behind and prying them apart. He felt something wet and warm against his hands and prayed he wasn't too late. Wrestling Carl over, he knelt on Carl's chest, binding his right hand to his side, yanking the tiny, razor-sharp blade from Carl's hand. Carl fought like a beast then collapsed, panting. Jordan was glad for his own wrestling experience. Carl was covered with sweat and blood, and stronger than he looked. Jordan checked Carl's wrists. They were fine. So where had the blood come from? He check Carl's body methodically. Carl gave no further resistance. There was blood spattered everywhere, but he quickly found the wound on Carl's belly, where Carl's hand had been when Jordan had grabbed for the blade. Jordan blanched as he saw how low on the abdomen the cut was. That swipe could easily have done damage to what most men considered a very important part of their anatomy.

"Leave me the bloody hell alone," Carl hissed, staring at the wall.

"That's not you talking, Carl," Jordan answered, holding Carl down with one hand as he looked around for something to stop the bleeding.

"I haven't been myself for months. Just … Let. Me. Die."

"If you meant to die you wouldn't have hired me. I intend to understand this before I let you go making permanent plans for a temporary mood. You're going to take at least a few days to think it through."

Carl didn't speak for a while. "I'm tired of it all, Jordan," he murmured finally. "I just want to get it over with."

"If you die I'll have to hire a lawyer to get my pay. Plan on living, even if I have to chain you up."

"No!" Carl yelped and wrenched free of Jordan's tight grip. Jordan grabbed Carl's arm and twisted it behind Carl's back.

"Agh!" Carl exclaimed. "Jordan, let me go! Set me free. I can't stand this. I feel – trapped."

Jordan assessed Carl thoughtfully. "So, this is about being caged? Have you felt this way before?"

Carl glared at the wall, his blue eyes fierce in the harsh laboratory lights. "I've never been insane before!" he gritted through his clenched teeth.

"Have you ever been caged before?" Jordan asked. He could make no sense of the physical transformation, but he'd seen it twice now, once in each direction, so he had to accept it until he found a better explanation for what he'd seen. The man, however, he was sure he could figure out. And he'd better figure him out, his life might depend on it. "You're not insane, Carl, or we both are, despite your promises that it's not contagious."

Carl continued to glare.

"You're... a," Jordan whispered, "... a werewolf," Jordan shuddered as he heard the nonsensical words fall out of his mouth.

"Bullshit!" Carl shot back at him, with a look of revulsion. Jordan wondered if Carl was possessed by a demon. It seemed just as likely as lycanthropy. Carl had never been violent before, even on the football field. His classmates called him 'The Earl,' with his British accent and civilized way of handling the game. The Carl he had known had been a calm, gracious person, if somewhat ignorant about other lifestyles.

"I watched you. You changed into a... a wolf," Jordan said while fumbling for his phone in his back pocket. He paused to fight down his own revulsion at the same time he retreated logically into a more academic view of the incident.

"Do you know how many different cultures have myths about shape-changers?" Jordan remarked slowly, hoping to calm Carl. Carl continued to stare him right in the eyes. Not like a lunatic, not like a demon, more like an angry young man, a side of Carl he'd never seen in several years of shadowing him in the school halls and the football field. "Apparently... there's some truth to it ... and you're the proof. Whatever happened last night it's no excuse for dying," Jordan paused, thinking for a moment that, actually, it might be. "Not until you know why. If you can't stand it, cure it. And tonight you might not want to stay in the room." Jordan saw a hint of relief in Carl's eyes, confirming his suspicions. Jordan recalled hearing somewhere that a wolf denied its freedom would die. Maybe it was true.

Carl hadn't struggled for a while now, and the bleeding seemed to have stopped. He was still naked, which Jordan found disconcerting, as Jordan had never cared to be seen naked at all, by anyone. He had very little lighting in his room for that reason. The closet he'd lived in under the stairs in L.A. had been ideal.

"Are you actually hungry or was that just a ruse?" Jordan asked.

"I'm hungry – starving, really. I'm always ravenous on these mornings. Except at times when I wake up with the taste of . . . blood . . . in my mouth and bits of . . . something like fur on my face." Carl looked sick.

Jordan felt his gorge rise, but he kept a straight face for Carl's sake. "Let me take care of this cut, then I'm going up to the kitchen and you're going with me. And for Christ's sake, you're putting some clothes on!" Jordan lifted Carl to his feet. Carl wobbled. "You have a first aid kit here somewhere?"

Carl pointed to a drawer and Jordan found it stocked with alcohol, swabs, gauze and tape. Jordan swabbed the cut with alcohol and Carl's abdomen tightened in shock. Jordan noted the apparent tone of Carl's muscles and he began to devise a workout plan for upper body as he folded gauze and taped it down. "That'll hurt when you rip it off," he remarked.

"It's only fuzz – it comes out a great deal easier than the hair on my legs." Carl was leaning against the counter, his legs trembling. Jordan helped him to the steel room, which Carl refused to go into. Carl stopped to grab the hen off the floor in the hallway while Jordan picked up the quilt. They went upstairs and Carl began to rip hunks of meat off the bird, chewing briefly before swallowing. Disgusted, Jordan wondered if Carl would choke, but it didn't happen. This was not the fastidious Carl he knew from the high school cafeteria. After devouring the meal, Carl turned to go up the next set of stairs, yawning. Jordan grabbed a loaf of French bread and followed him up to his bedroom where Carl collapsed, immediately falling asleep. An exhausted Jordan remained to watch him, cramping himself into an uncomfortable position so that he wouldn't fall asleep himself, ripping chunks off the loaf of bread and chewing. He felt himself drifting off soon after and stood to pace back and forth. He finally decided to lean up against Carl's bed and sleep.

The next thing Jordan knew, something had moved and he was on his feet, whirling around in a crouch. Carl was awake and rolling over to put on a robe. "Where you going?" Jordan growled.

"I'm going to the john. Is that all right with you?"

"I'll go with you."

"Have it your way, then."

Carl made no attempt to take his life with Jordan watching him closely, but he didn't make any apologies either and his mood hadn't improved. He went to a room on the main floor which had a two-story curved wall covered with ornate, wooden bookshelves and a ladder on wheels. Carl sat down in a recliner. Jordan sat in another. Carl pulled out a remote control and a modern, roll-top, mahogany door on one of the flat walls slid away to reveal a large television. Carl flipped through hundreds of channels three times before Jordan reached over and took the remote control away.

"Are you interested in my notes? Or the video I took?" Jordan asked. Carl shook his head. Jordan was sure, now, that this was a sudden difference. Last night Carl had hardly been aware of the world for his interest in his notes, but his attitude had changed since the transformation. Jordan flicked the channel switch a few times and landed on a *Three Stooges* show. He hadn't even had a chance to settle in before the horrific events of last night interrupted the tour Carl was giving him. He wanted to check out the house, unpack, look at supplies, start writing lists. Looking over at Carl, he sighed inwardly. Jordan wasn't going anywhere until Carl's eyes focused again. Of course, since Carl wasn't wearing his glasses, he probably couldn't see very well. The screen was most likely a blur.

Jordan looked around to see if there was anything Carl could use to hurt himself with here. Carl had only slept for two hours and Jordan was still utterly exhausted. He had to sleep even if Carl didn't. He noticed a tiny sword on a small figure in the bookcase and got up to look at it. It was a letter opener. He took the sword from the scabbard and tucked it into his pocket sideways so it wouldn't stab him when he sat down. He found no other obvious hazards and went to lie down against the door and fall asleep.

Four hours later something suddenly dug into his back. He sprang up, knocking Carl against the wall behind them in the process. Carl must have been trying to open the door. Jordan grabbed Carl's shoulder, pinning him against the wall. "You could ask," he hissed, his face barely six inches from Carl's. Seeing Carl's pained expression, Jordan stepped back, exhaled, and decided he was done trying to sleep for the day. Carl walked through the doorway, down the hall, and out the front door. Jordan followed. Rain was falling softly, shrouding the trees in gray, and turning the rich lawn into a diamond-studded emerald carpet. It was impossible to tell the direction of the sun in the overcast sky. Carl stepped down the staircase and headed toward the tree line.

Jordan wished he had left the sword in the library before following Carl. It had slid down in his pocket and was now jabbing his thigh. He caught up with Carl at the edge of the forest and found him leaning into a tree, his forehead against his arm. From the shaking of his shoulders, he must be crying. Jordan hadn't the faintest idea what to do about that since he himself couldn't remember crying more than twice in the past twenty years. Not publicly, not even in front of his own mother. It made him uncomfortable to watch Carl like this, but he couldn't leave him by himself. He wasn't ready to trust the young man with his own life yet.

The rest of the day was just as disturbing. Carl wandered listlessly in the rain, resisting Jordan's attempts to get him inside where he'd be dry. At six o'clock that evening, Jordan stood in the front doorway and looked over at Carl, who sat at the base of the front steps getting wet. Jordan had thrown a jacket over his shoulders again, and it hadn't fallen off yet.

"Carl, you're not staying in the room tonight," Jordan stated.

Carl nodded.

"That means you could be anywhere when you wake up."

No response.

"There aren't any phones out there."

No response.

Jordan cursed under his breath. Carl was not interested in helping, obviously. How could Carl let Jordan know where he was? It's not like he could take an air horn with him as a wolf. But, if he howled... Jordan would have to stay up all night again, listening. And if Carl didn't howl, well ...

"Carl?" There was no response, but by now Jordan didn't expect one. "Think about howling up there so I can find you in the morning."

Of course, if Carl's mood didn't change by then, it probably wouldn't matter.

CHAPTER 5 – COME BACK

Carl was still on the front steps as the shadows fell that evening and Jordan was getting nervous. He started edging toward the front door, ready to dodge behind it and slam it shut if Carl suddenly turned into that damnable creature of the night before.

Finally Carl shuddered violently, then clutched his gut and bent over his knees in anguish. As soon as Carl's features began to change Jordan dashed for the front door, slamming it behind himself and throwing the deadbolt. He felt his arms shake as he braced himself against the door. He hoped the residual depression, if that's what it was, wouldn't affect the wolf . . . Carl. He watched what little he could see from the edge of the window, lights off inside with a bright floodlight shining across the yards outside.

Carl hadn't taken his clothes off, so all Jordan saw was writhing under the material. He focused on Carl's face as it gradually extended into the wide-mouthed, long-nosed creature with black lips that had taken Carl's place just before the wolf took over. Jordan's attention was on Carl's face, but it was turned to the side this time so he saw the profile of the forehead flattening out, and it swiveled on the neck so that the neck was coming straight out the back of the head, like a wolf's might. In a few minutes, there was a wolf in Carl's clothes. It tore the clothing off in a frenzy of shredded shirt and faded denim that gave Jordan a great deal of respect for the power of those teeth. Then, the wolf looked back at the house briefly before bounding toward the forest with several high leaps, like a puppy.

*   *   *

During the night, Jordan wrote up his notes on the events he'd witnessed the previous night. He found Carl's journal on a printout beside a computer in what appeared to be a den he discovered by walking through a set of sliding doors in the library. Another set of doors led to the living room. According to the diary he found, Carl had noticed some strange abilities in himself early on, such as rapid healing and heightened sensual perception. These abilities were noted on files that had a later date at the top. He apparently hadn't considered them part of the same illness until just recently. After the first month, however, there was a steady degradation, showing the loss of those abilities he had just gained, as well as loss of weight in a steady, downward curve. The graphs attached to the diary showed several things, but what caught Jordan's eye was the projected weight loss graph. There was a red line drawn straight across the graph at one hundred and thirty pounds. The line was labeled "critical weight – damage to internal organs begins." This line intersected the weight line on August 28th, a month from now.

Jordan put the pages down for a moment, overwhelmed. His first job, it appeared, was simply to keep Carl alive long enough to figure this thing out, and to do this mostly by helping Carl gain weight.

Why hadn't Carl taken this to his father? The man was a distinguished surgeon who had pioneered research on several obscure diseases long before he started acquiring hospitals, and the money he had invested in those hospitals had come from that career. So why didn't Carl want him to know? And Jordan was sure Carl didn't want his father to know.

Jordan shuffled through the stack of documentation. He found a penned list, or at least the start of one. It was titled, "Possible Initiating Events" and there was only one entry: "Wolf bite, May 7." Down below there was a note, crossed out: "No known transferal of similar illness between wolf and man. No known illness involving predictable memory loss. Prognosis: Mental illness." Was this why Carl didn't want to tell his father about it? Below these crossed out lines was the message, "Yellow amoebic cells in blood sample. Unable to determine nature. Virus? Too large. Blood sample sent July 18."

Jordan put the paper down and rubbed his eyes, which were getting heavy from lack of sleep. He switched the computer on and it automatically brought up a window showing pictures of gates. Below each gate was a label, many of which ended in "website", but another caught his eye. It read "library". His fingers struck the table as he snatched the mouse from its place on the mousepad, he was soon tapping keywords for the computer to look up in a search bar, including "werewolf". He was disappointed to learn that most of the books he needed were unavailable electronically. Carl's library gate was primarily a list of the names of books on the subject, what library they were normally hosted in, and whether they were currently checked out or not. "Guess money only goes so far," he muttered. He wrote the names of several books on a piece of paper and jotted the address of the nearest library next to them, along with several phone numbers.

After checking to see what else the computer had on it, much of which amazed him though little truly surprised him, he stopped to look at the piece of paper that read "Prognosis: Mental Illness." He turned the computer off and went to the kitchen to make coffee. He hadn't had coffee for years, out of a distaste for artificial alteration of the body's natural capacity.

So, Carl had considered the possibility of insanity before. Jordan had witnessed the transformation twice now and he still questioned his own sanity, but the only way to deal with this situation was to assume that what he saw was real. If it wasn't real it didn't matter, and if it was, he needed to be prepared. Once he had a cup of coffee, he went back to the den and started another list.

     1. Neck pack for blanket and cell phone (& Food? Size?)

     2. Signaling method? Check GPS signal in various locations.

     3. Blaze trees?

     4. Buy groceries.

     5. BAR WINDOWS!!! (steel rebar, MIG welder, torch)

*　*　*

Early the next morning Jordan was pacing the field outside the house, several layers of clothes bundled on, adrenaline pumping from nerves and the coffee he'd taken after he woke up. He was afraid to fall asleep in case Carl howled, which he hadn't. It wasn't until 7:15 a.m. that he heard the howl -- a drawn out, chilling sound. He looked up at the peaks from where it seemed to be coming, made a point of checking the landmarks to either side for bearings, and headed in that direction.

There were trails most of the way, making travel rapid until he had to go a different direction. Two hours later he heard another howl and came to a halt, checking his holster to assure himself that his gun was there. Carl should be Carl by now. The hell if Jordan was going to come face to face with a wolf, natural or supernatural. He said a quick prayer, not to any god, but to whatever force watched over fools who tried to help others. Jordan hadn't believed in a benevolent god since he was six.

It was taking too long to hike, even at the rapid pace his legs could lift him up the sections of the trail he found. Jordan decided to start taking shortcuts straight up through the switchbacks, where the trails zigzagged because the slope was too steep. He ended up panting heavily, nearly twisted his ankle twice, and slid down a less than solid embankment for twenty feet before grabbing a tree and reconsidering his options. He chose the trail whenever he could. Fifteen minutes later the point was moot. The trail clearly went the opposite direction, even after accounting for switchbacks. He heard another howl, this one rather weak, but closer, and he aimed straight for it, gun in hand. It still took him another full thirty minutes before he arrived at a rockslide where Carl sat naked, just above a path that cut through the precarious slope. Jordan re-holstered the gun while Carl disappeared into the forest after giving Jordan a brief wave. Carl appeared on the trail below, limping slightly. There was a trace of something brown and dry around his mouth that left Jordan disinclined to ask questions.

"Thanks so much, mate. I was considering the trail, but I eventually didn't know in which direction to go, and I didn't want to run into some poor hiker looking like this."

Jordan pulled his coat off and handed it to Carl, then nodded, turning to lead the way back.

Carl stopped him with a hand. "And for yesterday... thanks... for putting up with me, and ... for saving my life."

Jordan looked back at Carl, who was covering his naked form with the coat, then shook his head. "Don't get used to it. It wasn't in the job description."

Carl gave him a questioning look and Jordan turned away. He'd told Carl he wasn't taking the job as a friend. He didn't need another friend. Especially not one whose life expectancy was in question.

Over the next few months, Jordan and Carl worked out a method for dealing with the transformation. By time they were six months into the contract, they had remodeled the garage as a stable, bought a sturdy horse, and roughed out a routine. They also came to an understanding: Jordan did his job and Carl kept his distance. It took Carl some time to stop making overtures of friendship, but Jordan aided the process by being as difficult as possible.

Reversing Carl's weight loss was another matter.

CHAPTER 6 – LUKE FINDS NOTHING

Luke counted off his steps, walking silently west-by-northwest, from the large granite boulder at the base of the cross while the early morning Nova Scotian fog covered his path. He listened carefully to the sound of bird calls, squirrel arguments, the breeze through the tree branches, and the other little murmurs that told him that the animals hadn't noticed him. When he reached the right distance, he searched in a southward arc to find the square hole in the ground that was the entrance to the secret passage. It didn't seem to be disturbed, despite the excavations taking place throughout the rest of the island. He looked around slowly to be sure he was alone, then he knelt on the damp mat of dead leaves, the rich smell of decaying wood filling his senses with every cool, humid breath.

He jumped into the artificial depression, then reached a finger into a crack between the rocks on the sidewall, which released a latch so he could remove an entire set of stones in the wall. He dropped onto his belly to squeeze himself into the tight passage. A twig dug into his hip and another into his shoulder as he slid into the dark passage, arms stretched forward as if it were a pool of water.

Wriggling forward, he finally found himself in a small granite cave. He came to the designated location and reached straight up into the ceiling of the tiny cave to find the alcove where there was ... nothing. Alarmed, he pushed his hands higher and grunted in pain as his knuckles scraped on the rock and one of his fingernails tore to the quick. Nothing. With both arms and hands, he felt around every inch of the jug-sized space. Nothing. The crystal skull was gone.

Luke pulled in a deep lungful of air and immediately let it out in a whooshing howl of agonized despair. He was tired, so very tired – nearly three millennia of tired. His responsibilities throughout the world had grown too much for one old wolf to handle, no matter how genetically fit and skilled he was, and he was just so damned exhausted. And now he'd lost one more tool he needed to retrieve his own memories when he became forgetful of a language he'd once known, or the location of a weapon he'd hidden, or, more personally, to keep alive the memory of the one person who had ever fully understood him and loved him anyway. He reminisced briefly about the exquisitely beautiful black-haired woman his heart had been faithfully married to for several thousand years. It was the one luxury he allowed himself in this difficult and nearly thankless job.

Now there was only one crystal skull left that was sufficiently accurate for clear memories of her, in the jungle thousands of miles away, in a country wrought with fractious guerrilla warfare. The other skulls had all been found and placed in museums, or private collections, and making new ones was always dangerous, leaving Luke open to discovery while the artisan crafted a replica decent enough that he could place it in the ark, then condition it to store and retrieve sharp, clear memories. He also had to mind the laws – even as the oldest member of the species, Luke had to answer to someone. And they would be coming, soon. His use of the skulls for personal memories was questionable. *They're my memories, dammit! I have a right to keep them alive,* he thought.

Luke took a moment to consider what other memories were stored in this skull, in case whoever had taken the skull knew how to decipher them, as was most likely the case if it was the witch he'd locked horns with long ago. Most of the memories were old codings, but what had been on his mind when he engaged with it for his latest journal entry? He had just learned of a newly infected werewolf in Washington that had been abandoned by the pack responsible for him. He'd marked the pack for a justice tribunal. His contact, Sarah, had been watching him, and said the cub was wasting away, which meant he would have to be executed, and soon. If left alone, there was a risk he would learn that a steady diet of human blood would keep him alive, though he would lose the ability to transform.

Luke considered the possibility that he would be unable to get the skull back. If the one remaining anatomically correct crystal skull was lost before he could make another good replica, his bright memories of his beautiful Julia would slowly fade as they were transferred from one hazy memory to the next, losing resolution every time. In time he would be completely alone in this world, a place he hadn't belonged in since the death of the Roman Empire. Luke stifled a sudden urge to howl again. He crouched back through the tunnel out of the cave and made the journey through the labyrinth and up to the surface of the earth. Luke had nothing to show for his trip. Nothing at all.

He reached into the medicine pouch that hung around his neck and pulled out his cell phone to dial his regional assistant.

"Hey Luke, what do you need?" Dwayne asked.

"Dwayne, the skull is gone. Did you come here since I showed you where it was?"

There was a moment of silence, then a panicked voice, "Oh no, Luke, how could anyone find that? I could barely get in there myself, and there's a latch that's damn near impossible to locate! Who–"

"TACIT!" Luke said, sharply. "It is gone. Have you come here since I showed it to you?"

Another brief silence. Luke didn't need to hear the next words, he already knew. "Yes, I went there to test myself and make sure I could access the memories without you. Oh God – you think someone followed me?"

Luke closed his eyes as his vision went red with rage. "*Did* someone follow you, Dwayne?"

"Oh God, Luke," the shaky voice answered. "There was a car behind me, but it went and parked at the museum."

"Was it daytime?" Luke asked.

"Yes, museum hours–"

"Vae!" Luke spat, cursing in his native Latin. "Why would you come at a time when people are likely to be about?"

"I wasn't thinking–"

Luke cut him off. "Think now!" This could be disastrous. "What type of car?"

A short pause, then, "It was... it was black–"

Luke cursed again. "If you do not know the make or model, just describe it."

Dwayne's voice had crept up at least an octave and was still shaking as he continued, "It had a weird grill with a line down the middle of it. It didn't have a bumper. Two headlights each side of the grill, separate, oval, more grill where I expected a bumper, and the license plate hung down, it was really weird ..."

Luke clenched his jaws together, then asked, "Do you know what a Bentley sedan looks like?"

"A what?"

Luke felt the cell phone dig into the base of his thumb as his grip grew tight. "Are you at your computer?"

"Yes."

"Google images of a Bentley," Luke prompted him.

Keys clacked, then, "That's it."

"Faex!" Luke swore. "Never allow a Bentley to follow you when you are working for me! It is not a common car, certainly not on this continent, and it is a car one of my enemies, a clan in England, prefers. It is a high-end luxury car. No one would choose to drive a high-end luxury car on the dirt roads of Oak Island. You were being followed." Luke cursed again. "Learn to recognize all models of Bentley and report to me immediately if you are ever followed by one. That damned witch is on my trail again. And she has resources to rival my own. Gods, she has resources I will never dream of." Luke scrubbed a hand through his hair.

"Can she read the skull?" Dwayne asked.

"Yes. Her people created them. She is the Sh'eytan Imperial Commander, though far more a witch than she is noble. We must track the skull down and get it back; it is dangerous to have that information in her hands. If she wanted the skull enough to drive a Bentley all the way out there, or more likely have one of her minions do so, she must have a very good reason. She's looking for something. And if she reads the memories, she will gain far too much knowledge about the location of packs ... the Skykomish pack, for one, and she will know they are on the verge of going rogue, if they haven't crossed that line already. I must get out there. They are due for a reckoning."

"You mean about that guy that got transformed? The one who's dying?"

"Yes, that one. He should never have been infected, but being infected, he should not be on his own. He should not even be alive at this point. There is no good prognosis. He will waste away soon enough, unless he discovers the blood cure and becomes a vampire. Deos. I will have to take that into my own hands. You are on notice, Dwayne. I am not sure I can work with an assistant who cannot do as he is told. I told you to see that you were not followed."

"Oh God, Luke, I was sure that car wasn't following me! Give me a chance to fix this. I'll find them – I'll get it back."

"No, Dwayne. You will find it, and I will get it back. The skulls are off limits to you until I can trust you again. Do not even think about touching one, or going anywhere near it. I will be checking your memories every time we meet until I can trust you again, and you had best stay in alignment with my orders." Luke took a moment to consider executing Dwayne immediately, and decided he needed time to think about it. Dwayne's ability to manipulate information over the internet was hard, perhaps impossible to replace, and it gave him an edge he couldn't afford to lose. He continued. "I need you to use your hacking skills to get the information I need to track the thief down. This most likely occurred immediately after you left the island. You will review all flights from the nearest airport to Seattle – that should be Halifax International. I'm sure she sent someone who could read the skull; it has ever been her desire to find our people. That's the only pack clearly identified, recently enough to still be where I located them when I encoded my local annual update. She's clever, she knows me well enough to move quickly to stay ahead of my actions. She will want to execute them all … or worse, and perhaps more likely, turn them against me. Futuo, I should let her, then destroy them all!

"And find me a flight to Seattle. Bump a passenger, put me on first standby and email a boarding pass to me. By the time I touch down I expect you to have a list of names and addresses: anyone who came into Halifax between the time I showed you the location of the skull and the time you returned yourself, then flew to Seattle within a week … three weeks … Deos! Since then, but record the dates, I'll have to check them all, though surely by now someone is there. And God help us if the thief is not the same person as the one who hunts the Skykomish pack. This will be difficult to track if that is the case."

"Got it, Luke. I'll have that for you by the time you arrive. Give me fifteen minutes and I'll have a flight for you."

"Good," Luke replied. "Call me when you have it, I've still got work to do."

"Yes, sir," Dwayne's voice was almost back to normal when Luke hung up the call.

He tried not to let his fury get the better of him. His new batch of assistants was less reliable, less aware of danger. It was hard to find good help anymore. He had to think about whether he was going to end Dwayne's service to him. It was problematic; Dwayne was a liability with all the information he had gained as Luke's assistant. If Luke didn't watch over him, his existence would be too tempting for Luke's enemies. Obviously the enemy knew Dwayne now. If he kept Dwayne he would have to find a new identity for him, a new home, and get him relocated. If he decided to find a different assistant, he would have to execute Dwayne, and he would no longer have an assistant who could break into and alter computer data anywhere in the world in a matter of minutes. And he had to keep in mind the two primary laws that his species was judged by; do not allow humans to discover you, and do not harm humans. Of course, Dwayne was not a mere human. Like Luke and all Luke's people throughout the world, Dwayne was Homo lupanthrus: a werewolf, though not like the horror movies cast them. Shapeshifter. Huma-animal hybrid.

Since Dwayne wasn't mere human the second directive didn't apply. Luke was free to injure or execute any Homo lupanthrus that was a threat to the species, or to either of the two laws. Dwayne was pushing it with this transgression. The crystal skulls held enormous amounts of information Luke had used, over the millennia, to do his job as chief protector, commander, and judge of all the werewolves throughout the world. To have that knowledge fall into the wrong hands would be disastrous. Luke would have to get the skull back, then eliminate anyone who had learned of its contents. He would suspend judgment on Dwayne – for now – and wait to see how well his assistant handled this crisis. For now, Luke had a witch, a werewolf cub, and a disobedient pack to deal with. The wayward assistant would have to wait.

CHAPTER 7 – WAKING UP

Carl awoke slowly to the sensation of intense cold, twigs, and stones pressing into his naked body where it contacted the damp earth. Eyes closed, he resisted the strong urge to shiver, remaining still for a minute or two. Hearing nothing but bird calls and a squirrel scurrying across tree limbs, he slowly opened his eyes to find himself looking into the face of a wolf sitting no more than ten paces away. He stared intently as it sniffed the air, staring for a moment before lowering its ears and looking down in submission.

"Sweet sister wolf," he whispered, "where have you brought me this time?" According to texts he had read, the wolf had already made the first dominant overture with her insolent stare, and in his physical state of vulnerability he couldn't afford that. He stifled another shiver and rolled his body over to face her; patches of gray fur fell off his shoulders, arms, legs, and side. The wolf dropped her ears to half-mast and let out a low "whuffle" sound as he stared at her, then slowly rose to her feet and turned to lope away through the trees. Carl relaxed. It was the second morning in a row he'd found her up in the mountains. His recent study of wolves hadn't fully prepared him for the subtle hints of aggression or submission in the social creatures, and it seemed lately that his life might depend on such subtleties.

He unsnapped a collar-bag from his neck, which was the only thing he wore, and pulled out a heat-reflective blanket, moved over to a tree and rolled himself in the blanket, glad that he had let his curly blond hair grow beyond his shoulders. He finally indulged in the shiver that would have betrayed him to the wolf. He was beyond the forest area where he had sprayed distinctive blazes on the trees, and he didn't know which direction he'd find the house in, so he tilted his head straight back, set his hands on either side of his mouth and howled. There was no response after several seconds, so he tried again. The sound died away before he heard an answering note from a bugle, then sat back to wait, hunger gnawing at his belly like a stray cub.

*   *   *

Miles away, Jordan stood over a workbench. He was looking, with dark, narrow eyes, at an open-bottomed, birdhouse-like box. In his latest battle against insects, he hoped to increase the bat population of the area by giving the small, winged creatures safe places to roost. He listened to the wind. Jordan was on-call for the second of three days this month and he was looking forward to ruling his own mornings again, rather than rising at four a.m. to pack saddlebags with dried beef and cheese, clothes, and wool blankets while a concoction of cider, honey, and spices heated on the stove to be packed at the last minute.

From a distance, up the side of a sheer mountain cliff, the wolf's howl drifted down to him. His broad hands reached for a bugle from the workbench and he jogged outside. The howl came again, and he squinted up at two peaks to either side of the strongest echoes. Once he had his bearings, he lifted the horn to his lips and blew a long shrill note, the only one he needed to know. He jogged over to the laden mare, strapped the horn to the saddlebags and swung himself into the saddle. Lifting the reins, he kicked her with short, black boots and she leaped through the open gate.

Minutes later Jordan felt the horse's hooves slipping and swung down so he could walk her across a rockslide, then got back up on the other side of it. He swore elaborately at the sharp grade. He gripped the saddle horn when she shifted her footing, then guided her past a boulder and drew the reins to one side, kicking gently this time. She surged like an ocean wave up the slope and Jordan swore again as he gripped her sides with his knees, grabbing the saddle horn with his free hand. On the crest of the hill, he pushed her into a gallop. He knew the terrain well and raced against time. It was late autumn and snow had already fallen at higher elevations. Carl would have to remain still under the blanket until Jordan arrived. For the next twenty minutes he guided the horse up between the slopes of the two peaks he was using as landmarks. He finally stopped, lifted the horn and blew again. The sound echoed back to him for several seconds, then a long, drawn-out howl gave him time to pinpoint the caller. He headed that direction and soon heard Carl's yell.

*   *   *

Jordan glimpsed the back of the Mylar-draped form through the trees. Carl must have heard the rustle and thud of horse hooves trotting through damp leaves because he rolled over and looked at Jordan, his gaze emanating from above the silvery plastic of the heat blanket. Jordan slowed the horse to a walk, then slid off and led her while she tossed her head and rolled her eyes. She strained against the reins, trying to stay as far as she could from Carl. Her reluctance forced Jordan to stop a couple of yards away, snatch a flask from a saddlebag and toss it to Carl, who whipped his arm out and grabbed it from the air. Carl shivered again, uncapped the thermal container, and tipped his head back, pouring the hot drink down his throat. Rummaging in the saddlebags, Jordan pulled out jeans and sweater and dug for more items in the other bag.

Carl slowly eased himself up the trunk of his tree, and nearly dropped into a faint. "Food, Jordan," he gritted through clenched teeth.

Jordan saw pain in Carl's blue eyes and swore, "Oh, Christ! I thought you'd . . . uh . . . eaten . . . something. Here!" He ripped a plastic bag from the saddle horn and yanked a hunk of white cheese from it, tossing it to Carl's shaking hands. Carl tore off a large corner with his teeth and nearly choked while swallowing it, then bit off another stringy hunk of the mozzarella, devouring the block as Jordan yanked dried meat from one of the saddlebags. After Carl finished the cheese and went through half the meat at a slower rate he finished off the juice, then took the clothes Jordan handed him and put them on swiftly, remembering the cold only after his belly was full. Carl sat down on the blanket, folded it over himself, curled up into a ball and fell asleep.

Jordan pulled the bedroll out from behind the saddle and draped it over Carl for additional warmth. He sat down, leaning against a large fir tree as he looked at the blanket covering Carl's bony back, then closed his eyes. If Carl was skinny, it was Jordan's fault. He mentally reviewed Carl's weight loss, tremendous on the three consecutive nights a month that Carl went through the supernatural transformation. The trick was not only getting enough food into Carl between those nights and the next cycle, but also getting him to work out enough to make sure it went on as muscle. His body was cannibalizing muscle tissue, particularly during the transformation. But Carl was so damned focused on collecting and analyzing data, looking for a cure, it was a battle to get him to step away from his microscope and computer to lift weights. What he needed was a treadmill instead of a chair, and weights hanging over the computer so he could be lifting while he stared at the screen. And discipline to do it.

CHAPTER 8 – GOING HOME

Carl woke up and looked over at Jordan, who seemed to be lost in thought, leaning back against a tree with his eyes closed. Knowing better than to pry into to the internal workings of Jordan's mind, Carl pulled the blankets around himself and stood up. Daisy was straining her neck to reach the nearest leafy bushes. He took a deep breath of mountain air into his lungs, filled himself with the rich scent of pine trees and dark earth.

Jordan cracked an eye open, shook his head and stretched, then handed Carl a pair of hiking shoes from the saddlebags at his side. Though Carl had bought the damned horse, she would kick him if he came too close, so he would walk. Carl set off down the nearby path on foot while Jordan swung up on the mare and walked her around in front, the wind blowing against their backs. They spoke little as they found their way down the steep slope.

"How far do we have to go?" Carl asked while

his blue eyes searched the terrain for familiar landmarks.

"Just five miles or so, if we follow the trails most of the way," came Jordan's reply. "Are you okay for it? There's still some meat and another flask of enerjuice." Jordan didn't seem to be listening as he braced himself fluidly, swaying with the horse.

Carl was concentrating on his footing. "I'd prefer a steak. I believe I can wait until we get to the house." Carl had learned that his body needed a great deal of protein over the past three months, to replace what was lost when fur fell out after each change.

They moved on in silence for a while. Jordan took every opportunity he could find to force Carl to a faster pace. He seemed to take his job as Carl's trainer seriously, and Carl was always reluctant to work out on mornings after the transformations. He felt it was more important to catalog his pulse rate, his weight, and any other test he could think of to give himself.

Carl's stomach growled loudly as Daisy stepped delicately across a clear, rocky stream.

"Will you be waiting 'til we get to the house, or can I expect you to drool all the way down? I've got more meat in the pouch."

"Meat? That cardboard stuff has all the flavor of kidney pie! I never did understand what my father saw in odd bits of internal organs." Carl watched as Jordan swung down off the horse to lead her across the rockslide, anxious to get back to the lab. "I think we're getting closer to a cure, and my weight is surely on the increase soon enough. Maybe we could broaden my diet a bit."

"You really think you're that close?" Jordan asked skeptically, flicking the tail end of the reins against the horse's rump as she slowed down. She tossed her head and sped up.

Carl wondered if he was just trying to convince himself. According to the data, they'd managed to extend his weight loss curve for another few months already, but it wouldn't last forever. He was on the downslide again. He only had a few more weeks before it became critical, and that would be right when another devastating transformation cycle occurred. Jordan hadn't said anything about it yet.

Carl took the crisp air into his lungs as he stood on the slope, hand braced against a tree for a moment while he nodded, catching his breath after half-sliding down the last hill. Carl started moving down the slope again and tried to make conversation. "You said yesterday we need more meat. I wish we could fit more than a week at a time of groceries in the Jag."

Jordan stopped the horse and turned around to face Carl. "I'm not the one that brought a sports car into the mountains." Carl looked up at Jordan, who stared back at him from his higher position on the horse. Jordan continued, "I'll get your groceries, cook your food, clean your house, do your endless digging for clues, and track you down at ungodly hours in the morning, but I think it's time I had a truck. I could stock up for several weeks at a time, make fewer trips into town."

Jordan was right, of course, but Carl didn't like the image that came with trucks. Jordan eventually turned his eyes back toward the house and got the horse moving again. Carl took a deep breath, releasing it slowly. Wolf or man, he couldn't seem to win today.

*   *   *

After several hours of traipsing down the path, they came down the last rise to see the three-story stone house, with two floors above ground and one below. From this angle, it looked as if it were carved out of the mountain it-self. Carl saw Jordan pause when it came into view, as if out of reverence. The bars Jordan had fashioned and placed over the windows were in keeping with the European style, and the front door had a silver doorknob and strips of silver beaten into it like runes on a magic tome. Carl had watched Jordan go out with a blowtorch and hammer every so often to correct a curve in a window grate or to reinforce a bar. Of course, upkeep of the house and was another part of Jordan's job, and Carl paid him well for it.

Jordan nudged Daisy toward the stables with his knee, tossing the key in Carl's direction. It fell several feet short, and Carl glared at him, but Jordan wasn't looking.

"Did you write up that report on the books I'm looking for?" Carl asked Jordan's swaying back.

Jordan spoke without turning around. "It's on your desk. If you want it in triplicate, I can print it out a few more times."

Carl had to remind himself that Jordan had never asked for this position, like other servants that he'd known. Jordan's most important job was as a physical trainer, and he did it well. Carl went up the curved stone steps, pulled on the glove that Jordan had left on the landing, and opened the door by its silver-plated serpentine handle. He shucked his shoes in the entryway, more to get the wet things off his feet than out of any concern for the slate floors that Jordan kept clean. He went through the living room, then the sliding pocket doors to the den, where he saw the printout sitting neatly on his desk. Skimming it, he wasn't surprised to see that nearly all the books he wanted were long out of print, but he was taken aback by the large number in the next column over that were still unfound. He decided to take that up with Jordan later. For now, he strolled through the library to the kitchen to warm up a steak.

He saw a pink sticky note stuck to the phone and pulled it off to read it. "Damn!" He swore. "Why didn't he tell me my father called?" He looked at the clock. "Hours ago." Carl crumpled the note and tossed it away. "Undoubtedly long gone or having dinner by now."

He finally headed toward the refrigerator, asking himself one more time whether to reveal his problem to his father or not. He passed a mirror in the hallway, one of the many that had appeared since Jordan arrived, and paused to look at his face. It was gaunt and bony; he almost didn't recognize himself. He frowned and turned slightly, trying to see his profile. His nose rose off his face like a cliff, and his cheekbones looked so sharp it was almost eerie. It wasn't the face he'd grown up with, and it wasn't a good sign. Scowling, he continued into the kitchen. He didn't like the mirrors, the constant reminders where he least expected them, but Jordan had insisted. Carl had seen Jordan looking back over his shoulder periodically whenever they were outside, even in the mountains, and he knew Jordan wanted eyes in the back of his head, but the mirrors were almost too much. He thought again about breaking them, but he knew they would just be replaced. With a sigh, he resigned himself to seeing more, or less, of himself than he wanted. Then, with another sigh, he lifted the receiver on the desk phone to call his father. He hated to disturb his father at dinnertime, but he still wasn't accustomed to the loneliness of his exile, and it would be nice to hear the voice of someone who cared about him for a change.

"Hello?"

"Father?"

"Carl! I was afraid I'd miss you. I can't talk to Jordan for the life of me. I've never been known for my bedside manner, but he always seems to have gotten up on the wrong side of the bed."

"Tell me about it." Carl leaned against the wall.

There was a pause, then Carl's father resumed the conversation. "I need to tell you there's a visitor arriving soon; she should be there at about two o'clock. She flew in from Nova Scotia, ten got on a train from the airport."

Carl stood straight up. "A guest? Father, I can't have a guest coming here today! Why?"

"Her name is Diana, and she's made me a business proposition regarding our property there. We don't really have much use for it anymore and she believes she can turn it into the Aspen of the Cascades. I met with her boss and spoke to her over the phone. I must say I find it unlikely, but she's quite a go-getter, and has offered to make a proper market analysis with no financial support from me. I told her she could have use of our cabin; she had to pay for her own travel, and she's on her own. If you want to share your groceries with her it's your choice. I expect her to prove herself; she's too young to have much in the way of credentials, but I was impressed with her knowledge of marketing and finance. I think she's worth giving a chance."

"You're just letting some stranger in then?

Without any references?"

"Carl, she's young. Someone has to give her a chance or she'll never get references. I hope someone at some hospital will do the same for you when you're out of school."

"But Father, now is really not a good time for me," Carl protested.

"Why?" His father asked with audible concern.

"Well, it's just… I have things to do…"

"She promised she won't get in the way of your studies," his father said, reasonably.

"But…"

There was a pause. "Is there something else Carl?" His father sounded a little hurt. "Are you okay? I understand you're on a lighter schedule at university due to this long virus. Are you sure it's just the flu?"

Carl couldn't think of an answer.

"Carl, I'd like to think you could tell me anything. I'm your father. You know I'd support any decision you might make, whether I agree with it or not."

Carl's mind raced. This was not a direction he had expected the conversation to go, and deception was not one of his finer skills, especially with his father. He had always been able to tell his father everything, and this was new territory for him.

"Carl? Are you all right?" Pause. "Is there something I should know? If there's anything wrong, I'd really like to know. Maybe I can help... Is it really the flu, or is it something else? Is Jordan all right? He seems to be a little stressed out himself. More than usual. Rather prickly."

Carl went cold, as it seemed clearer where his father was going with this line of questions. He'd been questioned before about Jordan's presence, and it all clicked. The questions about his weight loss, the questions about him living in seclusion with Jordan. Carl felt sick. Clearly he needed to head that insinuation off, and buy himself some time.

"Okay," Carl said quickly, "to be honest, my doctor is also concerned so he's running some tests. I should get the results soon, and I'll let you know. It could just be that I've been too stressed out to fight it off, or maybe not, but we'll know soon enough.

"But Carl, I have to wonder, and I'll refrain from all the questions I have about your lifestyle for now, but... what does Jean think of all this?"

Carl went limp and his back hit the wall behind him. He slowly slid down to the floor. Jean, his fiancé. The lovely woman with the warm brown eyes and long blond hair, whose laugh filled him with joy, and whose mischievous smile filled him with passion. He groaned quietly. "We've broken up. It was a while ago, I'm sure she's moved on by now. That's part of the stress. Wait, Dad?"

"Yes?"

"Will our guest have a car?" Carl asked. "Does she know how to get here?"

"Oh, for goodness sake! That's what I called about. No, you need to pick her up at the train station at two. Can you do that?"

Carl thought for a moment. If he could say no, it might help, but if she was the "go-getter" his father mentioned, she'd find a way. Better to have her under their control from the beginning.

"Yes, of course. We'll pick her up at two."

"Right then. Well, I'm glad we talked. You know you're my favorite son."

Carl smiled despite himself. This was an old game. "I'm your only son."

"Well, of course! Once we had you, we had no reason to try again. We got it right the first time. All right, now. Take care, Carl."

"And you, Dad. Give Mum a kiss for me."

"I'll get right on it. Look after yourself. And let me know the results of those tests as soon as you get them."

"I promise." Carl sadly hung up the phone.

CHAPTER 9 –
OF WOLVES
AND MEN

Carl sat in the parlor studying printouts of his graphs of variables, symptoms he had kept track of once he was aware of his disease. Just as Jordan arrived, drying his hair from a shower, the door-bell rang.

Carl raised an eyebrow at Jordan. Jordan went to the door and opened it.

"Game Warden John Samuels, here to see Mr. Carl Sanders." The warden's voice had a softly musical lilt that offset the gravel in it. His short hair was grey and his face was lined and leathery, like an old cowboy. Carl could see Jordan crooking an eye at the man.

"Christ! Delightful butler," Carl swore under his breath. He slid the papers into a drawer in the end table and went to the door where the thin man stood in the doorway in a green uniform.

"Carl!" The warden was craning his neck slightly to see around Jordan, who stood like a statue.

"Warden Samuels, it's so good to see you, " Carl beamed from around Jordan's broad back. "Make us some coffee if you would, Jordan," Carl ordered, slightly annoyed at Jordan's stolid posture.

Jordan turned and gave him a calculating look before he strode away.

Carl turned back to the warden, swung the door wide open and offered his hand. "Come on in, Mr. Samuels. Have a seat. Please join me for a cup of coffee."

The warden shook his hand. "Good to see you again, Carl. You know I'm always ready for a cup of coffee." He stepped through the doorway and followed Carl into the living room.

"How is hunting season coming along?" Carl asked over his shoulder.

"All stupidity and no crime at this point. The usual weekend warriors shooting without identifying their game, but so far it's just the wrong animal, not another human, and nothing endangered."

Carl shook his head in disapproval. "I don't understand men who fire before they know what they're shooting at."

The warden sat down in the chair Carl offered. "Fortunately it's rare, and generally they're just ignorant. At least, I always hope so. Poaching is despicable. How are you doing since that bite?"

Carl grimaced, sitting down on the edge of the couch. "I'd always heard how painful the rabies series was, but until I went through the shots myself, I had no comprehension. Next time something bites me, I'll wrestle the bitch down and bring in the carcass for testing."

The warden shook his head. "If you don't own a rifle you're best off leaving it to us. I'm just sorry we couldn't find it for you."

Carl shrugged. "Well, it's behind me now."

"Now that's what I came to see you about. It's probably nothing, but there's a guy down the road who found one of his cows dead and partly eaten about a week ago. He claims it's the wolf that got you, and he's raisin' hell. Personally I think the thing died, became carrion, and he wants someone to pay. It'd been dead two weeks when they called me, so it's hard to tell. I just thought I'd check it out, get some information for my report."

Carl's mind raced. What if it HAD been a wolf that killed the cow? What if it had been Carl? "What can I do to help you?" He asked as he stood to pace. They both waited when Jordan brought a tray with two large mugs of coffee and set it down on the coffee table. The scent of a rich, earthy Ethiopian brew wafted through the room in ribbons of steam. Jordan had thought to put milk, sugar and a spoon on the tray as well, and pulled two coasters from a stand on the end table to place them on the mahogany coffee table.

The warden nodded at Jordan, then stared at his back as he left the room. He picked up a mug and turned back to Carl. "What I need from you, Carl, is any news you might have or might get on the presence of a wolf, or wolves. Seen any tracks or scat out there? You hike, don't you?" he asked, taking a sip of coffee.

Carl began to pace again. "Yes, Jordan and I have both been up and down these peaks a few times in the past few days, for exercise. Since that wolf had a bite out of me, I've looked for signs. I haven't seen any," he lied. "And I'm not sure I'd know the difference between wolf scat and any other kind, but I haven't seen much other than our own horse's."

The warden nodded. "I've got copies of the files on the wolves they brought into the Northern Cascades National Park from Wyoming. Since it has to be a descendant of one of those–"

"Why does it have to be one of them?" Carl sat down on the chair across from the warden.

The warden leaned back into the recliner where he was seated. "Because we haven't had wolves in these mountains for several decades, except the ones that were brought in way north for relocation. So it's got to be related to a wolf from that project, in which case it's still come a long way south, and that's the bad news. One of them must have left their pack, for one reason or another, and come this direction. Since wolves are pack hunters, it may not have been eating as well as it would with its packmates. It could've had just about any illness or disease. Course, you would've shown signs by now."

No kidding, Carl thought. Then, without missing a beat, "I'll certainly keep you in mind if I find anything. Do you plan to shoot any wolves you find at this point?" Carl drummed his fingers anxiously on his coffee mug.

"Not unless we have solid evidence that it's a danger. We'd need another documented case of a bite, or to actually find a wolf with identifiably odd behavior. Despite their rarity, we still can't guarantee that any wolf we find is the same one that bit you, and I really don't think this other thing is a case of predation. I had Dr. Schilling do an autopsy, which showed that the cow wasn't well – course, that's exactly what a wolf would be interested in – but it's more likely the cow got sick and died, and scavengers got it. The ranchers are paranoid about wolves. As soon as they hear about one, they think they're going to start losing calves, and they start pulling out their rifles and patrolling the area. At a minimum of $900 a head for a good steer, I can understand why. The complaint would be legitimate if there was reason to believe it. Wolves and men have never cared to coexist. I think they'll stay deep into their territory for the most part. It's really unfortunate you cornered that one."

Carl nodded tensely. "If I'd known it was hiding in those bushes I wouldn't have been sticking my hand in there. I would've left the damn flask I dropped." He was shaken by the thought that, beyond the usual hunters, the farmers might be out looking for a wolf to shoot as well. "More coffee?"

The warden smiled and nodded. Carl poured him another cup from the insulated pot on the table, then refilled his own.

"The people in Baring are holding a meeting, if you're interested, at the town hall, eight o'clock Sunday. They're gonna talk about this wolf problem they think they have. Scheduled it when they know I'll be out of town, and the local environmentalist types weren't invited." The warden gave Carl a knowing look.

The last coffee Carl was pouring splashed from the cup as his hand spasmed. "Oh, well, maybe I can..."

"No, no, I wouldn't want you to spy for me. Hard enough to get their trust as it is. But if you just happen to overhear anything around town I wouldn't mind knowing about it." He paused, then inquired, "Hey, tell me, how are your parents doing? I haven't seen them in years."

"Quite well, thank you. They have a lot a lot of business to take care of in Europe since my father just acquired another hospital that needs updating. Regional. It needs a lot of polishing, he says. Mother's been taking care of Grandmother since Papa died," Carl said, dropping into the lilting cadence of the warden's voice without noticing.

"Sorry to hear that," Samuels said, the harsh

lines around his eyes softening.

"It was time," Carl sighed.

"What about you? You were studying medicine, last I heard. I was too busy filling out forms when I caught up with you in the hospital. Still studying?"

Carl cracked a grin. "Oh, well, on and off. Been a bit stressed out since after the bite, you know, so they've given me a hiatus for the summer and fall, but I'm doing some research on my own."

"There's the Sanders work ethic for you." The warden paused, then added, "You've got a good heart, Carl. Don't let the books bury it."

"Well, thank you," Carl said, trying to think of something more to say. The warden finished his coffee and stood up.

"You're not leaving so soon, are you?" Carl asked. He missed having a social life. Jordan was poor company at best.

The warden nodded. "Really oughta be going. Got paperwork up the ying-yang to turn in at the office. Our new secretary's a real stickler for deadlines, and the boss is behind her one hundred percent." He stretched his back. "This job isn't what it used to be."

Carl put his hand out again. "Thanks for stopping by. Sorry I couldn't be of more help with the wolf problem."

The warden shook his hand with a firm grip. "I doubt there is a problem. Thanks for the coffee. Let me know if you do see anything . . . well . . .

unusual. Just for the report, you know."

Carl walked him to the entryway and moved to open the large door, then stopped himself and stood back from the silver handle. The warden grinned at Carl, put a finger to his hat, then opened the door and left. Carl stood for a moment by the open door, then carefully pushed it shut with his stockinged foot. Jordan had gone into the parlor through the den to pick up the tray. "Jordan!"

Jordan stopped and looked up. "What?" his voice grated.

Carl turned to him. "I think I'll answer the door from here on, so we'll need to do something about this silver door handle. I'm getting tired of having to ask you to open the door, aside from which it would raise eyebrows if anyone caught me doing it."

Jordan appraised the door, then the entryway in general. "How about an end table or something right there, with a – one of those throw rag kind of things on it."

"A table scarf?" Carl said, quizzically.

"Yeah, one of those. Antique mahogany, with a . . . red rag."

"Not a rag, Jordan," Carl said, exasperated. "And Queen Anne style to match the living room set."

"Certainly. I'll make sure it's a pretty rag, just for you."

"Just do it," Carl said through a clenched jaw.

He decided he could use a workout, and strode down the hallway to the basement stairs, where he came to an abrupt halt.

"Jordan!" He turned to see Jordan looking back at him. "We've got a problem. My dad scheduled a visitor, and she's arriving at two."

"And?" Jordan responded with impatience. "What's your plan, genius?"

"We pick her up at the train station, treat her like a guest, and get her out of here by any means, and as soon as possible. She's here to convince my father of a business deal on the property, and he's giving her some latitude. We're going to make the deal look like a bad one. She'll leave as soon as she believes there's no money to be made, or a security issue that could tie money up in lawsuits, or legal restrictions. Something."

"Okay, so what's your first thought on how to make it seem worthless?" Jordan asked.

"I don't know yet. It's a piece of land; start brainstorming. She wants to get my father to develop it. Maybe we can find some unusual animal that lives on it." Carl turned to go down the steps.

"No problem," Jordan answered. "We've got you."

CHAPTER 10 –
THE DOWNTURN

Carl looked up to see Jordan a few minutes later as he stepped into the weight room. Jordan's glare reminded him why he'd come down, and he turned on some music and finally started working out. An overhead fan kept cool air circulating in the room, blowing invisible fingers through the hair curling at the back of Carl's neck.

"Jordan," Carl said, breathing heavily as he lifted a dumbbell repeatedly, "am I losing it?"

Jordan eyed him speculatively. "You mean form, mass, or mental stability?"

"Mass," Carl breathed, ignoring the bait. He looked at himself in a wall-length mirror as he continued the exercise.

Jordan appraised him carefully from a distance, then came over to sit behind him on the workout bench and place a measuring tape around Carl's biceps. He started wrapping it around different parts of Carl's body, making marks on a sheet of paper on a clipboard after each assessment. Carl twisted, trying to see how the present data compared to yesterday's, but Jordan grabbed his shoulders and turned him back around. Carl figured he wouldn't know anything until Jordan was done, so he relaxed, lifting an arm when asked, standing, flexing what little remained of his once athletic body.

Jordan set the tape down recording the last bit of information, picked up the clipboard, and looked at the results.

Carl finally lost his patience. "What?" he barked. "What does it say?"

"You're losing too much mass," Jordan said under his breath, checking the figures on the chart again.

Carl had been lifting weights for two hours every morning and evening, alternating between upper and lower body, and his diet was carefully formulated for bodybuilding, with extra protein to replace what seemed to be lost in the transformation. He knew there was a point at which muscles could be damaged by overwork, and he was treading the thin line as it was.

Carl took a deep breath, counting silently. "Where am I losing it?" Carl was looking directly at Jordan when Jordan looked up, and he saw Jordan's hands shake slightly out of the corner of his eye.

"Everywhere," came the quiet answer.

Carl sat for a moment, then got up to check his weight. "One fifty-eight." Jordan wrote the number down as Carl went back to the machine, leaned over and lifted the dumbbell again. As he started the mesmerizing motion of flex, down, flex, down, he spoke quietly. "Take the data and run it through the computer. It's just a couple of pounds, it could be a normal fluctuation, but we can't risk it. Alter my diet." He knew the weight loss graph like the back of his hand, and this marked the new loss as part of a downward curve. Apparently his weight would continue to come off at a steadily increasing pace unless he could find a way to stop it.

Jordan set the chart down on the seat. "Christ, Carl," he swore, "you're taking more protein than is wise already, the maximum in carbohydrates for what you're burning... we should add more carbs on your transformation days, but you won't take them then. Adding more mid-month will just increase your fat level. Muscle takes time, and you've lost more than you can replace in a couple of weeks."

That scared Carl; after plotting the new weight graph today, he wasn't sure he had a couple of weeks. "My body's handling the protein," he objected. "As you witnessed, I'm not human anymore. I want you to reconsider my plan." Carl pulled out the calipers and measured the skin under his arm. He held the calipers up to the measuring gauge. "See, my fat level hasn't changed. It's protein I'm losing, in the form of muscle tissue."

"But you're losing it on the three nights you

change!" Jordan exploded.

"Oh no, Jordan, that's not all and you know it. It simply goes faster then. I'm losing it constantly again. I need more than what I'm getting. Look at me," he added fiercely. "Look at my face!"

Jordan stared at him. Carl wondered how much longer Jordan could ignore the evidence in Carl's cheekbones. It stared him in the face every morning when he shaved, and had begun to think he should stop shaving, or risk taking skin off as well. It was no longer just his jawline that he had to be careful with. It was his chin, the hollows of his cheeks that he'd had a hard time reaching over the past few days, and his cheekbones themselves, standing out like tombstones. Always robust and healthy, Carl now saw the form of a desperately skinny man in the mirror. Soon enough, it would be a wraith.

Jordan finally answered, "Let's start with the extra carbs. If we add everything at once and get results, we won't know what did it."

Carl fought to keep his fear at bay. "On the other hand, we don't have forever," he argued. "If we add it all and there's an effect, we know it's one of the three or some combination, and we can narrow it down from there. I hired you to tell me what to do, and I'll do it, but I'm asking you to widen our options." Carl carefully considered what Jordan was saying, despite his own feelings. Jordan's size and abrasive personality made it easy for a person to mistake him for a fool, but Jordan had matched Carl's GPA in advanced classes.

"Dammit, Carl," Jordan swore, tossing the clipboard onto the weight bench, clearly annoyed. "You don't know what will happen to this curse thing if you jack up your steroids, and too much protein can damage your brain."

"According to studies done on human beings," Carl answered pointedly, picking up the chart as his heart drummed against his ribcage. "And just how much protein do you think it would take to hurt me? I couldn't eat that much if you held me down and force fed me. In case you hadn't noticed, my body does odd things with protein, like grow a full coat of shaggy gray fur every twenty-eight days. The protein's got to be replaced." Carl would have given his right arm to know what was going through Jordan's head right now.

"Too late for your damn brain anyway," Jordan muttered, yanking the clipboard from Carl's grasp and walking away. Carl grabbed the curl-bar off the floor and started lifting again, his pulse throbbing in his ears. He counted out his second set, paused for a few moments, then went into his third. He realized he hadn't taken a blood sample yet, the warden having interrupted his usual routine. Cursing, he rose and strode down the hall to the lab.

CHAPTER 11
– FINDING
ANSWERS

Carl sat down at the computer in the den. Tropical fish swam lazily across the monitor. He tapped the keyboard once, then reached for the mouse as the screensaver disappeared, revealing a list of selectable files. An arrow sped across the screen as he moved the mouse to the left, and he selected several of the files in succession. Four graphs appeared across the top of the screen labeled, "weight," "health - subjective," "blood pressure," "food intake, by type".

Carl chewed his bottom lip as he stared at the data. He selected another file and a diary page appeared, filling the entire screen. He scanned the words rapidly, clicking the 'Page Down' button on the keyboard every few seconds, then finally pressed his forehead into the heels of his hands. "God – these bloody variables. There are too many of them. How do I separate the blasted data?" He looked up, hands still cupped to his face, then minimized the diary to fit on the lower half of the screen. He pressed another button and a menu screen popped up. His hands went to the keyboard, and he typed in several commands in quick succession. The five graphs disappeared from the top of the page and coalesced in a larger window centered on the screen, each graph's line showing up as a different color on a single grid. He chewed his lip again as he stared at the image, then selected another file. A photographic image of cells of various types moving slowly to the right appeared.

"I need more images," Carl muttered, then pulled up a communications program and set it to receive and record data before standing up to go to the lab.

*   *   *

Carl whispered to himself as he turned the lab computer on, then pulled a microscope from a cupboard and set it up. Reaching into a large drawer below the computer, he lifted the computer's "eyes" from it and screwed the lens gently onto the larger optical tube on the microscope. He then slid a cheap slide of paramecium under the lens. Using the optic lens on the side, he checked the focus, then turned to the keyboard and tapped out several commands. This projected the paramecium on the specimen plate onto the monitor. Satisfied, Carl pulled the slide out and put it back in a drawer, then pulled out a strip of rubber tubing and a hypodermic syringe.

"Father's going to think me a junkie the next time I visit, all these holes in my arm," he muttered to himself, then stood up abruptly. "Only crazy people talk to themselves," he said as he switched on some music on his computer. His shoulders dropped as he turned around. "Much better. Now I can talk to the music." Pulling his sleeve back, he reached for rubber tubing, wrapped it deftly around his arm and pulled it tight. By the time he had the hypodermic in his hand, the vein on his arm had risen like something undead. He pressed the needle into it, filled the syringe halfway, released the rubber strip, and withdrew the needle. Then, he grabbed a cotton ball to press tightly against the tiny wound.

Reaching into the drawer again, Carl pulled out several dishes in succession, each marked with a different label. Carl had been testing his blood for everything he could think of every time he withdrew any. With great care, he injected a single droplet of blood onto each, then set them under a Plexiglas cover on the counter.

Carl placed a drop of blood onto the final slide, placed the slide under the microscope, then turned to watch the computer screen, watching for the quasi-amoeboid yellow cells that had invaded his body. They were like nothing he'd ever studied, moving slowly across the screen as he moved the plate under the microscope. He tapped out a command to record the images, then stared at the lifeless cells. Leaning forward, he studied the cell structure again. He was positive that he saw a tear in the cell wall, an indication of damage. The innards were jumbled rather than orderly. Every cell in the world had certain parts in common, and though he'd never seen anything quite like this, he was sure that what he was seeing was a dead cell. Many dead cells. Nothing but dead yellow cells, populating his bloodstream and causing him to lose weight. Were they taking the energy his body needed to survive, then expiring and being passed out of his system somehow? Urine and fecal samples had been higher in protein than they should. Were the cells parasitic or symbiotic? They seemed to operate parasitically, killing him slowly, but Carl had to question that hypothesis considering that his health had improved slightly right after he was infected. The creatures appeared to be unsuccessfully symbiotic, dying, and taking him with them.

Carl set the mechanical slide controls to automatic and the microscope continued maneuvering the slide slowly across the viewing area with the record feature on, and walked away. He wanted desperately to send an anonymous sample to his father again, but he didn't dare. The first and only test his father had time to complete was DNA, since Carl specifically asked him to test this first. When Carl asked the team to check for variations and cross-contamination in the DNA, they found nothing at first. But, several weeks later, after Jordan had witnessed his transformation, Carl called back to have the lab check for the addition of wolf DNA in the sample. At that point, it was identified and confirmed: wolf and human. Wolf and human DNA. In his blood. Carl then retained a PI who removed the sample from his father's lab and destroyed all the records. Carl wanted them out of his father's hands on the off chance his father could somehow identify the human portion as fifty percent identical to his own DNA. Was he being a fool or not? He only suspected his Catholic father's reaction, but so far that had been enough to deter him.

He looked at his watch and cursed. It was time to pick up their guest at the train station. He thought of Jean and felt like he was poleaxed. He didn't want to see a woman at all right now.

CHAPTER 12
– FETCHING
DIANA

Jordan sat down at the den computer where he had just entered the new data on the spreadsheet. It came out to a solid twelve-pound loss from three days ago, size loss nearly equal everywhere. Carl had been running the data for over nine months now. The initial loss curve stopped plummeting when Jordan was hired on and even rose briefly, but it soon showed a second steady decline, and the rate of it was increasing. The catabolic wasting of muscle was draining Carl's body, more so this cycle than ever before. He pressed his head against the computer and thought for a moment. In high school he had known more about physiology than Carl did, with his independent research on building muscle mass, but the tables were turned now. Jordan wasn't sure he knew what he was doing anymore. What if Carl died and it was Jordan's fault? He couldn't ignore it much longer. Carl's clothes, once a fashionably good fit, were now hanging on him like loose sacks. Jordan put his hands to his head and massaged the furrow of his brow as he evaluated the information. He closed the weight file window and opened the diet file – the full, unabridged one. He'd just about decided on an extra-carb/extra-protein diet. If Carl wanted steroids, he could set it up himself.

Carl strode in, hair wet, in jeans, shirt, and socks, a sweatshirt in his hand. "On your toes, Jordan. She'll be arriving soon. I've decided to have you go down to pick her up. You should probably buy the groceries first."

Jordan looked at his watch, feeling his jaws tighten. He tried to speak nonchalantly. "You should have told me earlier. If I leave now, I'll get to the station right before the train arrives. I'll have to get her, then the groceries."

"No. You can't be getting groceries while Diana sits in the car. Even if her presence is inconvenient, she will be treated as a guest until we find a way to send her back home. I'll open a tab for her at the station, she can have a cocktail and something to eat while you're gathering groceries." Carl pulled the sweatshirt on over his head.

Jordan suspected Carl's calmness was an act, there had to be a reason Carl was backing out of his obligation. Regardless, being late was a pet peeve of Jordan's, and he had no desire to pick up Diana and make a bunch of excuses. "What if she doesn't want a drink?" he growled, slamming the wireless mouse against the wall and standing up to face Carl, his broad shoulders thrown back. "Maybe she doesn't drink. Why didn't you just come in here a little earlier? I thought you were going, or I'd have left eons ago. Months ago. Why in hell did God give you blond hair when you could have had a brain instead?" Jordan leaned over the computer, banged a few keys to save the data and strode toward the door.

Carl stepped into the doorway as he finished pulling the sweatshirt on, stood up straight and looked the short distance down at Jordan as only Carl had the guts to do. "Are you going like that?" Carl asked, folding his arms and leaning against the doorjamb.

Jordan looked down at himself. "Like what?"

Carl waved a hand at Jordan's clothes. "Like ratty T-shirt and faded jeans."

"Don't have much choice on short notice, boss," Jordan answered, staring coldly into Carl's steady blue eyes. "My only good pair of jeans is in the laundry, and I don't wear silk. I'll get a newer T-shirt." Jordan turned to brush past Carl.

Jordan felt Carl grab his sleeve and seethed with rage but refused to turn.

"What in the hell are you doing with all that money?" Carl released Jordan's shirt a moment later, and Jordan brushed it flat, his face a storm. Carl continued in the same tone of voice, striding through the doorway ahead of Jordan. "Dammit, let me get you something of mine. I may have an oversized sweater that'll fit, but the pants..."

Jordan hissed, "What is your problem? Who needs fashion up on the side of a mountain where you never see anyone?" Carl showed no intentions of responding. "Fine. Get me a shirt, if you can find one big enough," he growled, "and let me go do your job for you. Lazy-ass prima donna." As Carl's steps sounded up the stairs Jordan grabbed the upright bar of a weight machine, pressed his head against it and squeezed it until his knuckles turned white, regretting his hostility. Carl's size, right now, was Jordan's fault if it was anyone's. He wished he was back in his tiny closet in California, seeing women on the weekends, writing a letter to his mother in his spare time. He barely got a chance to call anymore. Maybe Carl would just die of this thing.

Shocked, he opened his eyes and thought for a moment about Carl dying. He let go of the bar, stood up straight, and dismissed the notion. It was a comforting thought only when he was angry, and it shook him that he thought of it at all. In high school, Carl had had a reputation for diplomacy that Jordan had seen only traces of since the unexpected visit in California. It might be that Carl had changed, but it was more likely the stress that made him unpredictable and short-tempered.

Carl came back with a large polo shirt an aunt had given him. It was much too big for Carl even when he was healthy, but it would be tight on Jordan. Jordan stripped out of his T-shirt to show a broad, wedge-shaped mass of pure muscle fiber, his back crossed with scars that became visible as he turned slightly and started walking toward the laundry room. He almost expected Carl to ask again about the scars, but it seemed an earlier tightlipped silence had made the message clear: don't ask.

Carl crossed over to him and took the big T-shirt from his hand. "Just go."

Jordan stared at him a moment, then left. He stopped at the doorway and bellowed over his shoulder, "Up your protein twenty percent." He hoped his voice sounded confident.

*   *   *

Jordan slid into the smooth leather seat of the sporty little yellow coupe and took a deep breath, trying to clear his thoughts. He felt like ripping Carl's head off and dealing with the consequences later. He took another deep breath, put the keys in the ignition, and his foot hit the floor like a jackrabbit. The engine roared into life and Jordan yanked his leg up, letting it slow down to a gentle thrumming. He took another deep breath and counted to five while he released it, closing his eyes and listening to the deep growl of the car he so loved to drive. The idea of losing control over himself while he was driving the beautiful machine put him off more than the thought of ripping Carl to pieces. He forced himself to calm down. His anger wasn't getting him anywhere, as usual, and he had a job to do. He shifted into gear and crept down the gravel drive, careful to keep the tires from spitting the gravel onto the car's enamel skin.

He knew Diana's presence was a threat to Carl, and he tried to think through what Diana would see, and what she would think of it. He wasn't happy that he had a tight shirt on. He didn't like drawing attention to his muscles. He focused on the house, on Carl. What would seem normal, what would seem out of place? He tried to remember what had seemed normal to him and shook his head. The house had changed since then, reinforced with steel bars and silver hardware. It might not seem normal, but it shouldn't be alarming.

Arriving late at the lounge in the train station, Jordan saw the back of a head of long, black hair at the bar and assumed it was Diana's. Other than that, the lounge was empty. He walked up, feeling awkward. "Diana?"

She turned around and caught him off guard with the intensity of her striking blue eyes. He felt himself falling into them and focused his mind sharply. She was stunning in a slightly exotic way, could have been a supermodel. He hadn't expected that at all.

She measured his expression coolly. "Were you expecting someone else?" Her glossy, thick hair was feathered around her face and her full lips and dark eyebrows intensified the deep-blue of her eyes, which looked irritated.

Many typical lines came to mind and he quickly rejected them. "Would you like to finish your drink?" He reached for a barstool – she had chosen a seat that stood alone.

"Hmm . . . the first thing he does is quiz me. No, the first thing he does is tell me he can't arrive in time, so would I please be so kind as to get drunk so that I'll be ready when he gets here." Her gaze penetrated him as she tapped her fingers on the varnished wood counter.

Jordan pulled up the stool and sat down at an arm's length from her. He would have liked to have gotten closer and that bothered him. "No, the first thing he does is find out whether his boss' instructions have made her as mad as they made him." He paused so the next words would sink in. "I'm Jordan, the houseboy."

Diana appraised him coolly. "In that case, let me finish the drink, Jordan the houseboy." She stared at him as she lifted the glass to her shiny red lips.

Jordan felt her stare measuring him, and he wondered how he looked to her. He thought his dark features, while not particularly handsome, were well-balanced. He was clean-shaven, but his face had a hardness to it that was intimidating to many people, and in pictures he noticed his eyes were always narrow, as if he were squinting. Or as if he'd seen enough of life and was trying to filter out any more of it than absolutely necessary.

"So, you're just a lackey working for an arrogant master?" she asked, her lips parting slowly in a sensual smile.

Jordan looked down for a moment and shook his head. She flustered him as if he were still in grade school. "He just got back this morning, and he had a lot on his mind. We're sorry you had to wait, it wasn't intentional."

"Don't worry, I'll reserve judgment until we meet. I know I'm more impatient than I should be. Actually, I've really been enjoying the view." Diana stared at him as she gestured out the large picture window at the river that wound through a steep, rocky valley.

"If you think this view is nice, wait 'til you see the castle."

She raised her exquisite eyebrows. "The castle?"

He grimaced. It was his own private term for the house. "It's a bit grander than what I grew up with. It also has a beautiful view of the valley and a private stream of its own." There was no point hiding from her what she'd see with her own eyes soon enough. "It's not a bad place to spend a few days."

"Well then, a couple of weeks should be just grand," she said, twirling a cherry from the condiment rack by its stem.

"Don't settle in until you meet the master of the house. I made that mistake myself, and I'd hate to see you lose all your hair. You must have had it your whole life."

He watched a smile spread across her face as he realized how lame his attempt at humor sounded, and it chilled him. He wasn't sure if it was just that he was too attracted to her, or that she seemed the type to use it against him. "Where's your luggage?" he asked, looking around at her feet.

"I had it put in a locker when I got the message." Diana's dark brows framed her question. "Does he own these people? I haven't experienced such solicitous attention since I won a first-class ticket to Maui."

Jordan shrugged. "He might. He can afford it." His eyes narrowed almost imperceptibly before he changed the subject. "If we can't get your bags into the car I can have someone bring them up. You might want to bring just the things you need."

"It'll fit in the trunk of a standard car, I'm sure. I didn't expect to be picked up in a van."

"You won't be disappointed; it's not a van. But your luggage probably won't fit."

"Hmmm. Well, let's see what we can do." She stood up and stretched languorously. His breath caught at the sight of the long, shapely legs utterly exposed between the black miniskirt and the high T-strap leather stilettos.

Diana's short jacket had been hanging over the low back of the bar stool, obscuring the view, and Jordan took the chance to appreciate the swelling curves under the creamy silk blouse. He told himself that he was simply starved for the sight of a sophisticated woman after several months of forced hermitage. It would be a shame to let her go. He followed along behind her casually swaying hips as she led the way to the locker.

"How many of these do you have?" he asked as she turned the key in the lock.

She turned around and let her gaze slide slowly over his face. "I have one. This is it." She slid a suitcase over to him, then reached in again and pulled out a carry-on bag. "I didn't think I'd need much, which is good because airlines discourage baggage. Perhaps one of you could lend me a few things to wear until I go shopping if I find I need anything," She added flippantly.

Jordan lifted the heavy suitcase and led the way toward the car.

"Sorry about the... oh, I guess you didn't notice, did you?" she asked, following him.

"Notice what?" he answered.

"No, you wouldn't," she said. "The suitcase weighs a ton. But then, with a body like yours, what's a ton?"

Jordan smiled to himself as they stepped through the automatic doors and walked toward the Jaguar. He tried not to think about how he moved but he was afraid he was strutting.

"Is that yours?" She asked when he set the luggage down. "I see what you mean about fitting. These cars don't even have back seats, do they?" She leaned over to look inside the small, two-seat compartment.

Jordan almost missed his cue as he stared at the heart-shaped curves of her backside. "I think we can fit the suitcase in the trunk, but you may have to get cozy with the carry-on." He opened the trunk and stashed the suitcase next to the groceries, then closed it.

She was settled in snugly, bag on her lap, by the time he slid behind the wheel. He pointed out the views as they drove into the woods, forgetting to dissuade her. He loved the scenery. She rolled the window down and breathed the pure, cold air, tainted with ice and fallen leaves.

"How much farther are we going?" she asked.

"It's just down the other side of this hill. But it's a long hill and the road isn't paved, we'll have to go slow."

She looked out the window again. "I knew it was in the mountains, but I didn't realize it was quite so remote."

Jordan belatedly realized this was as good an opportunity as any to start convincing her not to stay too long. "We were surprised to hear you wanted to stay here. I don't know about that shopping you wanted to do. We might be able to get out in a week or two, if the snow holds off.

Otherwise we'll be trapped in the mountains for the season."

"Hmmm. I hope you have several spare shirts." She gripped her seat, looking straight down the cliff at her right. "What size is Carl? Is he another Goliath?" Her voice sounded strained despite the attempt at humor, and Jordan assumed it had more to do with the sheer drop off than Carl's possible size.

Jordan shifted into a lower gear. "He's tall but slim."

Diana sighed with relief as they passed the cliff. She shook her head and stared up at the tall peaks, laughed under her breath, then said, "Wonderful. I'm going up into the mountains beyond the limit of standard telephone wires, to be trapped in a castle with a couple of giants."

Jordan pressed the accelerator as they approached a hill. "We're a lot like humans, if you ignore our diet of Englishmen."

She grinned. "Yes, but it's the human part I'm worried about."

They came around a corner and the huge house came into view. Out of the corner of his eye he saw her frown; not the response he had expected.

"Why all the grills in the windows? Surely you don't have to worry about gangs up here?"

He looked up at the house. "No, just wolves," he said without thinking.

Her glossy black hair flew as she turned to

him. "Wolves!"

"And bears, and rabbits," he responded quickly.

"Wolves and bears and rabbits! Oh, my," she laughed.

Jordan slowed as they hit the ruts of the graveled drive. "The rangers are reintroducing wolves up north of here and we don't know what it'll do to the rest of the wild animals' behavior." It sounded lame to him but she seemed willing to accept it.

He pulled around the circular drive, right up to the front steps, then got out to come around and help her, but she was already standing up. He quickly opened the trunk and pulled the heavy suitcase out, then closed it. She was looking at the door. "And why the silver artwork on the door?"

"Decorative," as well as functional, he thought. "Can I get that for you?"

She appraised him. "Yes, I'm sure you can." She handed him the bag.

"Why don't you just come inside and get comfortable? I'll . . ."

The big door opened. "Diana– " Carl was standing on the dais holding the silver door handle with a towel.

Diana looked up and smiled.

Jordan sighed inwardly. Carl had looks and a charisma that he would never match. He could write Diana off as Carl's, unless she disliked skinny boys.

Carl stood for a moment, then his good grace took over. "You must be tired; let me show you to your room. Jordan will bring your luggage." He dropped the towel, took her arm and swept her through the huge metal-clad doorway and up the stairs to the guest quarters. Jordan followed a few paces behind with the luggage, stepping to pick up the towel as he passed the doorway.

CHAPTER 13 – ECO-TOURISM

Carl paced the kitchen floor while Jordan unloaded the groceries. "Jordan, Diana smells dangerous."

Jordan gave him a disgusted look. "That's rude, Carl."

Carl paused and looked up. "No, really." Carl rubbed his hand through his golden hair. "I can smell things in a way I can't explain, ever since that first transformation."

Jordan shuddered and stopped with the groceries. "You mean to tell me that you can smell me, too?"

"Yes, of course, I can." Carl stopped pacing for a moment. "I didn't know what it was at first, but now it's part of you, like your face, or your voice."

Jordan pressed the heels of a hand against his forehead and turned away. "Jesus, Carl! Why did you have to tell me! That's . . . unnatural. I don't suppose showering helps?" He glanced at Carl as he lowered his hand.

"For a minute or two." He walked over and put

a hand on Jordan's shoulder. "Come on – it's not all that horrid. Actually, you smell quite . . . well, good, I suppose. Not so much as a woman does, but much better than the horse!" Carl grinned.

"Well, that cheers me right up." Jordan swung out from under Carl's hand and left abruptly, passing Diana on his way out.

Carl frowned and began to pace again, shaking his head, averting his eyes quickly as Diana walked in the door.

Diana looked behind at where Jordan had been a moment ago. "What's wrong with Jordan? He looks sick."

Carl looked up at her with his most charming smile. "I couldn't tell you." Which was true, technically. "He's not in a pleasant mood very often," he said, dismissing the incident.

Diana focused her long-lashed eyes on Carl. "That's strange. He's got quite a . . . dry sense of humor."

Carl considered her words for a moment, then shrugged. "So, tell me more about your task here." He leaned back against the counter and crossed one ankle over the other.

Diana started opening and closing cupboards.

Jordan won't be too happy about that, Carl thought as he watched her.

Diana answered blithely, "I made your father an offer he couldn't refuse. I can turn $500,000 worth of property and an equal initial investment in cash into millions of annual revenues in the long run by developing the property into an eco-tourism resort."

Carl watched her methodically search through the kitchen. "Why would wealthy people drive all the way up Highway 2 when they can go to Aspen and have prime shopping with their nature experience?"

"Where they drive all the way up I-70, then Highway 82, and don't get to feel like they're making a positive difference." Diana's lucid blue eyes measured him with condescension. She had found a bag of pretzels and pulled them down. "Mind if I have some?"

With a nod at the pretzels, knowing he'd receive several rounds of verbal abuse from Jordan, Carl answered, "But there's already infrastructure there."

"There wasn't when it was built." Various locks of her hair brushed her shoulders as she shook her head, a wry smile forming. "Carl, trust me, I've done feasibility research already. It will work. I've checked it all out. I just need more specifics, like an inventory of the species that can be seen on the property, some quotes from local construction companies, things like that."

Carl watched her fingers and lips almost tease the small pretzels into her mouth, then realized he was staring. "Why don't I take you to the library." He led her toward the far corner of the house. "That's as good a place as any to start. You'll probably want to go into Seattle tomorrow to meet with local businesses. And with traffic being what it is, it would probably be best if you just stay there in a hotel tonight. Why don't I have Jordan take you in? I'll get you a room."

Diana grabbed his arm and pulled him around, frowning. "Don't be ridiculous," she chided. "I've got to check out the lay of the land first and have my numbers ready before I ask for quotes."

"But surely…"

She gave him a calculating look. "You don't want me here."

"No, no, that's not it. I just have some business to take care of tonight."

"And I would be in the way?" She frowned.

"Well, to be honest, yes, you would," Carl tried to think of a more compelling reason to get her out. He would be transforming again tonight.

"Live with it. I told your father I'd get here, get the job done, and get out. That's what I plan to do. If you have a problem with that, talk to your father." She turned away from him and walked into the library, where she stood seemingly stupefied for several moments as she gazed up at row after row of books from all eras and subjects. Her jaw dropped.

Carl stepped just outside the library and opened the back door, where he found Jordan blanketing the car with a heavy cover that defended it from windblown objects. The weather report had said to expect winds overnight. He called to him. "Could you bring some..." he turned back in Diana's direction and suggested, "Coffee, tea, brandy?" She shook her head as she chewed pretzels, still looking up at the books. He turned back to Jordan, "One coffee. A French roast if you would."

* * *

Carl was looking for a book on genetics and didn't notice that Jordan had entered with the coffee until he realized Diana was staring intently at the weightlifter. He waved Jordan in, and Jordan stood by while Diana walked out. She turned at the doorway and her thick black lashes lowered as she asked Jordan, "Can you come up and help me in a few minutes?" when he nodded, she left. Carl watched the exchange with mixed feelings.

Jordan turned to face Carl. "What?" he asked.

Carl clenched his hands on his hips and stared at Jordan's implacable form. "I trust you aren't thinking about getting involved with her. She has to be out of these mountains before I alter again."

"No, really? Tell me, is the sky blue? Fucking hypocrite." He put the coffee down. "If that's all, I should get dinner started," he lowered his voice and it cut sharply as he finished, "and Diana wants me."

Carl cursed silently, then picked up the mug and paused, trying to get a grip on his emotions. He was beginning to think he'd have to go through this transformation phase with her in the house, and it terrified him. The last thing he needed was to imagine her working Jordan over for information while he was indisposed.

"God, Jordan, if I had your nerves I'd be a surgeon. Is there anything in this world that moves you?" He took a shaky sip of coffee before setting the cup down, then pulled a slim wallet from his pocket. "Take this," he spat, as he drew a card out of the wallet for one of the more expensive stores on the more expensive end of town, "and get yourself some clothing tomorrow. Oh, what the hell; redo your wardrobe – say, $2000. Some slacks, jeans, definitely shirts, maybe a tie or two..."

Diana strolled back into the room. "You're going shopping?"

Jordan jerked around to face her, his attention seemed to be drawn like a magnet to the way her blouse clung to the S-curves of her shape.

"Could you take me with you?" she continued.

Jordan turned back to Carl who gave him a hard look. "Sure," he said, staring at Carl. "I don't see why not." He turned to Diana. "What did you want?"

"Oh, a few sweaters, some jeans..."

"I meant now!" He said sharply.

"Oh! I'm sorry..." Diana leaned back slightly, looking confused for a moment, then replied, "I need you to bring my suitcase down here for me, if you could. It's quite heavy, and the wheels don't work right. I left it at the top of the stairs."

Jordan walked out before she finished, and her eyes followed him as he went.

"He's kinda weird," she observed, turning back to Carl, her big blue eyes widening. "Jordan mentioned wolves that are being relocated. How far away are they doing that?"

Carl was still off balance, trying to analyze the body language. Jordan was enough of a challenge alone, and Diana was a problem not only to interpret, but to avoid being interpreted by. If she was an entrepreneur she was likely to be very perceptive.

"Oh, perhaps 150 miles as the crow flies," he finally answered.

Her brow furrowed. "With this kind of country, you shouldn't be seeing wolves anywhere near here. They wouldn't go toward civilization, and I understand that the mountains become less and less inhabited as you go north, so that's where they would head. The animals in this region shouldn't be affected by wolves, really. Have there been any reports nearby?"

Carl was at a loss. Apparently, Jordan had started the subterfuge, but he didn't understand wolves as well as Carl, and apparently Diana, did. Carl could tell her about the bite, but if the news got back to his father, he'd have to explain why he hadn't said anything in the first place, which could unravel his carefully woven deceit. "You have an interest in wolves?"

"Oh, absolutely," She answered as a sensuous smile spread across her face. "I'm interested in turning your father's property into an eco-tourism resort, with viewing towers and high-powered telescopes. I hadn't dreamed of wolves, though. That would clinch it. Are you sure they're that far away? Maybe someone thinks they saw something near here?"

To cover his alarm and gain some time, he turned and slid open a drawer in the end table, lifting a sheet of paper from it. "Maybe you'll be interested in this," he said, holding it out to Diana. It was the book inventory of his current library on wolves and wolf-like creatures that Jordan had put on his desk this morning. She studied it, and her eyes opened wide. He took a long swallow of coffee as he watched her.

Jordan was back shortly with the suitcase. She opened it, provoking an exclamation from Carl. It was packed almost entirely with books, primarily on wolves. Diana watched him when she spoke. "This might interest you. It's all the books on the upper part of my priority list. Oh, here," she handed him a piece of paper and he scanned it intently, catching his breath at one of the titles.

"You brought the entire lupine series?" he asked, eyes wide in disbelief.

She shrugged as she leaned a delicate arm on a shelf.

"Not the whole thing. I have 'Vocalization', 'Gestures', and 'Scenting'. I'm still tracking down the others. I've always been fascinated by them. I didn't dream of being so close to them . . ." her voice trailed off as she looked intently at him, pushing him again to tell her where they were. No doubt she had noticed he'd dodged her question twice. But then, he'd noticed she had asked twice and now implied the question. He found that strange.

Carl dodged her eyes, and couldn't resist looking again at the list again, trying to suppress his excitement at books he'd been trying to get his hands on for months. Especially with the wolf showing up in the morning, he felt like he needed to understand them better.

"Where did you find these?" He forgot himself for a moment as his eyes ran eagerly over the page.

"I have a few sources who know I'm looking for scholarly books on nature, with a particular interest in wolves . . ." her voice trailed off as she stared intently into his eyes. What was she trying to find?

Carl lost himself for a moment as he re-focused on the titles eagerly. Many of the volumes would be immensely helpful in his studies of wolf behavior.

"If that's all you need me for, I have a trout to net," Jordan's voice broke in on Carl's thoughts.

"A trout to net?" Diana inquired.

"We have a farm in the back," Carl answered absently, still perusing the list. "We're beta-testing it for an associate."

Carl and Diana started an exchange of information that would have lasted long into the night if Jordan hadn't interrupted them for dinner, which was unusually spectacular. Although Jordan and Carl didn't normally dine together, they decided to do so for the sake of hospitality, and to remain aware of what each of them was saying to Diana.

"Jordan, I never knew you could cook so well," Carl commended after taking a bite of the trout.

"You never gave me the impression you'd appreciate it. Anyway, it's hard to ruin good trout."

Diana nodded, "It must be wonderful having control over the pollutants that wild fish get into."

Carl raised his eyebrows. "I'd never thought of it that way. It does taste better than the average trout, doesn't it?"

Jordan grinned mischievously. "No, it's just my experience as a chef."

"You? A chef? I don't recall seeing that in your work history." Carl looked surprised.

"Prep cook, actually, with the title of dishwasher, but I learned fast."

"It didn't work out?" Diana asked.

"Inferior appliances." Flexing his biceps subconsciously, he explained, "I can be hard on equipment."

Carl took a bite of the pilaf, chewed then spoke slowly. "Hmm... remind me to have you list all that you can do."

Jordan groaned, putting his head in his hand. "Mother of God, no more lists. I know nothing."

When Diana laughed, Jordan turned to her with a mock-serious look. "You think I'm kidding? This guy would list his unmatched socks, if I didn't hide them from him. I'm amazed at how many things can be listed – I learn something new every day." Carl laughed, finally, and the three of them spent the rest of the meal talking and appreciating Jordan's culinary skills. They had several cups of after-dinner coffee, cider in Jordan's case, before getting up from the table.

*   *   *

As Jordan cleared the dishes off the table and the other two walked down the hallway, Diana said to Carl, "He's really interesting."

Carl stopped. "Jordan?" He'd learned a lot about Jordan in the past hour.

"Yes. He hasn't had it easy, has he?"

"No, but who has? He's got flaws he managed to hide tonight. There have been times when I'd rather be stuck in a room with a mother grizzly."

"I think the feeling is mutual."

"Yes, I imagine so, but he's certainly the best man for the job." He stopped at the stairs. "Well, this is where I leave you, unless you care to sweat in a small room with me." Diana's lips parted as her dark blue eyes flared open, and Carl held up his hands, "No, no – I apologize, that's not at all what I meant. I lift weights twice a day. Maybe if I get to Jordan's size I'll get the respect I think I deserve. Do you work out?" he asked conversationally, wondering for a moment what it would be like to sweat in a small room with her.

"No," she slowly answered. "I probably should, but I get too bored. I'd rather be out with the scenery, riding a bike or a horse or something."

Carl paused, his hand on the doorknob. "I should introduce you to Daisy, then. She can take you just about anywhere up here."

"Daisy..." she paused.

"The horse. She's part Appaloosa. It's been said they can dance on a mountaintop. That's why we have her."

"That would be fantastic." She gave Carl a pleased look that immediately reminded him he was supposed to be encouraging her to leave soon. "Is Jordan busy?"

"I'm afraid so. He'll be with me for the next two hours, spotting me. But he could take you – no, you'll be in town tomorrow. After you get back?"

She beamed. "I think I'll spend the evening in the library, then, if that's all right. There's a lot to catch up on in there." Carl remained standing at the door as she left, wondering what to do about her. Her company was more than pleasant, and she was beautiful and intelligent as well. The silence of the mountains was no place for a gregarious young med student, and she could brighten the dull hours. Diana's presence wouldn't change his feelings about Jean, though. Wincing, he walked toward the weight room.

CHAPTER 14 – WASTING AWAY

In the exercise room, Carl grumbled as he folded his pants then pulled a loose tank and shorts on. "No kidding it's boring. We should have a Blu-ray player and screen in here. I could watch *Casablanca,* or *The Grey,* or the National Geographic channel – whatever."

Jordan was bench-pressing an incredible stack of weights. "You're the boss, but that'll decrease your performance. You need to concentrate on the muscle you're working for the best results." He completed his set and went to leg curls. Jordan worked his lower body while Carl worked upper, and vice versa, so they never needed the same set of weights at the same time.

"Can you prove that?" Carl asked, reaching over to turn down the music on the sound system. Jordan would count his repetitions with him, at the same time as his own, if there was no music in the background. Carl wanted to make sure he had a backup in case he lost count. It was too important to risk error.

Jordan snorted. "I don't . . . have to." His breathing was catching up with his words. "Someone else did." He waited until Carl started lifting weights before he continued repping out his own sets, at five times for every four of Carl's. He'd said once that he had composed a twenty-bar piece in his head and knew, by which bar he was in, how many reps they'd each done. "So, what happened up there?" Jordan closed his eyes as the room filled with the sound of the shuffling weights.

"You mean while I was out last night? How would I know? I might need to get a radio collar, or perhaps you should follow me – find out what I'm eating, when, where, how. Maybe the virus is mutating." Carl fell into his own rhythm as he lifted.

Jordan shuddered as he continued lifting his own weights. "Nnnno ... no. I'll track you down after the change. Hell, I'll even start looking before you change, but I don't want to be anywhere near you when you're not human. I could have killed you that first time."

Shocked, Carl dropped his weights with a heavy clunk. "You what? You never told me that!" He picked up the bar again and resumed lifting, looking at Jordan in consternation.

Jordan held his weights at halfway until Carl regained his tempo, looking impatient. "I was pissed ... and right next to a room with a wild predator. You gave me no warning whatsoever.

I mean, damn, Carl," Jordan nearly lost control of the weights in a burst of strength, then went on, "You took me downstairs, asked me to record everything I see, slipped into that room with the barred door, and started . . . changing on me. I thought you were some kind of demon, witch ... God knows what. But it sure didn't look like the reality I grew up believing in." Jordan paused, then started lifting again.

"Jesus." Carl was mortified. Though he had found the experience disorienting, he'd become accustomed to what was happening by the time he introduced Jordan to the situation, and he'd been so psyched about gathering data it hadn't occurred to him that it would be disturbing for Jordan. "I apologize. I guess that couldn't have possibly gotten us off to a good start."

"Not hardly. Keep lifting, Carl. You shouldn't be on your second set yet."

Carl was astounded. "How many did I do?"

"Eighteen, and you were lagging on the last three or four." Jordan paused for a few seconds again, then went into his third set. Jordan finished his set before Carl regained his composure.

"I was exhausted. I was sure I'd done the full set."

"You didn't have any problem yesterday," Jordan said with concern. He let his weights down gently and walked over to Carl, picking up the measuring tape and the chart. "You've lost six pounds, starting from day one of this cycle. You say you have no memory whatsoever of what happened up there?"

"No, just the ... the wolf when I woke up."

Jordan put the chart on the bench and straddled it again, tape in hand. "I look forward to the day you stop surprising me. What happened with this wolf?"

"She just–"

"She?" Jordan's hand dropped to the bench.

"Yes, it was a female."

"How'd you know it was a she-wolf?"

Carl cocked his head. "I can't rightly say. It was the way she smelled, the way she moved, I guess."

"You didn't, uh . . ." Jordan became very uncomfortable.

"I keep telling you I don't know! But she's been there every morning this cycle."

"You know they mate for life ..."

Carl gave the wall a disgusted look. "Yes, I know. This curse thing is worse than a bad drunk. But ... at least she can't slap me with a paternity suit," Carl joked, using humor to hide his concern. He rubbed his hand across his head as Jordan started taking Carl's measurements, beginning with the upper shoulders. They went through the process of recording physical findings again, and Jordan marked off each data point. Carl didn't bother even trying to look.

As Jordan made the last notation, he sighed and paused. Finally, he broke the silence. "I noticed you were off your feed at dinner."

Carl answered wearily. "I didn't know how Diana would feel about my eating several pounds of fish. I had supplements while you were gone, but I haven't adjusted to the new diet yet. It's an imposing amount of food."

Jordan gave him an incredulous stare. "You insisted yourself on getting more food, and I agreed."

Carl winced, then shrugged. "Are you going to tell me what the chart says?" He turned around.

"Thought you didn't want to know."

"I didn't, but I need to get back to the weights." Carl held out his hand for the chart.

Jordan ignored his hand. "So, start lifting."

Carl's hand remained. "Tell me."

"It's about the same."

"How close?"

"About the same--"

"Hand me that!"

Jordan passed him the chart, and Carl's stomach sank as he realized just what Jordan meant to hide from him. He had lost nearly half as many inches during the day as he lost during the night with the two transformations. He felt queasy. "Oh my God. What in the hell is going on?" He checked for an error, but couldn't find any. "Did you calibrate the tape against yourself?"

"I did this morning on three measurements. Mine haven't changed. Here," he flicked the tape over his own upper arm, snagged the end and pulled it tight. "Biceps eighteen." He released the tape.

"Jesus, I've got to check that blood sample."

Jordan clenched his fists onto the measuring tape and started folding it, the tail whipping back and forth against his arm. "You've got to eat, damn it, and you've got to work out."

Carl cradled his forehead in his hand. "Oh, come on Jordan. I can't do any more. I'm so tired of working out, and I'm just not hungry enough."

"If you work out, you'll get hungry, you idiot! Too bad there's no place to swim. Across a small lake and back a few times, you could dispense with the weights, and you'd be hungry enough when you got back to eat a whole rack of prime rib. Of course, at this time of year, you'd also have hypothermia."

"Who knows? Maybe werewolves don't get hypothermia." Carl surreptitiously glanced at the door. Even when they didn't have a guest they avoided using that word for fear of getting in the habit and being overheard. It also appeared to make Jordan queasy. "Hey, I'm sorry about the kitchen," he said, changing the subject quickly to distract Jordan.

"What? What's wrong with the kitchen?" Jordan stood up in alarm. "What did you do – you didn't move things around again, did you? I know you didn't eat anything, though it'd be a blessing if you did.

"No, it's Diana. I told her to make herself at

home, and I forgot to mention the kitchen . . . uh . . . rules."

Jordan's face turned to stone. A difficult task, Carl thought, when it normally seemed chiseled out of topaz anyway.

"I'll have to check it out," Jordan said angrily. He looked at his watch. "And after that, I'm on break. Keep lifting. And count your reps, dammit!" He strode from the room.

Carl turned and hefted the bar again. He had noticed that Jordan kept a running tally in his head, always, of exactly how much food there was in the kitchen, and roughly how much in the pantry. Carl could take food without it bothering Jordan as long as Jordan was notified, but when food disappeared behind Jordan's back it could put him in a black mood for hours.

Carl checked his watch; he still had an hour before he needed to leave the house for his last night of transformation this month. He had hoped to talk to Jordan about coming after Carl without making Diana suspicious, but Jordan would know what to do.

CHAPTER 15 – KEEPING SECRETS

Diana climbed the stairs half an hour later. Even though he'd mentioned that he was trying to build his physique, it was suspicious that Carl went off on long runs at night the past few evenings – and that he was up early in the morning coming back from an intense outdoor exercise session again the next morning. It seemed to fit with her suspicions, but she couldn't be sure yet.

She saw that Jordan's door was cracked open, a light, twanging metallic sound coming from inside. Curious, she tapped at the door, and it opened further to show Jordan reclining, eyes closed, on a plain bed, covers rumpled. Jordan had his broad shoulders and his head against the wall, one leg bent to help keep his body upright. His hands wrapped around the body of a red electric guitar, from which the barely audible twanging came. She heard only the sounds of the naked strings without the boost from the amp – only

Jordan could hear this through his headphones which were connected to the small box that the guitar was also plugged into. The amazing thing was the face; it wasn't his. At least, not the one she'd come to recognize from the short time she'd known him.

The furrow between his eyebrows had disappeared; his dark, slightly open lips were fuller, more sensuous. The tightness she thought was permanent in his jawline was gone entirely. He was a handsome man when he wasn't wearing his usual expressions of anger, frustration, irritation, suspicion, and skepticism. His eyes had never smiled, but with them closed he seemed lost in the bliss of a sound only he could truly hear. She tried to make out the tune, listening carefully to the faint twanging of the unamplified metal strings. She remembered the words first: "I close my eyes, only for a moment and the moment's gone..." then, to her surprise, he opened his eyes and leaned over to reach a knob, but his movement was arrested when he saw her staring at him. His arm remained for a moment in midair as he appraised her, then he turned away and made the adjustment, removed the headphones from his head and put them on the amp.

When his face came back around it was hard again. She was about to leave but he motioned her to a pillow lying on the floor. Other than the bed, several pillows on the floor, a nightstand with a radio alarm clock and a glob of clay presently affixed to the wall in a flattened lump (by the myriad blotches on the wall she suspected he threw it around a bit) there was nothing in the room. Even the wardrobe, half open, was well-organized but virtually empty. There was no dresser.

She realized he was staring at her and waiting, so she sat down on the pillow he had gestured at. He continued staring. "This is my break," he said finally. "By state law, an employee gets fifteen minutes for every four hours. I take it in a lump sum, an hour and a half a day, every evening. The door's usually locked, but it hasn't recovered from the last slam I gave it."

He was still staring, and she felt rather uncomfortable, as if caught in an act of voyeurism. "I'm sorry, I didn't know. I've interrupted. I should leave," she said, rising to her feet and turning to the door.

He was silent for a moment before he spoke. "That would depend. Are you work or pleasure?"

Diana spun around. His eyebrows had drawn together and his lips had narrowed further. Something that she couldn't identify drew her to the weightlifter, though she knew she didn't dare get involved with either of the men. She'd been sent to scout out the werewolf pack so they could be executed. She'd begun to suspect that there was another, right under her nose, but she wasn't sure yet.

She weighed his question as his eyes passed over her body like she was a painting at the Louvre. "I'd like to think I'm not work, but I ... I'm ... not sure if I want to call myself pleasure ..."

Jordan's head snapped back almost as if he'd been slapped. "I'm sorry. I'm not a good host, and that was rude. If you sit down, I'll try to be ... decent." He unplugged the headphones and smiled with half of his face, then shook his head. "I wouldn't blame you if you left."

She wasn't sure it was wise, but she had a job to do, so she returned to sit down. He motioned at the door and she closed it with the toe of her shoe, thinking she could scream, if she had to, before he could get to her. She was pretty sure Carl was a decent man, though what else he was remained to be seen. Jordan's hands were straying to the frets again as if he were unable to stop them, and she recognized the song this time.

"'Dust in the Wind,'" she said.

He nodded. "It's all I know." He continued playing while she watched and listened.

She watched his face began to relax again until she spoke. "Is the guitar all you own?"

Eyes closed, he nodded. "I try not to own things. They break."

She watched his hand change position with the chords as his right hand plucked strings with alternate fingers, like a dance. "And the guitar?" The music was still quiet, but distinct now.

"From a friend." His face continued to fall into

softer contours.

"He didn't want it anymore?" She asked.

Jordan didn't answer until he had segued into "Love Song" by The Cure. "He broke." She was watching his face when he said it and would have missed the slight clenching of jaws if she hadn't been looking for clues to his thoughts.

Jordan's eyes opened and he gave her a wry smile. "Like classical?" he asked.

She nodded slowly.

He adjusted the dial on the amp with a wry grin. "This is the closest thing I've got," he said, and launched into "Classical Gas". It sounded excellent up to the point in the piece where the orchestra normally took over. His fingers grappled with the fretboard, trying to get all of the notes in, and fumbled slightly. He watched his hands intently, then went into quick arpeggios, knuckles turning white. He shook his head with frustration, his lips thinned past visibility, and he put the guitar down.

"Giving up so easily?" She asked with a smile.

He looked startled, as if he'd forgotten she was there. "Uh, just ... my father was a perfectionist. He tried to beat it into me, and sometimes I think he succeeded."

He looked over at her then, his eyes an open window into a pain that looked as ancient as time itself. "Diana ..." he said slowly, then stopped.

"What?" She asked, puzzled by the change in

his demeanor. He had a primal quality, but she'd also noticed his mind was sharper than she expected in a man that seemed to live for nothing but bodybuilding, judging by the size of his muscles.

He looked into her eyes for quite some time, then looked down. When he looked up again his expression was a closed door. "What are you doing here?" He looked like the same Jordan that had picked her up at the station.

"First, tell me why you lied," she said with her most charming smile, buying a moment to think. She wondered how much he might have figured out about her. She arranged her body to show off her hips and legs.

Jordan raised his eyebrows, undistracted by her posture. *Damn,* she thought, *That usually works.* She tried to smile warmly, "You know quite a few songs."

He looked at the guitar, then turned back to her with a lopsided smile. "Oh . . . " he said mischievously, "I didn't lie, I was just speaking metaphorically. That flaw apparently didn't get beaten out of me." His eyebrows drew down further. He was leaning on his side now, and she felt his eyes wander over her body again. "Why are you here?" He asked bluntly.

She leaned back against the wall and nodded. "I'm here to see the lay of the property, what kind of animals can be expected to pass through, and how often. Viability for ecotourism and potential profit margins, after getting quotes for the work that would need to be done." She hoped that providing some details on her cover story would increase his confidence in her. Both Jordan and Carl were wary of her, and she had too much work to do out in the woods, hunting down the werewolves that were in this area. She was the hunter here, and she needed to make sure she didn't become prey.

CHAPTER 16 – HANDLING IT

The next morning Jordan's bare feet padded softly down the hallway. He paused at Diana's door to listen but heard nothing. It was five a.m., so he wasn't surprised, but he felt safer knowing he wouldn't have to deal with her as he got things ready to track Carl down. Carl had left the house in the evening, with black sweats on that would be easy to hide in the bushes when he changed. Jordan stepped silently down the stairway and into the kitchen. He set a pot of fresh juice, honey, and spices on the stove to heat. He'd packed the saddlebags the night before to avoid making enough noise in the kitchen to wake Diana up. He had grown accustomed to simply getting up and going out to find Carl in the morning, and Diana's presence was an intrusion to his schedule. Having prepared thoroughly the night before, while she was upstairs in her room, there was nothing to do now but wait for the juice to heat. He stared at the pot of liquid, willing it to boil. His jaw set slowly, and he finally reached for the thermos and set it on the counter without making a sound.

Restless, he went to the closet where he had placed a pair of socks and his boots. He pulled his gun down from its hidden perch on the upper ledge, put the socks and boots on, then, checking to see that the magazine was full, he slipped the gun back in the holster and strapped it to his chest before putting his coat on over it. He returned to the kitchen and poured the now-hot cider into the thermos, tossing several scoops of whey protein powder in as well, then sealed it and shook it before stepping softly across the slate-tiled entry to grasp the silver doorknob. Turning it slowly, he opened the door and stepped outside, carefully closing it behind him. As he headed toward the stable, he heard something move along the edge of the tree line. He pulled the gun from its holster, switched the safety off, drew the slide back, and released it to load the chamber as he crept quietly toward whatever creature stirred in the bushes, pressing the floodlight control as he passed the garage. He heard a groan and started running, lowering the gun so it pointed down and away from himself. As he neared the trees he saw the naked body and swore.

He dropped to his knees next to the man. "Carl!"

Carl rolled over slowly, gasping in pain. He was naked, pale and covered with goosebumps in the chill of the early morning.

Jordan watched in shock as Carl's hand fluttered across a deep wound in his upper thigh. Blood seeped from the ragged hole, painting a brick-red path down his leg. Jordan couldn't tell if there was a rhythm or not, which would indicate an artery, but he was grateful to see the blood seeping slowly. "Carl – talk to me! What happened?" Jordan put the gun back in its holster while Carl's eyes rolled slowly upward and he collapsed against Jordan.

"Shit!" Jordan swore, then peeled Carl's eyelids back to look into his pupils, which contracted slightly in the shadowy light. Jordan whipped off his shirt and tied it around Carl's leg. He checked Carl quickly for broken bones, then rolled him onto his side so he could lift him.

Carl stirred again. "Jordan," he rasped. "Put me in the car, get some clothes, and . . . drive me down. I've lost... a lot of blood. I don't ... know how much time I've got. An ambulance will . . . take too long." Jordan paused to take a deep breath, then went to the car and carefully set Carl down in the passenger seat. "And–"

"I got it! Shut up and stop moving!" Jordan barked, trying to control his panic. The blood seemed to pulse with every word Carl said. Sprinting to the back door of the house, Jordan grabbed a towel and some clothes from the laundry. He ran back and Carl tried to take the items from him, but it seemed that the pain stopped him. Jordan growled, then pulled a pair of shorts on over Carl's legs and pressed the folded towel over the wet shirt that was already covering the small, round hole in Carl's thigh. Then he pulled his belt off quickly and slid it around Carl's leg, moving the end around to the front and holding the buckle against the towel as he slipped the end through the buckle and drew hard on it, to press the bundle tightly against the broken vessels. Without the belt that held his wide-legged jeans up he felt even more naked, on top of being shirtless. Jordan hated being naked, the feeling of being exposed and vulnerable, but Carl needed the belt more right now than he did. He got Carl to the car, jumped in the driver's seat and tore down the gravel road toward town.

*   *   *

At the hospital, one of the women at the desk was already busy filling out forms for a very pregnant woman, but her coworker looked up at him.

"Is this for you yourself?" She asked as she reached for a form.

"No, it's my. . . friend. They just took him into surgery."

"Can I get your friend's name, sir?"

Jordan leaned over the desk, whispering. "Carl . . . Carl Sanders."

She looked up in surprise. "Carl's here?"

"Can we just keep that between you and me?"

"Naturally, sir, we don't announce when any of the family is here for treatment." She typed the details into her computer and glanced at the patient status. "I guess that explains why he's headed to surgery already. Should I call his father?"

"No, I'll do that. He'll want . . . more details."

She began a series of what Jordan considered inane questions 'for the record,' one being Jordan's full name and relationship to the patient. Jordan's answers came out in exasperated breaths.

An alert blinked on her computer screen and she shook her head. "Give me just one second – I need to double check his file." She nervously ran her fingers over the keyboard, and, after a few clicks, he saw her eyes widen with concern. "Oh no."

"What is it?"

"He's O-positive."

"So? ...What?" Jordan blurted out.

"We're out of all O-positive blood. There was a big wreck on Highway 2 yesterday, as well as a number of people who suffered an unexplained blood loss. We used what we had in multiple surgeries and the bank won't deliver more until three today. We'll have to find immediate donors. What blood type are you?"

Jordan stared at her for a moment. "Are you sure he needs blood?"

She gave him an exasperated look. "With that

kind of wound of course he does. What type are you?"

"O-negative."

"Universal donor, perfect! How would you feel about saving your friend's life?"

Jordan felt fingers crawling up his spine. "You mean ... let someone slide a needle into one of my veins?"

Tilting her head, she sized him up. "Well... only if you want him to live."

Jordan crossed his arms tightly over his chest. "Where do I have to go?"

"Down the hall and to the left. Go to the desk, someone there will be able to do your intake and get things started."

Jordan soon found himself in a room where an attractive young woman with short, strawberry blond hair had him sit down and give her his name and date of birth.

She smiled at Jordan as he sat in a chair equipped for blood donation. She quickly had him lying down and hooked up to a plastic bag. She handed him a sheet of paper with a list of questions.

"I have to ask you these questions verbally as well as having you look at the sheet," she smiled, and her smooth cheeks revealed a dimple.

"I'm on file as a donor. My blood's been tested already," Jordan interjected.

Looking back at the records on her computer, she replied, "Ah... I see that. Looks like it's been about six months since you were screened. And anyway, we have to ask these questions every time. Protocol, you know?"

Jordan nodded.

"Have you ever had sex with someone known to test positive for H.I.V?"

Jordan paused and studied the shape of her face, her breasts, her hips, wishing the girl's scrubs were a little more form-fitting since he could tell she was hiding a fit figure beneath them. "No. Is there someone less attractive who could ask me these questions? An ugly man... anything?" Jordan asked playfully, in an attempt to release some of his tension. Aside from Diana – and the lady at the registration desk – this girl was the only woman he'd seen in months.

She blushed "No. Have you had sex with a member of the same or opposite sex since the last time you were screened as a blood donor?"

"No," he admitted. "Not for too damned long," he answered.

Her face turned red and she gave him an admonishing look. "Okay. Let me have your arm."

Jordan lifted his arm to her. She swabbed it, waited briefly for the alcohol to evaporate, slid the needle into his vein, set up his IV and left the room, but walked back through the door a short while later.

"Wow! It's a good thing I came back so soon. You've almost filled that bag already."

He grinned at her again, but she was reaching

for a clamp and didn't notice.

"Well, this ought to do it. They've given him plasma already, of course, but his RBC count is way down as well, so they'll be needing blood." She clamped the tube and drew the needle from his arm, placing a cotton ball on the tiny puncture and gave him the usual instructions on after care.

"Don't I get a cookie or something?"

Her dimple reappeared again as the sides of her mouth curled upward. "That's the blood bank. This is a hospital. Cafeteria's that way, if you're interested." She pointed down the corridor disappearing through the door with the blood. Jordan's body didn't care for blood donation, and it usually left him weaker and dizzier than he thought it should, so he gingerly moved himself to a padded bench from the donor chair, taking a moment to regain his bearings. After a few minutes the girl returned.

Jordan inquired, "Is he all right?"

She smiled reassuringly. "Your friend's got the best doctor here working on him. I just handle blood samples and IVs but it looks like they've got everything under control."

It was the third time Carl had been referred to as his friend. He wasn't sure if it was an appropriate word, but it seemed the safest way to describe why he was here.

Jordan left the blood donation room and made his way to the surgical waiting area. He had flipped through every magazine twice by the time someone came out to see him.

"You're the man who came in with Carl?"

Jordan dropped the magazine and jumped to his feet. An older man in scrubs, covered by a loose, white coat stood before him.

"I'm Doctor Balboa, his surgeon. He's going to be fine. We removed the bullet and we have him in recovery now. He was lucky – it nearly hit an artery. We'll move him to his own room as soon as he's awake. We have express orders on how to handle an emergency for anyone in the family, so he'll be in a fully private room once he's ready, and you can see him then. What I need to talk to you about, however, is how this happened." The man looked at Jordan sternly, and Jordan felt his face grow hot. "How did he end up with a bullet in his thigh, and wearing nothing but shorts in this weather?"

Knowing how gossip could fly in a small town, Jordan was glad the waiting room was empty. "He went out early this morning to run and when I went out to see what was up I found him lying in the bushes with a bullet in his leg. That's all I know."

The doctor shook his head. "It was a lead nose bullet. They're designed for maximum damage. Usually used for deer hunting. I see it every so often during hunting season, when someone shoots without checking to see whether he's actually got a deer in his sights or something else entirely. Like his hunting partner. Have you reported this?"

"Not yet. I was too worried about Carl."

The doctor pursed his lips. "I'll have to report it, you know. Any suspicion of criminal activity has to be reported by the physician who treats it. Whoever shot him probably realized he'd shot a person instead of a deer and took off running. He might get a case of conscience in a few days and come in to report it, but the police will want to ask a few questions and investigate the area where you found him."

"Of course. I'll be glad to help any way I can." From what Carl had said, he was most likely in wolf form when he was shot, and beyond that it was unlikely they'd seen anything. If they had, they wouldn't be believed if they talked about it.

The doctor nodded. "Good."

One of the young men who wheeled Carl into surgery when they first arrived entered the waiting area. "Your pal's been moved to 215. He's come around and he's responding well."

The doctor looked alarmed. "On whose orders? He can't possibly be ready to be moved! Come with me." He strode away from Jordan, the younger man following quickly after him.

"He responded thoroughly, fully awake, procedure says..." the voice trailed off as the two took a sharp left out of the waiting room.

Jordan went to the desk. "Carl's in 215?"

The attendant looked up at him. "Why don't

we give the doctor a moment alone with him and I'll let you know when you can go up."

Jordan nodded and sat down.

*   *   *

Carl was looking right at the door when Jordan walked in. Jordan stopped short when he saw the accommodations. *So this is how the other half lives,* he thought with disgust. It was still a hospital room, but it had a huge pull-out couch in the corner along with a double-sized oak closet next to a mirror and vanity, over which hung Hollywood dressing room style bulbs. A 60-inch flat screen T.V. stared at him from the wall opposite Carl, and there was a control panel on a metal arm at Carl's side.

"Pleasant, isn't it?"

"You even convalesce in style man."

"I plan to convalesce at home."

Jordan shook his head. "You just had a lead-nosed bullet taken out of you and you have a pint of someone else's blood and a bunch of fresh plasma in your veins. You're not going anywhere."

"I beg to differ. I feel fine. Apparently my recuperative powers are beyond those of mortal men," he joked cheerfully.

"That's probably the morphine talking."

Carl shrugged, then looked serious. "I'm hoping you can help me out a bit here, Jordan. I don't want to be here. We have a guest I don't trust at the house, I'm doing quite well, and I need to leave before they take any blood tests."

"Didn't they do that already?"

"I don't know and I don't want to find out. As far as I can tell, standard typing and chemical tests will reveal nothing. As long as they don't put the blood under a microscope I'm fine, but there are some strange cells in my blood that might make them suspicious. You'll be answering the phone for the next week just in case. Switch the landline to voicemail when you're out. I'm leaving; they can't keep me."

"Okay, but you'd better do something about that I.V. first." Jordan shook his head in exasperation, then turned away. "You're the boss. You'll need to make a statement to the police, though, and they may want to question me."

"Yes, they told me that. I'll try to spare you – after all, you weren't there. Neither was I, exactly, but I'll tell them what they want to hear. Have you said anything yet?"

Jordan turned back toward Carl. "Just that you went out for a jog this morning, and when I went out to check on you I found you like that."

"Good. Perfect. I'll sort it out from there."

"By the way, what did happen to you out there?"

Carl frowned, his lips pursed. "Hmmm, I can't rightly say, but I recall an excruciating pain in my leg, then a foggy kind of run through the trees. I remember an urgent need to get back to the house, but it was more like a den – you know how things aren't always what they should be in dreams; it's like that. There was something crashing through the brush behind me for a short while and ... and I ... was on four legs." Carl paused, surprised. "I had a tail! Jordan ... I remember! Well, in a way ..."

Jordan's face contorted into a grimace.

"Never mind that for now," Carl said quickly. "Could you get me something to eat? I'm famished!"

Jordan acted as if he was going to say something, then turned around and left.

Carl watched him go, his mind racing for a moment, but he could remember no more about the wolf-dream. He turned to the IV unit attached to his arm and read the label. A moment later he pressed the button for the nurse. The young man who had brought the doctor in earlier came into the room less than thirty seconds later.

"Yes, Mr. Sanders?"

Carl knew other patients had to wait a while for a response and it irritated him that he was so coddled. "What do I have to do to get out of here?"

The young man looked puzzled. "Well, you should stay for a while yet – that's a serious wound you have, and you were under anesthesia far too recently."

"But I've been given antibiotics?" he questioned, motioning to the IV.

"Of course."

"So, what could happen?"

"Well . . . there could be complications with the donated blood or plasma, there could be a clot, the wound could start bleeding again–"

Carl sighed loudly. "Did you use refrigerated blood or fresh stuff?"

He paused. "I'm afraid we had to use fresh. We prefer to avoid that, but your type is rare and we had a universal donor we determined was highly reliable." He smiled. "Don't worry, Mr. Sanders. It's perfectly safe. We would never have used it otherwise."

"Okay then. I have an assistant, he can keep an eye on me and if anything happens I can be here in less than an hour."

"I can't make that decision. Talk to the doctor–"

"I'll do that."

A few minutes later Doctor Balboa walked into the room. "What's this I hear about you wanting to leave?"

"I make a poor patient and I'd rather be at home."

"Well, normally, I'd say that any patient who wants out is just about ready to leave but this is too quick. You just came out of surgery, and the anesthesiologist doesn't feel that you should be walking around yet."

"I know what signs to watch for ..."

"You're not a doctor yet, Carl. Don't try to act

like one." Dr. Balboa folded his arms and frowned down at Carl.

Carl shook his head. "I've got more sense than that, but you know how much better a person's own home is for a quick recovery, and I have Jordan."

"But he's not a nurse, is he?" the doctor answered, implacably.

"I don't need a nurse, I need rest. And I don't need what's in this IV."

"Yes you do. That's your antibiotic. After the IV's done I'll put you on oral antibiotic and some painkillers and reassess your progress. Talk to the police officer who's on his way, let the drip finish, and we'll see how you feel then." Doctor Balboa strode from the room, ending the conversation abruptly.

CHAPTER 17 – NOSING AROUND

Diana woke a little after 7:00 a.m. to find the house empty. Seizing the opportunity, she moved quickly through the manor to dig for clues. Ever since her commander, Jean, had directed her to find the crystal skull, she'd felt like she finally had a purpose in life. Jean had said there were records kept in the skull somehow, and given instructions on how to pull information out of it. She'd learned that a pack of werewolves were living in the Cascade Mountains north of Highway 2, just outside of Baring. She'd taken an alias while Jean negotiated with the man who owned what they referred to as a cabin. Jean had worked quickly to convince the man who owned it that Diana was the perfect person to do a market analysis for real estate development, appealing to his charitable nature after receiving a full bio from her team. That Diana had clinched the deal was impressive, considering how little she knew about real estate before accepting this campaign. She was told she was chosen because she resembled a woman whose images were buried deep in the skull, in case she ran into the man they'd stolen it from. The woman was important, somehow, and if she had an opportunity to pass as her she might be able to fool them long enough to get access to their lair. She'd had to change the color of her eyes, but aside from that she was a pretty good match.

When she'd first learned his son was staying in the house it worried her, but it was clear now that there was something of interest going on here, right where she was staying, and she wanted to get to the bottom of it. If she found the pack but missed a stray in the house where she was staying she'd never get another assignment.

She quickly rifled through the drawers in the huge master bedroom, looking for anything that would tell her more about Carl. She had noticed earlier during her stay that the door handles, from outside, were all silver, and he never touched them. It could be a coincidence or it could be a clue. What was she looking for? Fur? She had no idea and everything in this room looked perfectly normal. Clothes, books, a razor... she made sure she put everything back exactly as she'd found it, then went to Jordan's room.

The closet had shelves with very few clothes folded and stacked. Spare boots. The guitar. She moved to the nightstand and found the top drawer locked. There had to be something in there he was hiding. Pulling a small packet of tools from her back pocket she sat beside the drawer and set her ear to it as she teased the rotating tumblers into motion, listening for the hollow sound that said they'd aligned. She slid a thin blade between the drawer and the desktop, feeling around to determine how the mechanism worked. She thought she heard the tumblers fall into place and tugged the drawer, but it was still locked. She tried again. After several false attempts and more probing, she heard a different snap, and when she tugged on the drawer it slid right out. Inside there was nothing but a handgun, a spare magazine, and several boxes of bullets. She was astonished to see that they appeared to be a type that would explode on impact. With such bullets, this would be a wicked weapon. She wasn't even sure explosive ammunition was legal for street use. What was Jordan worried about? Regular bullets would be sufficient for most intruders. He seemed to be expecting something more dangerous. She slid the drawer closed and rolled the tumblers to lock it, but not before she memorized the combination.

From there she went to the basement; the lab was the next obvious place to tour. She wanted to find out what was on the computer. Carl's system upstairs had been password protected but maybe the one downstairs was open for convenience.

She listened at the front door as she passed, unsure of how much time she had... or where Carl and Jordan were exactly. Perhaps another early morning workout session outside? Those two were obsessed with their physiques, though Carl was clearly new at the fitness game.

She stepped into the white, sterile room and stood in front of the computer, bumping the mouse to wake the computer up. Immediately she saw images that looked like cells viewed through a microscope. She had no idea what any of it meant but that wasn't what she was interested in anyway. She slid a nearby stool over and sat down while she looked through the files on the desktop. There was a shortcut to a file folder named "biometrics." In it were many images like the one on the screen when she arrived, along with spreadsheets with temperatures, weights, and other biometric details. She opened a document simply called "data," and her jaw dropped as she saw that the date on the folder was shortly after the date specified in the file as a wolf bite. It looked like Carl believed something happened when the wolf bit him, which confirmed her growing suspicion. Further down the page, a journal entry about a visit from the game warden, noting that a local rancher believed his cow had been killed by a wolf. He hadn't said anything about that when she'd asked. On another line it stated there was a wolf present when he woke up in the morning, and the area he'd been in when he woke up. She made note of it so she could search the area later, then opened the spreadsheet and checked the dates. Flurries of data, three nights a month, with a 28-day cycle. Every evening at nearly the same time until day-light-saving time shifted it by an hour. The fol-lowing day, there was less data in the morning, more as the time wore on. Problematic weight loss, most intense on the three days of the full moon.

"Damn," She whispered. She checked the measurements and confirmed both the weight and girth of the torso, arms, and legs all pointed to Carl being the subject. This was it, proof that Carl was being affected by the cycle of the moon, and it had started when he was bitten by a wolf. She pulled a USB drive out of her pocket and cop-ied the entire directory onto it. There were others that would be able to get more knowledge from all of this. It might give them an edge in future hunts. This one was nearly over now; it shouldn't take long to find the pack, especially once she could use the horse to track them down. She knew they were close.

She went back upstairs to get the gun out of Jordan's nightstand. She might well need that if they figured out what she was really doing there. Jordan already seemed suspicious. She checked to see that the safety was on and grabbed the gun, along with a box of ammo, then slid the drawer closed, rolling the tumblers with her thumb to relock the drawer. Now she was committed to action before he found out his gun was gone. If she had to kill him it might be wise to bleed him first; it had been difficult to find humans to feed on in such a remote area, and she'd had to eat more food to compensate for the loss her body felt.

She needed to call Jean, but first, while Jordan and Carl were still gone, she wanted to find out if there was any other information in the library. The last time she'd been in the room she'd thought they were just two young men who were going to be underfoot while she tracked down the pack, but she knew better now. She wanted to see if there were any other journals, aside from what was on the computer, and, more importantly, records of other people, other werewolves. She had a chance to prove herself, and she wanted as much information as she could get her hands on. Was he connected to the pack? Would they come to the house at some point and make her job easier? Surely they were connected. Werewolves didn't spring from the ether.

So Carl was a werewolf. Was Jordan? It seemed unlikely, as there were no records matching Jordan's weight and size. That didn't necessarily mean he wasn't one, she realized. And Jordan was obviously involved. He was protecting Carl at a bare minimum. Could she win him over to her own side? What if he found out what she was? Most people associated her type with the devil. She should find out what his religious views were before she said too much.

She rifled through the drawers of the desk looking for notebooks, address books, anything. It looked like Carl kept everything on the computer. She should go back downstairs and check for names, phone numbers, addresses. She hadn't thought to do that. She wished she had a bigger thumb drive.

CHAPTER 18 – CONVALESCING

Carl limped out of the hospital on crutches less than a half an hour later. He stopped to see if anyone was looking and quickly switched legs, realizing he'd been pretending to favor the wrong one. He managed to get that mistake past Jordan who continued to walk toward the car.

"How'd you get out so quickly?" Jordan asked as he stepped toward the back of the car.

"I ran them out of excuses and made an incredible ass of myself. They say doctors make poor patients, but apparently med students can be just as bad. Oh no—" Carl exclaimed, stopping abruptly by the back end of the car. He set the crutches down and dropped into a crouch.

"Carl! You all right?" Jordan rushed over to him.

"Jordan! Look at what you did to the paint!"

"Paint? You son-of-a-bitch, you scared the shit out of me!"

Carl looked up at him. "You'll have to get a touch-up. This is horrible. Nicks all over." He appraised the fender. "Have you been scrubbing the wheel wells?"

"I'll scrub your fucking nose off your god-damned face. Get in the car." Jordan swung the passenger door open.

"You'll have to take it in, you know," Carl stated reproachfully as he stepped into the car.

Jordan closed the passenger door and went around the car to the driver's side. "I was in a bit of a hurry when I left the house." He started the car and pulled out of the parking spot.

"Watch out for the pothole!"

Jordan avoided the pothole and looked over at Carl. "Would you like your glasses?"

"Actually, I... Oh. That's odd."

"Your vision?"

"Yes."

"Sure as hell is. You're normally blind as a bat without your contacts or your glasses. I brought your glasses but I forgot about that and you never asked for them. And your leg is obviously not hurting," Jordan pointed to the way Carl had his right leg slung over the wounded left thigh. "What's the deal?"

"I don't know," Carl answered, trying to resist the urge to look at the wound.

"You recuperated awfully fast." Jordan turned onto the highway.

"Yes, I noticed that, which is probably what distracted me enough that I hadn't thought about my vision. I forgot that I didn't have my contacts in."

They continued in silence as Carl rubbed his chin.

Jordan cut through the quiet. "You know I had to give blood for you? The hospital staff told me I was saving your life. You hardly look like a man on your deathbed."

"I suppose not. Oh, by the way, you remember the blood tests we ran two weeks ago?"

"Yeah," Jordan answered as he shifted down to go around a tight curve. "You said we'd run more in two weeks," Jordan confirmed.

"Very good. I just thought I'd warn you."

Jordan scowled. "I just gave you a pint!"

"Why, thank you. I shouldn't need any more blood from you, actually, but I could use a hand in the lab. I've already set up the tests and I'd like to dictate my observations."

"Great. Now I'm a secretary."

"That was in the job description," Carl answered as he succumbed to temptation, slid his jeans down and peeled the edge of the bandage back. He stared at it for a moment, then looked up. "Pull over, Jordan."

Jordan eased the car over to the shoulder of the road.

"Take a look at this," Carl continued, looking at the wound.

Jordan tried to keep his eyes on the road, scowled, then pulled the brake handle before leaning over to gape. There were several seconds of silence as they looked at the fresh pink scar tissue where the bullet wound had been.

Jordan finally spoke. "What does the doctor think of that?

"He neglected to check it before I left. He'd only bandaged it a short while earlier and it hadn't bled through. I lied to him, told him the nurse had looked at it and it looked fine. I was trying to get out of there."

Jordan looked up at Carl. "Other than that, how do you feel?"

"Like I could run a marathon. I had to fake that limp. I'm ravenous, though. Could you stop at the store?"

Jordan looked up. "We've got food at home."

"I'm hungry now. Just swing into Rosie's, I'll get a couple of roast beef sandwiches and some bread."

"Bread! What's with the bread?"

"It sounds good. Humor me."

"I'd be glad to. Bread... " Jordan shook his head, hit the turn signal and pulled back onto the highway.

They picked up the food on their way and Carl ate voraciously through the half-hour trip home from there.

When they walked into the house Jordan saw Diana came jogging out of the living room and down the hall to meet them, but she stopped halfway, looking at Carl. "What's up?" she asked stiffly.

"Just getting back from a little jaunt," Carl answered.

"Well," she smiled nervously, "I've been cooped up in the house all morning. I think I need to go for a walk."

Jordan nodded and watched her swift departure. He went into the den, where Carl was typing notes into the computer.

"Too bad I don't have a vision chart. I believe I'm twenty-twenty right now, but I'd like to check. Tell me, can you read this?" Carl got up and placed a magazine on the windowsill, then backed off. "I mean the third line, there to the left."

Jordan stood next to him. "Yes."

"How about below, under the picture?"

"Mmm, it looks like... something about... bacteria?"

"Uh huh. What's your vision Jordan? Is it twenty-twenty?"

"Last I checked."

After a moment Carl asked, "Where's Diana?"

"She left."

"She left... really... " Carl tapped his fingers against his elbows. "Jordan, do you think... is it possible she's... a werewolf?"

Jordan eased into the chair next to Carl's at the computer. "That seems pretty unlikely. She's a real estate developer and she's also a werewolf who coincidentally ends up here? I doubt it. What makes you think so?"

"There's something about her that's off. I'm trying to place it. It alarms me, but maybe it's just that I'm recognizing my own kind. I've never met any. It's nothing I can put my finger on, but I thought maybe I was picking up on something."

"And there's been a female wolf when you wake up—"

"After I've changed back. So... if she were that werewolf, she should have changed back by then as well. If she's a werewolf, she's not *that* wolf. Unless, somehow the curse plays out differently in different people... I hadn't thought of that... What would that mean?" Carl started pacing.

Jordan found that thought extremely disturbing. If what little they knew about this virus, or whatever it was, only applied to Carl, then they would have no clue what to expect from any other werewolf they might run into. If they ever did. "I'll keep an eye on her, see how she responds to other things that affect you. Maybe there's something that will give us a clue. If she's a werewolf like you, she shouldn't be able to open the silver-plated door handles by herself, and she's had no problem with that."

Carl nodded. "And she's not much of a meat-eater, though she goes through a lot of carbs." Carl sat down in his chair and began to enter these facts on the computer's notepad.

Carl paused, his hands perched over the keyboard, then stood up and started pacing back and forth again. "What if these specific traits are unique to me? We have a sample size of only one. That hardly counts as useful data in the scientific community. We're assuming all werewolves are identical to me. But a virus that kills its host is an unsuccessful one, evolution favors a non-lethal parasitic relationship. Perhaps I'm the rare failure, and other werewolves have a different set of symptoms."

"Still, if she's part wolf, wouldn't Daisy be afraid of her?"

"That's it!" Carl said excitedly. "Get her in the stall with the horse. If Daisy throws a fit we'll have reason to confront her."

"And if not?" Jordan asked.

Carl stopped pacing and frowned, one hand in his back pocket and the other on his chin. "It won't be conclusive. You can't prove a negative." He paced back and forth several times, then said, more quietly, "If she's not a werewolf, maybe she's some kind of cryptozoological hunter of some sort. Or a religious fanatic who hunts down demons. We'll have to make sure we don't reveal my identity."

"Oh, Christ, Carl!" Jordan exploded. "You mean her ruse may be that she's here to kill you?"

"Or exorcise me," Carl continued dispassionately. "Not that there's much difference, from what I hear." Carl kept pacing.

"How can you let her stay in this house if she's here to kill you?"

Carl grimaced. "We don't know that's what

she is. More likely than not, if she's not being entirely honest she's actually just checking up on me on my father's orders."

"Hardly a pure motive."

Carl shrugged. "He's my father. He's entitled to his concern. I just wish it didn't interfere quite so much with my research." Carl would have to tread very carefully from here on. He wanted to run, get away from her, but he couldn't leave his lab, his studies. They were more important now than ever before.

CHAPTER 19 – DEALING WITH DIANA

Jordan heard the front door open, then close. Carl looked at him and whispered, "Go check her out if you would. Make some sort of excuse if you have to."

Jordan nodded and walked into the hallway. "Nice walk?"

Diana whirled around. "I... yes. I had a nice walk."

"Hungry?"

"I... suppose."

"Why don't you join me in the kitchen?"

Diana nodded and followed him.

In the kitchen, Jordan pulled a lemon out of the refrigerator, then opened a cupboard and pulled down some honey. He halved the lemon with one huge whack of a large knife and Diana winced. He finally started talking without turning around. "Where did you go?"

"Out," she answered. "Why, were you worried?

"No, just curious. Walks usually last longer."

Diana leaned against the wall. "Is this an inquisition?"

"Not unless you're hiding something." He turned around, doing his best to hide the anger that rose like a tide inside of him. "Look, Carl just went to the emergency room with a bullet wound—"

Diana gave him a shocked look. "What? How did that happen?"

"He was in the wrong place at the wrong time, apparently. He must have been in a hunter's line of fire this morning. Fortunately it just grazed him. Then we come back from the hospital and you're acting strange."

"But he's fine, isn't he?" Diana's voice would have sounded forceful if it hadn't faltered at the end.

Jordan stared at her. "What makes you think," he said, walking toward her with the knife in his hand, "he's perfectly fine?"

She bridled, holding her ground. "Because you don't seem very worried about him. You might want to keep in mind that this house does not belong to Carl. It's his father's, and I'm a guest of his father's. Carl can't make me leave, and if that makes you uncomfortable it's not my fault." She glared at him, then looked down at his hand, which still held the knife, and finally took a hesitant step backward.

He looked down at the knife, then turned around and carefully put it down on the counter. He picked up the lemon and squeezed it into a mug. "You're an ungrateful houseguest," he said.

"And you're an inhospitable host! I know there's something you're not telling me."

Jordan obliterated the other half of the lemon over the mug, and muttered, "Hell, the recipe doesn't call for peel, but why not." He squeezed some honey into the mug, then lifted the water off the stove and poured it in. He paused for a moment. "Look, Little Miss Righteous, you're keeping secrets yourself. If you're telling me you want us to tell our supposed stories before you tell yours, you can forget it. If we have secrets, we're keeping 'em." He looked at her and saw her staring at the mug. "Are you hungry?" he asked, not recalling her earlier answer.

She looked up at him. "Starving. This mountain air really gives me an appetite."

He opened a drawer and pulled out an unsliced loaf of bread, paused for a moment, then handed her the knife and the bread, pointing to the breadboard on the other counter. He opened the refrigerator to pull out a plate of sliced roast beef, along with mustard and lettuce. He laid out a series of the leaves and put a squirt of mustard on each, topping them with a handful of meat before rolling them up, and securing each with a toothpick. She sliced several large chunks of bread off the loaf. He realized the box of muesli he'd left on the table this morning was gone. The milk level was also much lower; he'd noticed when he moved the carton to pull the lemon out. He wondered how she managed to eat like that and maintain a svelte figure – it had to have been four hundred calories in Muesli alone, and the day wasn't even half over yet. At the rate she was going, she'd have over three thousand calories today, and she had claimed she didn't exercise. He noticed she rarely seemed to sit still, though.

She sat down at the table where he had placed the bread. She ate several pieces before noticing his stare. She sighed. "Okay, I'll start, for the sake of diplomatic relations. I'm representing a very wealthy client who wants a cover for a retreat in an unpopulated area. I'm sorry I didn't say it sooner." She placed a hand gently on his arm. "I'm just trying to earn a paycheck here, and I think I can make a deal where everyone wins."

Jordan concentrated on her wide blue eyes in an attempt to ignore her hand. He wondered just how much she thought she knew, and whether or not it was a bluff. He didn't believe her cover story for a second. "I told you Carl's been shot. I think you owe me more than that."

She looked down for a moment, then released his arm with a sigh. "Okay, fine. I think there's something going on here that neither of you can handle." She looked back up at him and he thought he saw only concern now as she gazed at him, her eyes hypnotically pale against the frame of her jet-black hair. "Do you want to talk about it?"

He released a deep breath. "Not really," he answered. He stood for a moment, trying to decide what to ask next. He decided to organize his thoughts first and scooped whey powder into the mug, stirred it, then carried the concoction and the food plate down to Carl.

Carl took the mug, then whispered, "Learn anything more?"

Jordan braced his hand against his thigh and leaned over, speaking quietly. "Not so far. Not done yet."

Carl took a sip from the mug with his left hand as he stirred the contents of a dish with the glass rod in his right hand. "What is she eating?"

"She asked for bread. This morning she ate cereal, with milk. Mostly carbs, and a whole lot of 'em."

"Well, thanks anyway for the hot, lemony thing," Carl said absently, then looked into the mug. "Did you know there's lemon peel in it?"

Jordan shrugged. "It's good for the immune system."

Carl ran a hand through his hair, "Well, back to work I guess." He went back to stirring the dish.

Jordan grabbed a roll off the plate and shoved it into Carl's hand, then went back upstairs where he found Diana on her way to the library.

"Diana, would you care to go horse riding?"

She looked surprised. "That would be great!"

Jordan led her to the coat closet. "Are you gonna be warm enough?" he asked, looking at her light garb. "I suppose I could loan you a sweatshirt. You're gonna freeze in that." Something inside him said, *let her freeze*. He ignored it.

"Oh no, it's no problem. I have a high metabolism."

They went out through the back door and the wind bit into him. The stable was much warmer, insulated with stacked hay bales in the small area so Daisy's body heat kept it comfortable. Daisy's nose poked out from her stall. Jordan had picked up a carrot from the box by the back door, as always. He handed it to Diana. "Hold this." He went up and rubbed Daisy's nose. The muscular horse pushed against his chest, sniffing to find the treat. "Not the coat, Daisy. I'm gonna have to stop putting carrots in the pockets. Hey, girl, how ya feeling today?" Frisky, was the answer.

They usually set Daisy loose in the pasture the morning after the final transformation of a cycle, and Daisy knew it was time to get going. Jordan was more concerned about Diana's presence; if she were a werewolf, Daisy would be kicking down the stall by now. So she wasn't a werewolf. Maybe she was a hunter of werewolves.

He reached for Daisy's halter, unlatching the bar and lifting it out of the way so he could lead the horse out of the stall. Daisy knew there was a carrot here somewhere and started nosing Diana. "Hey! Stop that!" she laughed. "Guess she likes me."

Jordan looked over his shoulder at her. "No, she just wants that carrot. You've fed a horse by hand before?"

"Ever since I was five or so. I got bitten once, but it didn't stop me." She pulled the carrot out from behind her back on a flat hand and held it up for Daisy to lip off her palm. Daisy looked her in the eye while chewing, as if committing Diana to memory. "Boy, she never forgets a carrot dispenser, does she?"

"Never," Jordan answered. "Ever ridden an Appaloosa in the mountains?"

"No, but I was on a mustang one time."

"Is there supposed to be a similarity?"

"I hope not. It was miles before I was in control again."

"That's crazy!" Jordan revised his estimate of her skills. "You won't have that problem with Daisy. She's powerful but sweet. That's probably why she doesn't like Carl. But she can go vertical on steep slopes, and she'll lunge suddenly if she needs to, so make sure you've got a good grip with your legs and give her her head so she can move however she needs to. Grab the saddle horn if she lunges just for safety."

Jordan was turned to the tackle box as Diana queried "Daisy doesn't like Carl?"

"Not at all." Jordan unlatched the tall cupboard shakily as he realized he'd just revealed too much. "It's a real shame. She's Carl's horse." Handing her the reins, he advised, "That's the breaks. Hold this for a second," he pulled Daisy's head around so she could grab the halter and reached into a large locker-shaped box where he kept the saddle.

Diana held on to Daisy, stroking her nose as the horse eyed her curiously. She watched Jordan as he put the blanket and saddle on the horse's back and slipped the reins on, then got Daisy to open her mouth for the bit. Diana drew Daisy out of the stable and stopped so Jordan could hold her.

He held Daisy steady while Diana jumped up with the aid of a stirrup. "Here," he said quickly, handing her the reins. She took them and looked down at Jordan. Jordan turned away to open the gate. "Do you think I might bump into a hunter out there?" She asked intently.

Jordan rubbed his lip. "It's possible. They're all over the place lately. I think you're safe on the horse; that makes you too tall to be mistaken for anything else."

Diana's eyes narrowed as she grinned, then she directed Daisy down the driveway.

Jordan watched her long hair sway against her back as she trotted away, wondering what that was about, then went back inside the house to report Daisy's acceptance of Diana. He wondered whether it was wise to have let her leave on a horse that could carry her for miles. The clues were too tangled, he couldn't make any sense of the whole thing. He also berated himself for missing more of her reactions than he should have, in retrospect; all he knew, really, was that Daisy hadn't rejected her. There was a great deal more to know.

Jordan and Diana left for town several hours later, after she'd returned and he'd put Daisy out in the pasture. He vowed to watch her more carefully while they were together and try to get more answers.

CHAPTER 20 – SHOPPING

Jordan dropped Diana off to do some shopping then took the car to the Jaguar dealership, where they gave him a loaner; they were going to give him a newer model with all the bells and whistles, probably in hopes of enticing a sale, until he told them how the paint had been scratched. He pulled out in a Toyota Corolla from the back lot instead. As he pulled out he decided he had better seem to loosen up with Diana for a few hours while he reassessed her, so the tedious chore of consumerism was cut by the pleasantries of conversation. He was soon able to forget the constant stress which had become his life over the past few months. He even tried an espresso – decaf skinny latte, no frills. He had begun to accept her tale about metabolism, because she swept him through the mall like a small windstorm. He had to slow her down regularly by pointing out scarves and sweaters so he could secretly stop to catch his breath. He was strong, but clearly she had the aerobic fitness advantage over him. She tried to get him to try on some wild animal print outfits, and he shook his head with a grin. Then she went into a crystal store to browse and motioned him in. He backed off and waved his hands and told her he had no desire to go into a place where a misstep could cost a hundred dollars. She laughed.

He separated from her long enough to get what he needed. It was then that he noticed how little she had bought. *Had the trip to town been an excuse? If so, for what? Did she meet with someone while he was away?*

They decided to stop at a small outdoor bistro. It was much warmer at this lower elevation, though it was October and autumn coolness was creeping into the air. While they were eating their marinara sauce and breadsticks he decided to come right out and ask her. "What did you need to come here for if you don't want clothes?"

A tormented look washed over her face and vanished. "I'm concerned about Carl," she answered.

"Then what are you doing here?" After a full day of trying to be civil to her, he discovered he no longer held a grudge over her intrusion into his life, but he renewed his vow to keep her away from Carl and discover the depth of her secrets.

"Hoping you can help me," she answered tentatively.

"I'm not following you," he said as he pulled a piece of bread out of the basket in the center of the table.

Her face drifted into a troubled expression again, and this time she didn't try to dismiss it. She looked up at him. "Do you believe... I mean, are you at all religious? Do you believe in God?"

"I haven't reached any conclusions on the subject," Jordan responded, carefully.

"The devil?"

"No," he answered.

"Good and evil?" She asked.

"I don't know. I've seen some stuff that would be hard to explain if evil didn't exist."

"Can you keep an open mind?" She stopped and looked into Jordan's eyes for a moment, then said quietly, "I believe that Carl is in trouble."

Jordan felt a chill go through his body. It was so bluntly accurate that he didn't realize the two statements had no apparent connection until he reviewed what she said several times, then he shifted his gaze so that he saw her again. "And you're going to tell me that this has something to do with God... or the devil?"

"Or maybe the solution does."

Jordan mulled it over. He rubbed his chin as he considered how to handle her concerns. "So, why haven't you talked to Carl about it?" Jordan stirred the ice cubes in his glass with his straw. Clearly Diana thought there was something evil about Carl. He'd have to handle this situation with a great deal of care. More than anything, though, he realized he'd need to either be in Carl's presence or Diana's until they could get rid of her. To lose track of both at the same time could allow Diana to act on her beliefs, whatever they were, but what he'd heard from her just now alarmed him.

"That could be even more trouble. But I know he's trying to get rid of me, and if he does I can't help him."

"What do you mean?" He asked, focusing all his senses on the sound of her voice and the features of her face while rolling a breadstick automatically on a napkin to soak up the extra oil.

"I have some knowledge... some skills . . . that I'm not ready to discuss." Diana was still looking him right in the eye. There was something about this that smacked of an interview. He wasn't sure it was Carl she was concerned about – that could just be a pretense she was using to explore his beliefs.

"You're giving me a bunch of words without saying anything at all," he said, breaking off a small piece of breadstick and lifting it to his mouth.

She picked up one for herself from the bread basket and dipped it in sauce. "I don't think he knows what he's gotten himself into. He's obviously looking for information. I have answers to a lot of questions; his or yours. If I know what you're looking for, maybe I can help you. You and I are both on the same side."

Jordan finishing chewing and broke off another small piece. "You don't know either of us well enough to know whose side you're on, even if Carl and I weren't on the same side. And you're asking me to lay our hand on the table first." He dipped the bread in the sauce. *Bullshit*, he thought. *You're not here to help him, you're here to kill him.* He'd put a bullet into her right here, right now, if he thought he could get away with it. It was a pre-emptive defense of Carl. No one would ever die, or be paralyzed, on his watch again. Ever.

"Just to be clear, I brought books about wolves, and I didn't expect to find any," she let that sink in. "I'm here to help."

"And Carl's in trouble. And apparently, this is related to wolves somehow." Jordan was breaking his bread into numerous small pieces, trying to control his hands so they didn't shake. He knew now that if there were anything evil here it was her, and he was sure the type of help she offered was terminal. The last thing he wanted to do was take her back near Carl, but leaving her behind, unwatched, wasn't an option. He didn't know what to do with her. For now he'd just have to keep an eye on her, and stay between her and Carl until they came up with a better plan.

"If you believe nothing else, you need to know he's in trouble." She watched his eyes carefully.

Jordan considered that for a moment, chewing another piece of bread before speaking. "From who?"

"I'm... I can't tell you yet."

"Say it, dammit!" Jordan nearly shouted, and Diana jumped, but said nothing. After sitting in the silence for too long, he took care of the bill and they left.

CHAPTER 21
– THE HUNT

It was a cold wet night in downtown Seattle, like most other nights. A pair of eyes continued to watch the neon-lit doors that illuminated the dark street, down which Luke, in lupan form, had walked a moment earlier. His nose carefully sifted the scents of the city, irritated by the acrid scents of petroleum and filth. A steady drizzle of rain fell, but the city stench overrode the neutralizing effects of water. People stood shoulder to shoulder behind the luminescent signs in the windows of the bar, their musky libidos and perfume-laden aromas spilling like a stew into the narrow alleyway.

With a huff of breath, Luke backed into a corner behind a dumpster rose on his hind paws and transformed from wolf to human. Then he strode into the claustrophobic confines of the Mexican-style nightclub. No one noticed him as he passed through the crowd. A deft psychic suggestion reminded someone they were late getting home and Luke dropped quickly onto the vacated barstool, immediately forgotten as the crowd around him swirled. The men and women paired off for cursory inspections, then separated to check out other options. Luke's target was hitting it off well with a petite redhead. Luke took shallow breaths of fetid air as he overheard the infuriating, witless exchange of what passed for pleasantries in a dive like this. He knew he would have to listen to every inane thing the man said all night. He could nearly recite it by now.

"Oh Baby, it's been ten years since I've been able to do this. I can't believe I've found someone so wonderful. You are truly a miracle worker."

Luke couldn't believe there were humans stupid enough to buy into these lines. And the man's diction was atrocious. Luke spoke ten languages now, and he was more fluent in all of them than this idiot was in the single language he knew. The man spoke like a romance novel written by a twelve-year-old, and the women he hit on didn't seem to pick up on it. There were either a lot of unsophisticated women in Seattle, or this seducer was careful to select the less intelligent ones. Luke had been to Seattle before and knew it had to be the latter, which meant the man was cunning, at least on some level, which meant he could be dangerous if Luke let his guard down.

Luke was infuriated that he hadn't been able to narrow the suspect list down further from the Canadian travelers he'd told Dwayne to target.

He had transferred his latest memories onto the skull shortly before Dwayne's visit, while showing him how it worked and testing to see how well Dwayne could use the device. It was a difficult biological technology, created by the Sh'eyta for use by his predecessors, who also had a trace of Sh'eyta blood like the rest of his race. The overlords would be expecting a report on the situation that was developing in Washington. The thief had to have been in the car that followed Dwayne; he knew it hadn't been removed by the locals who were digging up the island looking for buried treasure. Everything the diggers found was inspected and documented by a small group of people with easily accessed, pliable minds, and none of them was vibrating with the excitement of finding such a rare artifact. As remote and tricky as the hiding place was, whoever found it was trying to find it. But what if the person who had located it wasn't then sent to track down the rebellious Skykomish pack? If that were the case, there was no way to know where the thief was, and he'd have to go after the powerful alien woman who had confounded and nearly killed him five centuries ago. That was a huge risk, and one he was reluctant to consider.

Dwayne had sent the requested list and Luke had visited everyone on it, quickly eliminating those whose minds were open books but showed no memory of a crystal skull. He was now back to the ones whose minds were compartmentalized in a way that hid their thoughts from him to the point that he would have to dig especially deep. This process could leave them with psychic lobotomies, which was a transgression of the law that said to never harm humans. Any transgression was a risk, so he had to minimize any harm that might come of his actions. He had to watch and wait, while time ticked away.

"That's a beautiful dress!" the slimy little man said to the redhead. "Where did you get it?"

She smiled as she took a sip from the glass the man had given her. "Jeannine's on Third."

Feigned surprise. "Really? I was just in there. I guess it just looks so much better on you that I didn't recognize it."

Titter.

The bartender handed Luke a glass of tonic water and he lifted it slowly to his pursed lips. He sifted the verbal exchange for any intimation that this man was the actual predator he was looking for, as he suspected he was not. If this was not the one, the last two days would have been for nothing. He would have to backtrack, find one of the last two potential adversaries and start the process all over. He took another swallow of water and settled in to watch and listen for a few hours.

It was only forty-five minutes before Luke stood up to follow the pair out of the bar. The man had scored already, and with his first play of the night, no less. Disgusted, Luke passed through the doorway and took a deep breath of wet, exhaust-laden air. At least it was a change from the sharp tang of alcohol and the musty bursts of cologne and perspiration. He dodged through the alleyway, shifting from man to wolf as he passed cement pillars in the ash and charcoal shades of the Seattle alleys at night. A quick scan told him no one had noticed the anomaly of a human going in and a long-legged canine coming out.

The man came around the corner with the redhead on his arm; she was laughing as if he had just said the most hilarious thing in the world. Luke had listened to the man and knew for a fact that he couldn't have said anything that witty. The man was the most boring creature Luke had ever known, and Luke had known some exceedingly boring creatures. He felt sorry for the woman. The man would be tossing her out of his room before the sun came up, and she would be surprised, just like the last one. That was the kind of woman this man liked. Luke was tempted to break the law and kill the man just to put him out of everyone's misery, but then he would never know if he had killed the right man or not, and worse, he might not be able to find the skull. Luke watched the man open the car door for her, just like the gentleman he most certainly was not.

But then, Luke thought, as he started to lope steadily after the car, the woman inevitably had at least five of the wicked slammers, rapid injections of mostly tequila, before the man took her home. Compliments of the man, of course.

Luke galloped down the city street, unnoticed by the clumps of people that flowed from place to place like jetsam on a tide. On occasion, someone would start to suspect his presence in spite of the psychic subterfuge he projected, then look but see nothing, shaking their head. Luke wasn't concerned if they caught a glimpse of motion out of the corner of their eyes, he knew he could blend into the greyness of the night. He'd been doing this for so long he didn't even have to think about it. There were many skills a lupan could develop over time, and he'd had more time than any other lupan on earth, by several thousand years.

The car had turned toward the piers and the smell of tar, salt, and dying fish assaulted Luke's nose. Almost choking, Luke dropped his head toward the pavement to get closer to the rubber scent of the tires he was tracking. Tall walls of cement rose up on either side of the street like cliffs and neon signs beckoned damp travelers. A young woman wearing combat boots brushed by Luke without seeing him, slapping his nose with a wet gypsy skirt suffused with the scent of cigarette butts and alcohol. He shook his head and turned to look at her as she swept around a corner. Luke saw only the bobbing of magenta hair as she strode into a tiny club that faced the low, dirty walls between the alleyway and the parked cars under the Alaskan Way viaduct.

The only thing Luke could find to admire in his latest prey was the way the man could disguise himself. He probably went to the same sets of bars every Friday and Saturday night, alternating through about a dozen that he would be back to visit every six weeks or so, and his past conquests never knew it. Despite his disgust, Luke knew better than to underestimate the man. He had done that with another prey, years ago, and it nearly killed him. The car passed into a parking garage, and Luke went to an alley to change form again, then walked through the front door of the building. A doorman let him in without knowing it, and Luke went to the elevators, where he stepped in. After the doors closed, he ripped the panel open, pulled some wires to force the elevator to let him out on the penthouse level, then shoved it back together so it looked nearly the same as before. It was going to be a long, miserable night.

*　*　*

Luke looked through the doorway to the repair shop, studying his new mark. The last one – the lothario – had proven to be a family-connected criminal with uncles in high places. After all the time spent in dank bars listening to bad pickup lines, Luke had finally dismissed him as a suspect and now studied the small, greasy man under the Pontiac convertible. It hadn't been a convertible yesterday.

Luke was beginning to get nervous. He needed to locate the crystal skull, and apparently the only way to do that was to wait and watch. He'd begun to think the suspect he was looking for was uncannily clever. Luke knew by now that his enemy would be trained to cover their tracks well enough to look nearly innocuous on the surface, sometimes hinting at underworld connections, but nothing serious. Luke chafed at the amount of time the precious skull had spent in the hands of the enemy. He needed to address the rogue pack, and he should also check in on the abandoned cub directly, but the imperative to get the skull back into his possession was too important to take a break from yet.

Luke reconsidered his tactics once more as he listened to the garage talk, barely decipherable even for his sharp ears.

It had been months since he'd made a face-to-face connection with anyone he knew. The enforced separation was distressing; both the wolf and the man in him craved company, but it was still a short time in his long life and he knew the thief would be looking over his shoulder, watching for someone like Luke. Not that there was anyone like Luke.

Luke had changed over the years. He had been brash in his youth. As long ago and far away as it was, he still remembered the dark hair and violet eyes of his first true love, though by now it was nearly all he could remember of her, and the way she looked at him the last time he saw her.

"Luciane," she had said, "Mi amor, noli abire. Hi homicidae sunt." *Lucianus, my love, do not leave. They are murderers.* He had brushed past her. It hadn't occurred to him, in his ego-ridden fury, that it wasn't his own life she was worried about.

He never saw her again. He only heard how she had died, weeks later, and how long it had taken. Four days. She had lived for four days through tortures relayed to Luke only in whispers, and only after Luke demanded to know, blade first. If she could wait four days to die, he could learn to be patient. And he had relived that lesson every day, for nearly three thousand years.

The new mark pulled himself out from under the car and wiped a grease-stained arm across his forehead, then walked around the side of the building to the bathroom. Luke had watched him drink six cups of coffee this morning so he wasn't at all surprised.

Luke also wasn't surprised to see another man rifle through the wallet that had slipped out of his co-worker's pocket. Men. Millennia after millennia, they never changed. What amazed Luke was that humans, every generation of humans, believed their generation was the most miserable. But time after time, there was no difference. There would always be holy wars. Where once there were Christian crusades, there were now politicians and welfare wars, both cleansing entire nations in the name of so-called ethics and decency. There had always been thieves, there would always be thieves. And war. Here in this relatively new nation of America, where officials were elected by vote, serfs still existed, only called by new names; minimum wage employees. Where once there were feuds, now there were Bloods and Crips. Subjugated, they filled the inner cities and perpetrated violence on the only opponents they could reach – each other. There would always be slavery and rape, too. These used to be more predictable because men who loved such sport would buy suits of armor and well-muscled stallions, then join armies and violate the women they found in towns they pillaged after murdering the men and enslaving the children. Such barbarians were still around, but they blended in more easily and found more underhanded ways to do the same thing, often using a position of public power to carry out their malfeasance. Era after era, nothing changed.

And nothing seemed to change here in the garage, either. The man returned to his work, stripping the Pontiac down for spare parts he was using to repair a different car. It seemed to Luke that there were better ways to fix a machine but it wasn't his place to point that out. It was his place to sit still and watch. Without even a sigh, Luke observed. Hours later, Luke followed the man home as a growl escaped him. He was nearly out of suspects. What if he was on the wrong track? It would be hard enough to defend his people from the coming judgment and subsequent genocide. Without this particular skull it might be impossible.

CHAPTER 22
– ANSWERS
IN BLOOD

When they returned from shopping Diana went upstairs with her small bag of new clothes while Jordan left his in the kitchen and went down to find Carl in the weight room. Carl jumped up. "Jordan! Thank God you're back. I've spent the whole day studying and eating. The scale says I've gained five pounds. Come into the lab with me, I need to ask you some questions."

They strode into the clean white room and Jordan looked at the main computer screen. "I want you to look at these two images and tell me what you see," Carl perched on the stool, bracing himself with his hand on the seat between his sprawled legs. He tapped several keys with one hand and two squares appeared on the screen, each framing a motley collection of alien images that reminded Jordan of what people called modern art. As Jordan peered at the screen he recognized the appearance of red blood cells, as well as at least two other types of cells and some random things that might or might not be cells. He realized he was probably looking at a comparison of Carl's blood from a week ago and the other from a few hours ago. A quick look at the image labels showing at the top of each frame confirmed it.

"I had some of my blood from last week and some from today. This is the fresh stuff," Carl said, watching Jordan's face.

"You mean this, on the right?" Jordan asked, peering at the image.

"Yes. The other is a week old." Carl kept watching him, apparently expecting a reaction.

Jordan glanced back and forth between the two. After a long moment, he sighed and shook his head. "It's Greek to me, Carl. They look the same."

"No, look closer at these yellow cells. See how this one in the new blood window matches this other in the same window – look here at the nucleus, see how it's approximately centered in the cell, and the edge of the cell is distinct? Look over here at the one from last week," Carl pointed to the other image. "The edges are often ragged, and the nucleus is frequently right up against the cell wall if not missing entirely. Then all this stuff in the serum, I believe that's the nuclei and other internal parts of these cells."

Jordan looked at what Carl was pointing to. "You said the second one is old?"

"Yes." Carl had one arm folded and a thumb

against his lips as he stared back and forth at the images.

Jordan's eyes narrowed as he looked carefully at the screen. "Looks like a mess, now that you mention it."

Carl dropped his arms and began pacing as he answered, thumbs in his belt loops. "Yes. That seems to be the problem."

"But that would mean something that happened since then has changed your blood?" Jordan looked at him, puzzled. "They both have the same cells, but the ones from today are in good shape."

"But why?" Carl asked, exploding with frustration. "And what is it that makes me a werewolf? The cells themselves, or the fact that they're broken and leaking some... I don't know... wolf's DNA into my bloodstream? How does that make sense?"

Jordan sat down on the stool Carl had vacated and watched him pace. "Well, what about that DNA test? Where did the wolf DNA come from, the yellow cells? Would the test have detected wolf DNA if the cells weren't broken?"

"I wish I knew, dammit!" Carl paced back and forth, hands now in his back pockets. "And if I ask my father, I'll have to tell him why I care."

"Why don't you tell him? It's not like you accidentally broke someone's window with a baseball. You're ... " Jordan's voice trailed off.

Carl stopped pacing and leaned against the

counter. "Dying. I know. But of what? What would I say? 'Hello Father, I'm a werewolf, and I'm dying. Can you tell me what you know about this?' My father's only lapse in scientific belief is his religious beliefs. He'd have me exorcised until the demon left me or I died. Better dead than possessed, you know." Carl shook his head. "He's . . . he's worried about me, Jordan. And Diana showed up just after his last phone call. He was asking me some uncomfortable questions." Carl didn't mention the possibility that his father might think he had AIDS, and where it might come from if he did. Clearly the man wanted answers.

"Oh." Jordan continued watching Carl as Carl began to pace again. Carl almost never talked about his family, that he could recall, and when he did it was often in anxiety or grief. It had to have been hard being raised almost entirely by servants as his parents were elsewhere nearly his entire life. He remembered Carl looking at the bleachers at football games, scanning as if looking for someone that wasn't there. Then he remembered Diana. "Oh hell, that might fit in with my latest theory on why Diana is really here. She was talking about God, the devil, good and evil, and it sounds like she's a spy of some sort and thinks you're in the devil's camp. I don't want you alone with her from here on out."

Jordan decided to keep his comments about Carl's family relations to himself, but it reinforced his view that the perfect family was a myth. He waited while Carl slowed to a near stop, then resumed pacing back and forth across the room.

"Jordan," Carl said finally, stopping in front of him, staring downward at nothing.

"Yes?" Jordan watched him, waiting for a reaction to what he'd said about Diana, but as usual Carl's mind was on the problems he could find answers for and left the rest of it to Jordan.

Carl looked up. "I need your blood."

"Why?" Jordan exploded off the stool.

Carl took a step back, then answered. "I want to—"

"Want? To hell with your want!" Jordan's chest was almost pressed against Carl's, his head thrust forward so that his nose was almost against Carl's lips.

"Shut up and listen to me for once! I need to infuse your blood with mine to see what those cells will do." Carl glared fiercely back, not giving an inch.

Jordan stood stock still, eyes barely visible behind his black lashes. He closed his eyes for a moment, then stepped back and looked down, cursing, "Shit! You said you wouldn't need any more!"

"The hell I did! I said I didn't need any for the standard tests. This isn't a standard test."

"Fucking vampire," Jordan clutched his arms in his white-knuckled hands.

Carl drew himself up. "Let's hope not," He answered stiffly, and Jordan's blood ran cold all the way to his toes.

"Is this something I can do myself?" Jordan asked.

"Not really, why?"

"It's just... your... " Jordan looked at the tracks on Carl's arms.

"You mean you're afraid I'll slip up and infect you." Carl stared into Jordan's eyes.

"Yeah, well, you know... " Jordan answered lamely.

"This must be what it feels like to have AIDs," Carl said, almost to himself.

Jordan winced. "I didn't mean—"

"Yes, you did, and I don't blame you, but I'm dying, Jordan. You said it yourself. This isn't some baseball-through-the-window variety of problem, and you're all I've got. Are you with me or not?"

Jordan stood for a moment longer, but he couldn't deny the logic. He sat down with reluctance and rolled his arm over so that the inside of his elbow was exposed, turning his head aside and squeezing his eyes tightly shut. "Don't slip."

While Carl slid a drawer open, Jordan faced the wall, eyes closed and trying to picture himself on a warm tropical beach. Carl found his vein, wrapped a piece of rubber tubing above his elbow, then reached for a needle and a small vial. Carl slid the needle in the projecting vein and filled a vial with Jordan's blood.

CHAPTER 22 – HUNTING THE WOLF

Jordan went to the living room to listen to music and write in his journal. A few hours later he ventured into the kitchen and found Carl by the back door putting his coat on. Diana had gone upstairs earlier and it bothered him to realize that he hadn't been between the two. He grabbed Carl's arm and pulled him around to look him in the eye. "Where the hell do you think you're going?"

"What's it to you?" Carl said twisting out of Jordan's grasp.

"I know that look. You're about to do something stupid or desperate, most likely both."

Carl straightened the cuffs of his coat sleeves. "I need another sample."

Jordan fought the urge to clutch his arms.

"Not you," Carl stated, noting the response, "the wolf."

"Are you insane? You're going to go out there

and try to find a wild creature in miles of mountainous terrain, get close enough to stick a needle in it, and then you think you're just going to walk away?" Jordan grabbed both of Carl's arms and held them firmly this time. "Remember what happened last time you cornered a wolf?"

Carl tried to squeeze out of Jordan's grip again. "This is a different wolf."

"You don't know that!" Jordan gave him a light shake. "Use your brain. The only way you're getting a sample off that wolf is if you kill it first."

Carl scowled, then looked Jordan straight in the eyes and spoke quietly. "I need that sample. There's something about that wolf or she wouldn't be hanging around me when I wake up. I've been reading the books Diana brought, I have my own observations, and I think the wolf is hanging out nearby. If there's even a snowball in hell's chance she's my connection to other werewolves I've got to know. We've been assuming what happens to me is representative of normal lycanthropy, but we don't know that. I'm working in a vacuum, I haven't got enough data."

Jordan stared at him a moment, then released his grip and turned around to get his double coat, putting it on before grabbing the gun that was tucked into the corner of the shelf above. "Well, hell. What is there to lose but life itself?" he said, slipping the gun inside the belt around his waist.

"Where's Diana?" Carl asked as he wrapped an orange scarf around his neck and handed an orange stocking cap to Jordan. During hunting season, wearing orange in the mountains was just common sense.

Jordan's lip curled, but he pulled the cap securely onto his head. "In her room with one of your books."

Carl turned around and grabbed the door handle with the towel that hung from a metal loop on the wall. "If I find those strange yellow cells in the wolf's blood we'll have to find a way to track it to its den. I'm not sure I can do that."

Jordan stepped through the doorway after Carl and closed the door quietly behind them. "One step at a time. We don't know what you'll find. If you pull this stunt off, my guess is it'll be normal blood and we won't have to worry about it. If it's still a wolf after you transform back, then it's just a wolf."

"Unless I'm not a typical werewolf. Do they all die after a few months? Seems like they shouldn't still exist if it's that fatal."

They went down to the stream where they'd found smaller wolf tracks on the hike home two days ago. Carl was acting a great deal braver than he felt but he was running out of time to find a cure, and this was one test he hadn't run. Jordan found the log he had placed at the ford, they crossed the stream and hiked up a small hill to a tiny clearing. He couldn't afford to leave any stone unturned.

They waited for an hour or so while the wan-

ing moon disappeared then re-emerged from behind clouds. Carl hoped the wolf hadn't come by
while it was too dark to see; even now it would
be difficult. He tucked his hands in his armpits
to keep them warm and tried to shift his weight.
They both sat crouched on their heels so they
could rise to their feet without making noise but
his legs kept trying to fall asleep.

Jordan looked back at the house and thought
he saw a shadow moving near the front door, but
by the time he pointed it out to Carl it was gone.
They continued to wait. Carl was getting dis-
couraged. He knew wolves didn't necessarily return to the same place every night, but he hoped
that this one sought him out more often than
he already knew of. Something told him it did; a
niggling sixth-sense awareness told him she was
near right now. A thought dawned on him and he
gestured at Jordan. Jordan nodded and covered
his ears. Carl leaned back against a tree trunk,
cupped his hands and threw out a long wolf's
howl. He had developed a knack for it since the
first transformation.

They waited for another twenty minutes, or
maybe it was an hour, before seeing a gray shape
by the edge of the stream. As it stepped out
from the cover of bushes they could see the wolf
clearly. Jordan pulled out the gun and motioned
to Carl to stay to the left. They crept forward,
Carl in the lead and Jordan silent behind him.
Once Carl got close he growled, and the female

lowered her tail and crouched, sniffing the air. He suddenly jumped on her and wrestled her to the ground, taking her ruff in his hands. It shouldn't have been easy, which supported the theory that she wasn't a typical wolf. He hoped she wasn't simply ill. She yelped when he cut her and tried to jump up, but he was straddled across her belly-up form and she was trying to prostrate and protect her neck at the same time, confused. He hoped her wriggling didn't hopelessly contaminate the sample. Unable to get the needle in, he swiped a slide across the cut as a last resort, knowing it would be dirty, then released her before she bit him. She lay there for a moment before jumping up and bounding away. He watched her go, sadly. If he was wrong, he may have ruined his relationship with her. Wolves did not hurt other wolves in their own pack without good reason, and this violent interaction had to seem totally random to her. He had just given her a clear signal that she had no value in his pack.

Carl and Jordan walked back toward the house without looking back.

*   *   *

Jordan slipped in the back door quietly with Carl, and Carl put the slide under the microscope, then looked at it. His eyes swept up to Jordan, whose gaze was fixed on him. "They're identical."

"Yours and the wolf's?"

"Yes. She even has the strange yellow cells

that don't belong in a blood sample. I'm guessing that means she transformed recently. That's the only time I see them in my own serum."

Jordan went cold all over. "But how can that be?"

"She's not a wolf, she's a werewolf." Carl looked back into the microscope.

"Can't be!" Jordan remembered aiming the gun at the wolf. "You're human now; she'd be human..."

Carl shook his head. "All I can tell you is that the same bizarre cells in my new blood are present in the wolf's as well, and healthy looking. I've seen a lot of blood samples at the University, studied blood, and I've never seen or even heard of anything like this."

Jordan stepped closer. "What is it?"

Carl looked back into the eyepiece. "I have no idea, but it's quite obviously three dimensional." He ran a finger along a small dial to adjust the focus.

"But the wolf's blood is like that sample I saw of your new blood earlier? What do you think it is?" Jordan asked, watching him intently.

Carl leaned back for a moment. "I really don't know. Perhaps we should ask what do I think *she* is? Maybe I'm on the wrong track and this isn't lycanthropy at all but something else, and it's just gone horribly wrong in me. For some reason itt was corrected when I went to the hospital. At least – let me check again." He looked through the microscope and started muttering, "No, I don't think so. I think – wait. Hmmm… " Carl got up and turned around. "Look through the microscope, Jordan. Tell me what you see."

Jordan felt his skin crawl as he considered the implication that it might be his own blood improving Carl's health. He set his revulsion aside for now, though, and sat down at the microscope. It was nothing like what they had used in high school. "I don't know," he answered, looking at Carl. "Where did you get this microscope?"

"From the hospital. It's on extended loan, since they upgraded to a newer model. My family bought this one, so in a way it's ours. I've been using it for a while now. Check her slide." Carl made an adjustment and Jordan looked again.

"Umm… " He leaned back and Carl switched it back again. He looked at it and looked up again. "I don't know, Carl. I'm not trained—"

Carl put a third slide under the eyepiece, "I'm training you. Look again."

Jordan placed an eye against the eyepiece and looked. "What's this?" he asked.

"That's yours, the plain stuff."

"Oh. Good looking blood, if I do say so myself."

"Yes – that's what the other two should look like." Carl switched back, giving Jordan a start. He'd still been looking in the eyepiece and the rapid rotation was disorienting.

"Hmmm. This has to be your old blood, with the broken cells, I assume."

"Apparently you can be trained."

Jordan gave a disgusted snort. "So, what's the deal, then? It all looks just like the pictures on the computer."

"But it shouldn't. I mean... my old blood... my new blood... the wolf's." Carl lifted his hands in the air and huffed in exasperation.

"But you already knew it would, didn't you?"

Carl's folded his arms across his chest. "I don't know what I expected."

Jordan leaned over the microscope again. "What about this other kind in yours. This is yours?" he looked up.

Carl responded affirmative, walking over to Jordan.

"Well, this looks like a crossover sample. The new sample has the well-rounded yellow ones like the wolf's, but I also see broken cells."

"Let me see that!" Jordan moved aside as Carl leaned over the microscope. "Damn. You're right. When did that show up?"

Jordan was silent for a moment. "But then... "

Carl looked at the wall, lost in his thoughts. "Does it explain the rapid healing? Is it going away? How long have I got?"

Jordan's head whipped around abruptly. You said you gained five pounds. Is that since before the change?"

"Yes, so it would be in spite of what I lost."

"And you've been eating and working out all day, right? Mainly eating, I hope."

"Yes, I have. And I've been doubling my usual limits on the weights."

Jordan frowned. "You should have mentioned that earlier. Shit, yesterday you were hardly able to lift what I assigned."

Carl grimaced. "I've had a lot of information to sift through since we got back home, and this bloodwork has me totally baffled, questioning what I'm seeing even, which is why I need your eyes right now."

"Well why don't we get back to the basics for a moment and check your weight again?"

Carl allowed himself to be pulled down the hallway and stepped onto the scales in the weight room gingerly. Jordan marked it down slowly and looked at the measuring tape.

Jordan measured and marked for the next several minutes. "Yeah, you're up by five pounds compared to the same time yesterday. What the fuck? That's more than 15,000 calories! You'd have to be wolfing shit down like a maniac. How . . ."

"And I've had tons of energy, all day long, like I used to have. Maybe I'm getting over it... "

"Think you'll stop turning into a wolf, then?"

"I guess we'll see in a few weeks."

Jordan was still thinking about the microscope. His curiosity fought with his pride, which lost. "Can I look at those slides again?"

"Please do." They went back to the lab, where Carl started pacing.

Jordan slid onto the stool, leaning over the microscope. He stared at the slide for a while, then looked up. Carl was still pacing, so Jordan picked up a slide sitting to the left of the microscope and slid it into position. "Wait! What's this?" He continued peering into the eyepiece.

Carl looked over at him. "What's what?"

"The slide to the left of the microscope."

"Oh, that. That's a slide I ruined, your blood and mine mixed."

Jordan jumped up in horror. "That's my blood?" he cried.

"No. I told you, my blood's in there. Don't worry, you're not infected."

"No, that's not what it looks like. You look at it."

Puzzled, Carl walked over and looked into the eyepiece. It was several seconds before he said anything. "Are you sure this was the slide to the left of the microscope?"

"That's where I got it. Are you sure that's the slide with both our blood?" Jordan tried to control his lurching stomach as he realized that, even if only on the slide, his blood had mingled with Carl's.

"Yes." Carl looked around the edge of the eyepiece to check the end of the slide, where he had used a pencil to scrawl several letters. "I marked it C, then circled the C and crossed it out." He looked at the slides on the plate that the eyepiece sat over. "See, this one is the wolf's, this is yours, this is mine, and this is... ours." He looked up at Jordan.

"You're sure?" Jordan looked hopefully at him. Carl nodded, and Jordan chewed his thumbnail, still feeling rather ill. "But... "

"I know. It looks just like the wolf's, and just like the new one used to. Not a single flat or broken cell to be found."

Jordan blew out the breath he discovered he'd been holding in a huff, frightened of what it might mean. What if his blood was the cure? Carl had gotten a little bit crazy lately, almost like a mad scientist. He started chewing his nail again.

"Would you stop that?" Carl snapped irritably.

Jordan looked up. "What?"

"Chewing your nails. It's like scraping your fingernails on a blackboard."

Jordan put his hands on the counter behind him and leaned against them, crossing his ankles in an attempt to keep his limbs from shaking. "Well, you want to try and do that again?"

"Good idea." Carl retrieved the ampoule of Jordan's blood from the refrigerator and set it in a stand, then pulled out another slide from a drawer. He rinsed the slide and let it air dry in a slide rack while preparing his finger.

It gave Jordan the creeps to see his blood sitting on the counter and Carl preparing to bleed himself again, so he decided to go upstairs.

His voice trailed back down the stairway. "Want some coffee?"

Carl yawned loudly. "Thanks for the reminder, mate. Now, you better get me some or I'll fall asleep."

"Right." Jordan was almost to the kitchen when a thought occurred to him. He turned around and went up the next set of stairs, then tapped quietly on Diana's door. There was no answer, so he tapped louder. Still no answer. He raised his hand to knock, then thought better of it and went downstairs to make some coffee.

For the next two hours Jordan made several large pots of coffee and Carl tried to reproduce the effect, but it didn't work. He looked up at Jordan finally. "No go. There's something different in this batch of blood."

Jordan frowned. "You're not gonna make me give blood again, are you?"

"Tell you what – let me re-puncture your finger and I'll give you an extra week off after this is over."

"With or without the truck?"

"Christ. The truck again." Carl sighed. "Okay, I'll throw in the truck."

Jordan felt better after this mundane argument about employment. It was as if things were going to be normal again someday. He considered visiting his mom again soon, and Kira. To avoid having Carl do it, he pricked his own finger and shed several drops of blood onto a slide. Carl added a few drops of his own blood after setting the computer up to record the results. Carl stared at the monitor for several minutes, but nothing happened.

"Let's give it some time," Carl said.

Jordan nodded and went to the kitchen to get more coffee. When he came back, Carl played back a video for him, and he watched as the flat yellow cells knit themselves back together and inflate to become fat yellow cells. Carl looked over at Jordan as he took a swig of coffee, then grimaced.

Jordan leaned back against the counter. "What does that mean?"

"I need another sample."

"We are not poking my finger again, dammit!" Jordan swore. Every cut he had – every time he bled – brought him closer to contracting this bizarre curse that Carl had.

"No, I'm not," Carl answered steadily.

"Then what?"

"Your arm. The only other thing I can figure is the refrigeration. I need to get enough to do another one fresh, and a second refrigerated from the same blood, to see if that's the difference."

Jordan looked sick. "So, refrigerate a slide… "

Carl shook his head. "The reaction has already occurred on the slide. I need your blood again."

"Why mine?" Jordan clutched his elbows.

"Because it works." Carl looked at Jordan's arms, considering where to place another needle.

Jordan shook his head. "Do you have any idea why it works?"

"Not yet. Give me your arm."

Jordan realized he'd just heard the front door open and close again. He used the excuse to go upstairs, his shoulders still shuddering at the thought of their mingling blood. Diana was taking tall leather boots off her bare legs, her cloak wound loosely around her.

He'd lost track of her, but he'd been with Carl, and now he knew right where she was for the moment. Just one thing he had control of at the moment, but he'd been between the two, and that was good.

"Coffee?" He watched her eyes, carefully.

She nodded, then went upstairs. Jordan caught her putting contacts in the upstairs bathroom as he brought her a cup. He'd continue to find excuses to check on her until she slipped up. The door was open and she turned to him, one eye blue and one eye brown. It was eerie. Obviously, she used blue contact lenses; it made her very strikingly attractive, but it wasn't real. The real Diana was the darker one, he thought.

CHAPTER 24 – REASSERTING DOMINANCE

Luke scanned the hillside where wide tire tracks disappeared into the tree line. He only had one more suspect to follow, but he needed a break. The mechanic had turned out to be another dead end, but he was close enough to the rogue pack that he figured he'd take a report from his informant now, when it wasn't as far out of his way.

According to the brief news clips he'd seen, this pack was also likely to be the source of the wolf-cattle incidents that had the local people up in arms. When they'd asked to locate themselves far from known wolf packs he'd been very clear with them, that, just like city packs, they were free to live in this area for as long as they could keep their presence entirely secret, according to the primary law of lupans. And he had been quite clear that any wolf sightings would be immediate grounds for withdrawal of permission. They had a lot to answer for.

Sarah, his contact in this pack, had told him that her sister had attacked a human and the pack had responded by executing her for her folly, but they'd refused to take responsibility for the cub, against law and common sense. She had deftly maneuvered them into shifting their territory enough that she could watch over him, but without the pack she could do no more and had sent a message to Luke to come help the boy several months ago. He had used the opportunity to teach Dwayne, his protégé, how to receive and respond to reports of mutinous behavior, while teaching him about the crystal skulls, but Dwayne was turning out to be insufficient for the job. Once again, the skills he looked for in the ranks just didn't seem to be turning up in the population. He shrugged off the weariness that always followed this observation and got back to the task at hand.

He had to tread carefully where mutiny was concerned, but he needed to talk to Sarah and find the boycub if he could. His stomach felt sick as he watched for any movement in the trees. He hated to face the possibility of executing pack leaders and was angry with the pack for putting him in such a position, but the existence of the entire species required absolute adherence to the laws given to them by their masters. Obey or die; sometimes eliminating those who couldn't stay in line was the only way to save the rest of them.

He rotated his position so that his left hip was under him rather than his right. Where was she? Or any of them,for that matter. They weren't cave dwellers, and he was nearly on top of them. He should at least hear something, someone moving around in the woods somewhere, bringing wood in or some other endless homestead chore. He didn't want to go into the woods without seeing at least a few of them first. He was a cunning old wolf with sharp senses, but even a cub could get lucky occasionally, and he hadn't grown to be so old by letting his guard down. He paused to listen while watching a hawk hunting small game. It came soaring from behind an outcropping of rock and circled the meadow between him and the dark forest on the other side of the clearing. Minutes passed by while Luke's attention remained on the spaces in between the trees, looking for the slightest shift in the shadows that would betray a living creature. There was nothing, though, and eventually, he had to shift his position slightly, once again, as he continued to watch. Rome wasn't built in a day, no one knew that better than himself, and miscreants were rarely caught in an hour. It chafed him that he must sit here and wait when the clock was ticking on the werewolf hunter and the cub that he would have to execute as well.

In addition to basic responsibilities, the pack should also be scanning the area at night to determine all life forms for many miles around them, and here was the loner, apparently living in a building by himself, right in the heart of their territory. He wasn't sure which was worse. Every single time that boy interacted with humans was a chance for information to leak, and those leaks could snowball. If the human population became aware of the existence of lupans, it was all over when the overlords returned to check on their creations. Luke had fought too hard and too long to see all his people die.

Luke brought his focus back to the trees once again. He had to fight for his concentration every moment, these days. He was a bit out of sorts from losing the crystal skull, and bad news on top of bad news was making him irritable. He took a moment to still his mind, breathing gently; in... out... in... out... and refocused on the spaces between the trees, watching for movement. The slightest change in the fall of the light. His nose sifted all the scents around him, but the air was very still today.

The hawk suddenly dove on a patch of grass, then rose back into the sky. A miss. Nothing was going right for anyone today, it seemed. He had to mull over the scent he'd caught while moving toward the ferals. She had brought them near enough the boy that he'd caught his scent, a sick odor of a failed transformation, the type that would kill the boy in the end. What was the loner doing in that big stone building that looked like a house? He should not exist at all unless he'd been vetted and adopted, but there he was, by himself, and he smelled morbidly ill.

The sick ones had to be shown the mercy of swift death. Letting such creatures live tempted fate, and they could be turned to dark purposes and adopted by the vampiric blood drinkers who defied the law in the dark corners of cities, far from the forests that the packs had to inhabit. The fact that the boy was alone in the woods was probably a good defense against that, but he would die a wasting death that no one should have to experience. No werewolf had ever safely survived more than half a year once the wasting began, except by consuming human blood, and that was something Luke would never allow. It turned a lupan; once a hybrid broke the instinctive taboo against consuming human flesh or blood, other laws fell, and soon their superior powers were controlled by nefarious motives.

Where were the damned ferals? Luke shifted his weight one more time, then caught the slightest movement through the trees to the right. That was it; a woman was walking through the underbrush and into the field. She wore a plaid shirt and faded jeans, with leather work boots. She looked around, then lifted a hand to place a blue and green stem in the crook of a tree. It was a stalk of purplish-blue flowers, each tipped with white; lupine. A safe signal. He tilted his head up and gave a quiet call into the air; not a full-blown wolf howl, he didn't want to alert anyone beyond the clearing. She stopped and looked straight at him, then walked back into the woods. He soon heard her coming through the brush behind him and turned to see her walk quietly toward him.

"Are you safe?" He whispered, and she nodded.

"They're assembling. I've been trying to get them to take responsibility for this youngling for months, and they have finally decided to follow the law. I don't know if they've figured out that you're in the area, but they certainly couldn't deny their responsibility when I had to report that a stranger has joined him and is living right under his roof, and he went to a hospital as well. He's not staying sufficiently isolated any more. It's finally too much for us to ignore. They're gathering their guns, making a plan, and they'll leave any minute to go kill him."

"Faex! The damned fools, they let this go too long. Finally they do what would have saved me the trip. They should know the law is not an arbitrary inconvenience. Follow the law or die!"

"They don't see you often enough. You are gone from us for so long, sometimes they wonder if you are still alive, even. They think perhaps we're on our own, perhaps we need to make new laws. They don't understand."

She was right about that. A leader must be seen occasionally, or anarchy would creep into the edges of his rule. It frustrated him that he had to be a dictator, but he was one of just a few lupans old enough to remember the last time the overlords came down from the heavens, as they did once every 500 years or so. He remembered with grief the decimation that ensued as they brought their creatures back into obedience.

"I cannot be everywhere on this entire earth at once. I am trying to find skilled and willing assistants who can lead and regulate, but technology is wreaking havoc with attention spans and this job takes relentless focus. My latest protégé should have had this under control. I could use you, Sarah, if you would step up—"

"Stop it. I'm not leaving Joe, and I don't want that kind of responsibility. I don't even like having to take the lead on this problem."

Luke shook his head. "You have the traits of a good alpha—"

"But I'm not one! This argument is old, and I need to get back to my pack. Tell me what you need from me, then tell me what you will do. I deserve, at least, to know if there will be death."

Luke closed his eyes and groaned silently. There was no way around it, there would have to be death, and one of those who must die would be the young man she had been watching out for, keeping safe at night during his first runs as a wolf while he slowly wasted away. Luke wasn't absolutely sure that he'd have to kill Gus, the man who was alpha of her pack. Most likely he would, and perhaps a few more, depending on how tight their allegiance was to him. There was no room for mercy when the existence of the entire species was at stake, and Sarah would suffer the aftermath of shifting power. If she would step up and lead, it would be better for everyone, but it wasn't her choice. He had always respected free will.

"Yes, there will be death," he answered, "but until I am face to face with Gus, I cannot tell you who else. If I can spare Joe I will, but until I see how he reacts to me I will not know whether I can trust him to change in the way he must if you are all to get through this. The cub, though… you know he must die."

She nodded, a deep sadness in her eyes. "Be careful. There is another man in that house."

Luke focused sharply on her eyes. "Another man?"

Sarah nodded, her wavy brown hair falling around her face and her brown eyes looked back at him intensely. "My messages had to be short, since we don't have phone service and it's hard to get away, but you need to know, there is a very strong young man who seems to be an assistant of some sort taking care of the boy. They came together when the cub returned to our area. I've often felt grateful that I can see his care pass from my own watchfulness to this other man. They seem to have a system. But you will get resistance there. He carries a gun, whenever he leaves the house, this other man. Watch for it and be careful."

"Faex. Is it not enough that I must face the sick cub and execute him while dealing with this moecha vilis, but I must fend off an innocent bodyguard as well? Deos, it will be hard to judge the pack fairly with this complication. They have forced my hand, let this get much too far. Do you know if there has been any leakage while the cub has been running around and piddling himself?"

Luke barely heard the groan, but it gave him the briefest warning before she delivered the last bit of bad news for him to endure. "Just the hospital visit and this new woman."

"Faex, that is enough. Did Gus do anything?"

Sarah shrank before him, but, true to her fortitude of spirit, she answered without a pause. "That's why he's gunning up now, I think. I also told him the boy cut me, for some reason, when I was in wolf form, and that infuriated him. But we have no one trained well enough to go into that hospital and find out if any tests were run that would reveal our nature – you'll have to do that. I should go," she said anxiously. "That is all the information I have, it's in your hands now. I need to be beside Joe when this goes down. I swear to you, if you can spare any of us, I will always be your voice wherever I am. But if you can't spare us, perhaps you can send me into battle on the streets of Seattle where the vampires gather and lurk. If my pack must go, I have no desire to remain. Let me at least take as many of the villains down as I can before my own blood leaves my body."

Luke put his hand on her shoulder. "If Gus were half the wolf you are, Sarah, this would not be happening. I promise you, if I am not able to spare them, you will be the first I send into those dens of filth."

She nodded, then swiftly left him with his bleak thoughts. Yet another task he must take on at some point.

It seemed like no time at all had passed when he heard engines start up and rev, then a series of pickups with large, deep-tread tires came grinding out on a broad trail that bordered the clearing. Luke shifted into wolf form and tore off after them, cutting down slopes to shorten the distance as the trucks followed the zigzag path of the old road down the mountain.

CHAPTER 25
– FACE OFF

Carl and Jordan looked up at each other as they heard several trucks with loud engines roaring up the gravel driveway. Jordan strode through the kitchen to the back entryway and grabbed his gun, then threw the back door open and ran out. He heard Carl follow right behind him. A series of pickup trucks were moving in a line to circle the side yard then, in succession, turn to face the house. Doors opened and men and women stepped out of the trucks. Jordan counted fifteen people with handguns and rifles.

"Carl, get back in the house!" Jordan bellowed, keeping his eye on the group in front of him as he ran forward, gun pointed down as he tried to identify a leader. They stood in a semicircle, in faded jeans and plaid shirts. The men were bearded and one of the women was looking past Jordan. "Get back in the house, dammit!" he yelled to Carl as he raised his gun.

He heard Carl's footsteps retreating as the men raised their rifles, all except for one man who drew a long-barreled pistol and said "stop," aiming the gun past Jordan. Jordan froze in place, legs in a wide stance and arms out and forward, gun aimed at the presumed leader, but ready to dive in any direction as he continued to assess the situation.

Shit, he thought. He had heard Carl's footsteps stop at the same time as his own. *What do they want?*

He heard the door open again – it wasn't Carl. From the sound of his footsteps earlier, Jordan was sure Carl was about eight feet behind him and slightly to the right. The door opening had to be Diana.

"Who are you and what do you want?" Carl yelled at the men.

The leader was still focused on Carl. "Apparently they want to kill you, Carl. You might want to ask why."

The leader answered, "We're here to do what we should have done a while ago. You're dying already, boy."

Jordan heard the click of Diana's boot heels on the narrow cement patio, then they crunched on gravel, and he saw Diana step forward into his peripheral vision to his left. With fury he realized she had his gun, the one he kept at his bedside, but he didn't move. The scene was explosive; one misstep and a dozen rifles would be firing until their magazines were empty.

On the other hand, there were now two of

the three of them with guns, against the twelve guns aimed their direction. "Carl, get back in the house," he said quietly. Then louder, "If anyone shoots him, I'll kill you." Carl took a step, and he saw the leader's finger move slightly. Then all movement stopped and he saw looks of shock register on their faces. He had no idea what had shifted the power until he saw a tall, broad-shouldered man with wavy gold hair and blue eyes step out of the trees and walk forward. No gun. No weapon at all. With panic, Jordan discovered that he couldn't move, except for eyes. He started breathing hard and his heart lurched.

"Who are you?" The man asked Diana, but it seemed less of a question than an imperative that she expose her secrets publicly.

Diana gasped, then answered, her voice an odd guttural sound, as if she was resisting a compulsion. "I'm Diana. I'm visiting the owner of this property to determine whether it can be turned into an ecotourist spot for viewing wildlife. Wolves in particular. I've heard there are wolves in this area."

The man laughed. "Wolves – I could tell you about the wolves, but that is not why you are here." The man's voice became low and menacing. "You are here to kill your host, as soon as you are sure he is the monster you think he is. But you are the monster here."

CHAPTER 26 – COMING AROUND

Luke grimaced in anger with himself. He could have saved himself so much time if he'd just come straight here to deal with the sick cub. Her she was, the woman who had lifted the crystal skull from its alcove under in the tunnels under the island. He'd let his ancient belief that men were usually the villains take him to one false lead after another. What had come out of her mouth was irrelevant. By asking the question he'd brought her thoughts forward, and in his urgent need to handle this quickly while he held the entire pack with the rest of his mind he'd plunged into her mind, much farther than he should, but the answers were there. The pack, the thief, and the cub were all right here, in one place, as if drawn together by the Gods, and he could kill them all in a heartbeat without even touching them, be free to get back to the rest of his work.

But executions couldn't be rushed. This was a perfect example of why it was unwise to let any matter escape oversight, for any amount of time; the hazards could snowball. The rogue pack had allowed the failed metamorph to live for too long, now he had to determine what his enemy had learned. Too bad this lesson would likely be wasted on the doomed pack.

"You're no match for Jean, you dog," the woman snarled defiantly, but her voice broke in fear. Perhaps she realized who she was facing; his name and current appearance were transmitted like an APB by his enemy. "Jean" was an interesting take on her current name; she'd changed it to Tam Djinn hundreds of years before, taking Tam as her family name and Djinn as her familiar name. The funny thing was that she'd done so as a play on her half-human son's name, Tam Lin, but she clearly didn't realize that, in Scotland, the name that comes first is the familiar name, while the second one is the family name. For that matter, Lin wasn't even the man's family name; it was a bastardization of "Glen" for the place he'd chosen to live for a brief while. The fact that she was a fool about so many things wasn't so much an indication of her intelligence as an indication of how alien her mind was. But never mind that, he had to get rid of this murderous woman quickly. If he paused, it was only because this black-haired thief reminded him of the woman he loved, and for a moment he enjoyed looking at her. But it wasn't enough.

"Djinn cannot help you now, you now, mo-echa putida, she is not here. You are, and you are no match for me, vappa."

Her jaw clenched then she spoke again. "I found your little head, and now I know where you've been and what you've been thinking."

"If you truly knew my thoughts you would not be so brave, little thief. You would see how easily I can turn you into a drooling imbecile, though some would notice no difference—-"

"I've already told Jean where to find all your friends—"

"Unimportant, they will be dealt with soon enough, though not so quickly as you." Luke needled her to see what more he could get from her before she died. Mind scanning was quicker, but not as safe as dialog; in spite of his threat, there was a slight chance he might wish to keep her alive and turn her back on her commander. He couldn't risk any more of his thoughts being revealed to her. One's own thoughts always bled through to some extent during direct mind contact. "Speak up for yourself, let me know why should let you live, if something comes to mind," he prompted.

Her eyes widened. Did she realize that not only could he could read her mind, but he could also paralyze her without touching her? Now she was scared. "I . . ." her voice trailed off.

"You have come far for such a useless little

thing," he finally said with disgust.

"I can help you," she gasped.

Luke snorted. "I have assistants, vappa. In every corner of the world."

"But not one with direct ties to her!"

"One I have no reason to trust," he waved a hand to dismiss the idea, having already discarded it half a minute ago. A weariness that had been building for millennia settling over him again. He wished he had an assistant he could trust with tasks like this. There were only twenty-four hours in a day, seven days in a week, four weeks in a moon, and thirteen moons in a year, and it wasn't enough time for Luke to monitor and discipline every single transgression. The directives were simple; don't expose yourself to humans, don't harm humans, but in the end there were too many humans, too many lupans, and not enough time.

He waited for her to raise a better defense in case he was wrong, gave her one more chance to raise a sufficient defense. But he didn't need her. What he really needed was a protégé: someone who could follow in his footsteps and orchestrate the work, someone intelligent, loyal, disciplined, and strong-willed. He didn't even have time to delegate basic tasks anymore, he was constantly responding to crises. There were too few faithful lupans he could fully trust. This pack was a perfect example; it was a total mess. This cubling had nearly made a full conversion to vampire. He should have been executed long ago, there was certainly no saving him. Sometimes he wondered why he even bothered to save any of them.

Her jaw was working, but she hadn't yet found any words she felt worthy of sharing with him. He could judiciously spare her another minute, then it would be over.

His focused shifted as he noticed the other pure human in this dynamic and wondered how he had missed the man. While not tall, he was clearly a physical threat were he to be released from the stasis Luke held over the entire group. A quick surface scan of his mind showed some subservience to the abandoned cubling and a fierce anger. There was a single-minded determination, an intense anxiety at his immobility, and a desire to obliterate all but the young blond man behind him. But there was something else about the man that eluded Luke. It seemed both familiar and alien; it drew him, but there was no time to delve further. There was too much going on here, he needed to get the immediate situation under control and get inside for the final task of execution.

He walked forward until he was two feet from her, grasped the barrel of her gun, used his mind to make her hand spasm, then pulled the gun away from her. He turned around to look at the pack of men and women. All eyes were focused intently on him. Good. At least they knew not to betray the laws here, when he was looking them straight in the eye. They had let the issue go for so long without handling themselves, forcing him to come, and he wanted them to be watching this disastrous outcome. Then he would have to deal with them later; he needed to get rid of the woman then handle the mess they'd made of this cub. He'd give them a task so they could believe he intended to let them live.

The mind of this black-haired man in front of him would have to be wiped, of course. Being human, the law said he mustn't be harmed, but the woman he was well within his rights to execute. She was no longer mere human.

With a snap, Luke used his mental powers to explode the vessels in Diana's brain. Blood trickled from her nose as she fell in a heap. He turned around and growled at the semicircle of men and women. Urine leaked through the jeans of several as he continued to growl. When he was sure they were sufficiently reminded who reigned, he released their muscles. Their bodies seemed to curl inward as they looked straight at the ground. One collapsed, and groveled, belly up, as if he were a dog.

Luke snapped his fingers to make sure, again, that their attention was entirely on him rather than their own fear. "You will take the woman and leave. I have killed her mind. Then you will go to the hospital and check for any loose information about us. If you find any, you will call me so I can do the erasure. Your existence depends on doing this well and quickly. I will be back soon to see that it has been done. Now GO! And take her with you!"

Several of the men ran forward, grabbed Diana's drooling body, and threw it in the back of a pickup like a bag of dog food.

Luke looked back at the two young men before him. This would not be a pleasant task, but it was time to read their minds and kill the blond lupan who was dying, then erase the mind of the other, as far back as was necessary. Then he would have to remain in the area and see that any threads remaining were cleaned up. The trucks had all rapidly disappeared down the road in a plume of dust that died down as the roar of the engines faded. With a sigh, Luke stepped forward, wiped their minds of the entire scene with the ferals, and released both from the paralysis.

"Hello," he said with a smile. "It seems I have become lost, and I saw your house. Can you help me? I'm thirsty and I need to use a phone."

Their confusion at finding themselves behind the house, with no memory of how they got there, should make them careless. Most people just acted polite while trying to gather their thoughts, which was good. The sooner they got inside, the sooner they escaped observation by people out hunting or hiking in the area.

The cubling nodded, and the dark, heavily muscled man lowered his gun with a puzzled look, then kept a wary eye on Luke. That was an odd thing. His brief survey of the blond cub's mind showed a definite dominance, but there was a curious dynamic. There was rancor, but the darker, surly man would throw himself in front of a bullet to save the cubling's life. Yet the man was not a bodyguard, nor a lover, nor family. His mind protested these ideas when Luke pushed the concepts into his thoughts.

He would need to be careful, but swift. There was never time for gentleness anymore. The dark one kept an eye on Luke as he went in, his body half turned and ready to fight at the first sign of threat. Luke was able to slip him a thought to leave his gun outside, and the man was so caught up in watching everything at once he didn't even realize he was setting it on the patio before he went into the house.

CHAPTER 27 – GAME CHANGER

Carl watched the stranger step across the patio toward the house. The man paused in front of the threshold as Carl walked in. Jordan was watching over his shoulder at the man as he stepped in behind Carl. Carl looked at the man and felt his soul searched out, judged, and laid back down again.

"May I?" the man said, motioning with his hand toward the door. Carl nodded.

The door seemed to slowly swing wider without being touched, and the man seemed to expand into his meager home. Surely the ceiling fell away for the great creature, then the sense of a huge space collapsed rapidly as proportions became normal and Carl breathed again. There was a relatively plain looking blond man before him, now standing in the mud room, and Carl looked down at the towel he had opened the door with.

Luke spoke. "You are allergic to silver." Carl nodded, unable to look the man in the eyes. "Cub," the man whispered, and the word twisted and sighed around his head and in his ears. He felt so relaxed he became sleepy. Carl could look at the man's eyes now, and they were blue like a glacier over water. He no longer feared the man; instead he was sure the man had come to protect him. He felt safe.

They all moved past the mud room and down the hallway. Carl stepped into the parlor first and looked back as Jordan stepped stiffly into the doorway between Carl and the stranger. The man peered into Jordan's eyes, then a look of surprise slowly dawned on his face.

Jordan apparently passed inspection because the man began to speak, looking at Jordan the whole time, though his words seemed aimed at Carl. "I am sorry for what I came here for. It is against the law to spawn a new lupan without the permission of an alpha. When it happens, by intent or accident, the newly spawned must be watched to be sure the metamorphosis will take correctly. Nearly one in three dies, some—" Luke glanced briefly at Carl, then back at Jordan, "become dependent on drinking the blood of others, and if the pack shirks the duty, it becomes my job to eliminate the cub and punish the pack." Carl wondered what the man saw in Jordan that fascinated him. Or was he concerned about how Jordan would react to what he was saying? It sounded ominous. He wasn't sure he understood.

The man turned to Carl finally, a sad look on

his face, but something had changed. Until now, Carl had felt so safe in this man's presence he hadn't even questioned whether to invite him in.

"No fear, little one, I will make this quick, but with more respect than I gave the killer who had come for you. Unlike her, your body can be returned to your family when I am done."

A rising panic gripped Carl by the throat. He could barely breathe, and it was impossible to talk. He gasped, over and over, trying desperately to fill his lungs but he couldn't seem to get any air. He became dizzy, and the room was getting darker. He sputtered and coughed, but he still couldn't breathe. *Oh my God*, he thought, *I'm going to suffocate! Why can't I breathe?*

Jordan's body shook, then he moved stiffly, launching himself at the stranger, whose look of shock was replaced by a mask of fury as he grabbed Jordan by the shoulders and threw him, hard, into the hallway. Jordan's shoulder hit the slate tiles with a loud, crunching thud. The man turned back to Carl, but Jordan rolled determinedly onto his side, clutching his left arm, and bellowed as he struck the man's feet from under him with a well-aimed kick.

The man tumbled to the ground, then rolled up and shoved at Jordan's head before rising, seeming to stop Jordan cold.

"Faex!" the man spat.

Carl sucked in a deep breath as Luke gazed at the now immobilized Jordan.

"What in Hades are you?" the man whispered to himself. "You are loyal, a defender, and you have an extraordinarily strong mind. You should not have been able to do that, not without an incredible will, and you seem to have greater concern for this man's safety than for your own. All noble. But there is something else about you, and I can't place it..." The man circled around Jordan, who barely moved his head so that he could continue to watch the circling man. The man lunged toward Jordan, but nothing happened and the man stepped back, continuing the circle. As he came past the front door and back into the parlor doorway he lunged toward Carl. Jordan gasped, then wrenched his body up off the ground awkwardly. The man stepped back and held up his hands. "No, I call a truce until I know what it is about you that baffles me."

Carl saw Jordan get to his feet with what looked like an incredible effort, then stand, gasping for breath. His left arm, which he still gripped with his right, appeared longer, the shoulder smaller, and pain laced his glassy gaze. "Leave him alone!" Jordan hissed through gritted teeth, eyes uncharacteristically wide.

The man still held his hands up. "I promise I will leave him alone this evening, from this point forward. We will discuss the future. I could be wrong about this execution."

Carl found himself fully released, and he stepped forward past the man to reach a hand out to Jordan, who flinched.

"What the hell is wrong with you?" Carl challenged the stranger, as he looked at Jordan's slack arm. He wanted to tell the man to leave, but it was obvious that the man would do as he chose.

"I am sorry, that was not one of my best entrances. It went astray. This is a difficult situation." The man was looking at Jordan as he spoke. "Just to be clear," the man continued, "I have released you from the coerce I used on you, and I have released him from what should have been complete immobility." The man shifted his gaze to Carl. "If I wanted to, I could coerce you both, but I will refrain because this little interchange has surprised me in a way that could be very important. After 2800 years, there is little that surprises me." The man paused for a moment, then began again. "You are dying, and the only way you can survive is to consume blood, which will make you a vampire. This is why I or the pack must execute you, as we do all those in your condition. That is what the pack came here for. They should have done it several months ago and saved me the task." Then he turned to Jordan. "And as rare as it is that I have to step in and perform an execution, it is you who are the enigma. If you are truly as surprising as you seem to be, I might have to strike a bargain, which is why I am putting this execution on hold."

CHAPTER 28 – RECOVERY

Jordan was so shocked that Carl could almost see the entirety of both his irises.

"You have no right—" Carl's voice stopped abruptly as he stood, gasping again. Jordan tried to lunge, but this time the man was ready and Jordan seemed locked in place. Carl found he could breathe, but he couldn't talk.

The man replied in clipped words. "I have far more right than you know, and I told you I could coerce you again. I can kill both of you without touching you. You fared well, for humans, simply because you astonished me beyond imagining, but if I have to demonstrate why you do not have a chance against me, let there be no doubt in your minds that *I will*—"

The last two words filled Carl's consciousness like air being forced into a balloon, stretching it to bursting, and Carl was afraid his mind would explode. Somehow. He motioned to Jordan. "STOP! Dear God, just stop!" he gasped as the two words were released from his head, and he fell to his knees on the carpeted floor of the parlor. Jordan moved, and Carl yelled "NO! Jordan, STOP!" Jordan stayed where he was. The man was staring at Jordan again, mouth open and eyes wide.

"God, this is *surreal!*" Carl whispered. "Who the hell are you and what the hell are you doing here?"

The man briefly looked at Carl, then back at Jordan. "I am called Luke. What you must know is I am literally the top dog on this planet, for lupans, and I have tracked you down because you should not exist. I am giving you a reprieve while we sort a few things out. I might let you live, but I will not make any promises beyond tonight. We will see how this goes." He turned to Jordan, who refused the man's offer to help him up, then back to Carl. "If you refrain from more foolishness while we talk, I will leave you free and unharmed tonight. But you need to understand this: I am in control, and nothing you do..." the man gave a puzzled glance toward Jordan, then shook his head. "No, nothing you can do can truly harm me, though I am surprised to find that you can even try. But if you try, I guarantee you will be permanently crippled before you can succeed. I have too many questions to want you dead. It is hard to get answers from a dead man." Luke looked at each of them in turn. "If I promise to sit down quietly and leave your bodies and minds alone, for now, will you agree to do the same?"

Somewhat reluctantly, Carl nodded. He felt

like a child being chastised by an adult, though he couldn't understand why. Jordan didn't move. The man glared at him. Finally, Jordan gave a minute nod. Carl watched Jordan rise gingerly, and it was clear his shoulder was dislocated, but he refused to let Carl help him. He was completely focused on Luke, who looked at him, then suddenly seemed to notice the arm. Luke stepped forward, grabbed Jordan's wrist, raised a leg and to place a foot against Jordan's hip, and pulled and twisted his arm, which gave a sickening pop. Jordan's face barely had time to register fear before the relief appeared. It was the fastest shoulder replacement Carl had ever seen, but Luke made no comment, just walked into the parlor to find a place to sit. In a few moments, they had all found the nearest chair. The tall stranger sat in the oversized, padded lounge chair that Carl usually preferred, right next to the fireplace. Jordan warily chose the wing-back tapestry chair his father had always loved, but only leaned against its arem arther than sitting down. Carl dropped onto the leather sofa. Slowly, Carl's sense of alarm retreated. If the man intended to kill them at this point, surely he wouldn't have fixed Jordan's arm. And whoever he was, he had answers, and Carl needed answers. There was something else about the man that made Carl want to trust him, but he couldn't put a finger on it.

"Who are you?" Carl asked.

Luke looked around. "Can I get a glass of

water? Mental work always makes me thirsty, and this could take some time."

Carl paused for a moment, then nodded at Jordan. "Tea would be good, too, Jordan." He felt a little chilled. Jordan slowly stood and stared at the man, then back at Carl questioningly. "I'm sure he's telling the truth about the truce." And also that there was really nothing they could do, but he didn't need Jordan thinking about that.

Jordan stood just a moment longer, then walked out.

"Remarkable," Luke whispered, watching Jordan exit, then he turned to Carl. "What is he, a servant? Friend?"

"Closer to servant," Carl answered, "but we call them employees here in America."

The man laughed with delight. "Of course. I lost myself for a moment—"

"What did you mean 2800 years? Top dog?"

Luke's grin turned into a coldly serious look. "I do not generally talk to… castoffs like you… let me think for a moment. There are things most of my people know but you are ignorant of, and these lessons haven't been my duty for ages. Do you know what has happened to you?"

Carl frowned. "What do you mean?"

"Let us start with you turning into a wolf three nights a month, in succession?"

Carl drew a swift breath and coughed. "Um, yes, I figured that out some time ago."

"Well, that makes this a little easier. There

are many of us human-wolf hybrids throughout the world. There are also rules that govern us, which are normally taught by elders, but occasionally a new cub slips through the cracks and is not taught what he needs to know." The man's lips curled, and the last words were tinged with anger. He went on. "Which means the cub does not learn how to hide himself, among other things. More importantly, one in three accidentally infected hybrids will start dying, and the only thing that will keep them alive is fresh human blood. Some figure that out, and of those, some get that blood by killing people. And that is why they must be terminated. It is unacceptable," the man finished.

Carl was silent. Luke resumed.

"And this is you. Once I learned about you from my sources, and that the pack was aware but refusing to take responsibility, I had to come hunt you down for termination, which is why I am here." He paused again, giving Carl time to absorb the information. "I do not like to take care of this task. Aside from the other tasks that occupy my time, I have been doing this job far too long. And that is what I mean by 2800 years. The hybridization also makes immortality possible, given a certain amount of discipline and training, which I have, along with wariness and luck. I have been alive and developing my skills for nearly three millennia," Luke explained and drifted into silence for a moment. Jordan walked back in with a glass of water, which he set down on the end table near Luke, and a tray with the steaming teapot and two cups. Carl also noticed Jordan had his gun tucked into the back waistband of his pants. It hadn't been there when Jordan left. Carl could see that Jordan was careful to face Luke.

Luke was gazing with great interest at Jordan, who slowly sat down, staring right back. "You appear to be fiercely loyal," Luke said, his gaze unmoving.

"You attacked us!" Jordan answered, incredulously.

"Granted. But I tested you, and you were unable to break the coerce when I attempted to subdue you with my mind. However, when I feinted at you, then Carl, you managed to break free only when I lunged at Carl, even when I was prepared for you. Which should not be possible." Luke picked up the glass of water and took a long swallow.

Jordan shook his head. Carl realized it was true: apparently, for all his surly demeanor, Jordan was even more protective of Carl than he was of himself, despite his refusal to accept the official title of "bodyguard."

"Furthermore, the incredible strength of mind you exhibited in doing so is astounding." The man paused again, as if allowing time for what he was saying to sink in. "All that remains of what I would need from you is a demonstration of devout discipline. The size of your muscles suggests it is possible that you possess such a trait."

Jordan's lips thinned, and his voice was low but intense. "Need? You don't need anything from me and you sure as hell aren't gonna get anything from me! Why the hell would I help you?"

Luke took another long swallow of water, then answered, "Because Carl's life depends on it."

Jordan looked confused. Carl heard what Luke was saying, and what it meant. He still didn't understand all of it, but a few pieces were beginning to fall into place. "You want to trade my life for Jordan's service to you?"

Luke looked at him carefully, and then gave a slight nod. "That is close enough to what I mean. It is more like he and I would both serve the world, as I do now. It is much more than that, even, and Jordan will probably have much more freedom, and even power, than he has now, though he would also have a list of responsibilities."

"I can't afford more responsibilities," Jordan interjected.

"Do not be selfish!" Luke exclaimed.

They eyed each other.

Luke finally swore. "I am trying to explain this to you, and you are not listening!"

Carl spoke. "We're listening, you're just not

making sense."

"And what has made any sense to you in the past few months?" Luke retorted.

Jordan shook his head. "That's not helpful."

"Listen to me." Luke stood up. "Listen to me… it is not going to make sense right away, but you need to keep listening until it does. I told you the normal sequence of events in these circumstances includes your death, if not by execution, then by the wasting." He looked over at Carl. Carl wanted to squirm but managed to keep perfectly still. Luke looked at Jordan. "But I need someone I can train to take over some of my responsibilities so I do not have to do all the work that needs to be done. It is getting out of hand. I have one apprentice in this region, but I must accept that he will never be good enough to replace me. I need someone who can work with me on the same level as I operate, but there are several traits that are required to reach that goal. I have been looking for a good man for a very long time." The last was clearly directed at Jordan, whose eyebrows rose slightly.

"I don't have time—" Jordan started.

"It will not take you more time than you are already spending, and Carl will not need you soon," Luke answered, apparently having anticipated this.

"What?" Carl said.

Luke turned his glance to Carl. "I can grant you a form of asylum, under house arrest, for your remaining days, but you are not far from your own end. There is nothing that can be done." He lifted the glass and took another drink of water as he thought for a moment, then continued. "You are forbidden to victimize humans to extend your life."

Carl shook his head in amazement. "Jordan has been giving me blood."

Luke looked at Jordan. "Your own blood will not be able to keep up with his need."

"I'm not giving him any more blood, dammit!" Jordan swore.

Luke's eyebrows rose and he looked back at Carl.

"Whatever," Carl interjected. "What's overwhelming me right now is finding a cure. And I'm close." Carl asked.

"There is no cure for what is causing you to waste away," Luke replied.

"You could be wrong about that," Carl replied, his voice cracking on the last word.

Luke rolled his eyes. "I think not. We have been looking for a cure for a very long time, and we have not found it yet—"

"But you haven't had access to the latest technology…" Carl cut in, as cold fear made his voice rise.

Luke slowly shook his head and spoke as if explaining a simple concept to an idiot. "Perhaps not. This current technology has only become available in this latest era, and, like all technology, only to the extremely wealthy."

"So there could be a cure that couldn't be found until now," Carl insisted.

Luke nodded slowly, but his lips were thin.

"And I need Jordan to help me with that," Carl finished.

Luke took another long swallow of water. Carl reached over and poured himself some tea. Jordan took the pot from him and poured himself a cup, holding it in his left hand without drinking any. He was probably keeping his right hand free at his side in case he needed to draw the gun. Carl didn't like the idea, but it made him feel a little safer. He looked at Luke and realized he was being measured. Did Luke know about the gun?

Finally Luke responded. "What if we all three worked at it until we exhaust the possibilities you have in mind now? Then, once you are out of ideas, will you let Jordan go? After all these years, perhaps I can wait just a little longer."

Carl considered. "I'm not sure I trust you," he answered honestly.

"That is fair," Luke nodded. "What if I win your trust?"

Jordan shook his head at Carl, but Carl wanted to think about it. He'd been developing an idea of what the next steps were, and he was pretty sure it would take more than himself and Jordan. He had no idea yet how to do it, but an additional assistant could make a huge difference, especially one with the type of skills Luke seemed to have.

He was far from ready to call Luke trustworthy, but he wasn't sure he had a lot of options, with time running out. He needed more information, which Luke clearly had, or could probably get. "Get me samples of blood from all of those were-wolf people we saw today."

Luke snorted. "How about I just sing down the moon for you? I can give you their names if you will guarantee it will be confidential. You seem to have some access to medical information, from what I read on the surface of your mind when I entered."

Carl thought about that. "It's a start," he answered. "I need to review medical data on a large number of werewolves to see if I can find any common threads that will tell me why one-third of them have problems."

"Lupans. Werewolves are monsters that don't exist; we're shapechangers, not monsters," Luke explained. "Okay. I will get you a list tomorrow, and I will see if I can get you a larger number of them so you have more to work with." Luke swallowed the last of the water, then stood. "Where was the woman staying?" he asked.

Carl and Jordan looked at each other, then Carl asked, "What do you mean 'was?'"

Luke brushed a hand through his hair. "My apologies. You do not remember. The black-haired woman who was staying with you was here to kill you. She is gone now, and will not be coming back. She stole something from me, and if it is here, I need it back. What room would her belongings be in?"

Carl looked at Jordan, then at Luke. "I don't have any reason to believe that…"

"Then go into her belongings. You will find a grimoire for a 'werewolf' hunter. That should help you believe. And while you are digging through her belongings, find the crystal skull. It is mine."

They both looked at Luke, clearly suspicious, and finally Luke threw up his hands. "Fine." He said, then placed one hand on Carl's jawline and forehead. Images of a large gathering of trucks and people flooded through Carl's head, men stepped out of the trucks and aimed guns at him. Diana came out of the house, then Luke arrived, everyone froze in place, Luke spoke to Diana, then Diana dropped to the ground, nose bleeding. He heard everything that was said, but he also knew the thoughts in Luke's mind, and he was aware of Diana's thoughts as well, and her intention to kill them all. Luke pulled his hand away from Carl, then did the same thing to Jordan, who flinched, then allowed it.

Carl was stunned.

"I told you she was saying some scary shit," Jordan said, dazed, as Luke pulled his hand from Jordan's head.

"How do we know these visions are real?"

"How do you know lycanthropy is real, or telepathy?" Luke answered.

"I'll go check her things," Carl said, and disappeared upstairs. Jordan and Luke followed him. Carl opened Diana's suitcase and dug through her books, but nothing was in there. He turned to her carry-on bag and there, at the bottom, was a large book in a velvet bag. He pulled it out and tried to read the runes on the cover, but he couldn't make any sense of them. He opened it and was relieved to find the words inside were in English, but then paled as he read the table of contents, which gave the names and pages of chapters dedicated to locating, identifying, and killing werewolves, among other legendary creatures. He wondered if all of them existed. Mermaids? Fauns?

"The bag to your right," Luke said. "Hand it to me."

Carl saw a second velvet bag, round, and lifted it. It was heavy. Luke stepped forward and grabbed it from him, then slid out a perfectly shaped skull that looked like it was made of clear glass with what looked like streaks of cracks running through it like cobwebs. Quartz crystal. He cupped it lovingly in his left hand and placed the fingers of his right hand along the jawline, up the cheek and at the temple, the same way he'd placed his hand on Carl's, then Jordan's face. His lips opened and his eyelids sagged. He stood unmoving for what had to have been at least thirty seconds, then his mouth snapped shut and he slipped the skull back in the bag, wrapping his arm around it. "Give me your phone number," he said to Carl. "I am unable to stay longer. I will connect with you this evening."

Carl recited the number for his cell phone, and the man let himself out through the front door. He didn't even look back as he broke into a jog and disappeared down the driveway and through the trees.

Carl and Jordan looked at each other for a moment, not sure what to do next after the strange encounter.

CHAPTER 29 – THE SOLUTION?

Carl stared at the spreadsheet on the computer screen down in the lab. A list of names ran down the left side, and traits were listed in columns across the top. "Dammit!" he cursed.

Jordan walked through the door and put the bowl of stew and cup of coffee he'd brought on the counter. "What is it?

"As I suspected, none of them have my blood type. Every other blood type is represented except O-positive."

Jordan walked behind him to peer at the screen. "So maybe it's not a big enough sample."

Carl thought for a moment, then shook his head. "Highly unlikely. It's the most common blood type; 38 percent of the population has it. Out of nearly 100 names, to not see even one is statistically highly improbable."

Jordan pulled a stool over from the steel counter in the center of the room and sat down. "Thirty-eight percent... Luke said one in three dies of this. That's close to the right ratio." He watched Carl stand up and paced back and forth. "If the problem is that you don't have the right blood type, there's no cure."

Carl glanced at the screen and continued to pace. "Yeah. The only way to do that is with a bone marrow transplant."

Jordan slowly stood up. "Excuse me?"

Carl stopped pacing and jammed his hands in his pockets. "Bone marrow transplants can change a recipient's blood type to the donor's type."

Jordan's eyes were staring into space. "So... what you need is a bone marrow transplant."

Carl shook his head with frustration. "That's for people with leukemia, and it's complicated and sometimes fatal. It also comes with a great deal of testing, monitoring, poking and prodding, possibly a lifetime of anti-rejection drugs that impair the immune system. And there's no guarantee it would even work. I thought it might work at first, but I'm not so sure."

Jordan turned slowly to look at Carl. "Or the lycanthropy could kill you. What if computer records show that you have leukemia?"

Carl shook his head, exasperated. "I don't see how that could happen, since I don't."

Jordan stared at him. "This, coming from a guy who used a back door past HIPAA. Records can be hacked."

"No... God no... that's an insane hack, Jordan! Beyond basic HIPAA security, false records would have to show I have leukemia to begin with, then I'd have to get my HLA typed, and the HLA typing would have to be inserted while covering the absence of leukemia, and this kind of thing would have to keep happening over and over every time a test is run to maintain the subterfuge. It's not a single hack, it's multiple hacks, with removal and insertion of data everywhere, repeatedly, without making anyone suspicious of recurring anomalies that are inevitable when electronic files are hacked. I can't even imagine knowing anyone who could do that."

Jordan dropped back down onto the stool. "Neither can I."

They sati in silence for several minutes, then Carl mused, "Or maybe I can."

Jordan raised his eyebrows questioningly. "Like who?"

Carl stared off into space as he answered, "Luke. If he can do what he just did, he can get a computer hacker to do this."

CHAPTER 30 – TRANSPLANT TACTICS

Several hours later Carl found Jordan in the kitchen, steaming chicken with a fragrant broth and chewing on a thumbnail. He had spotted Carl through the evening workout, as always, and neither of them had said a word about their earlier conversation. They couldn't afford to drop a single moment of the workout routine, no matter what else was going on.

Carl paced back and forth for several minutes, then spoke, finally breaking the tension. "A bone marrow transplant could work, but there's no guarantee, and death is a possibility. I'll also be taking a graft that might be needed by someone else. On the upside, apparently, I would just need to be within an hour of the transplant center, not in a hospital for months."

"Okay. But doesn't bone marrow replenish in the donor?" Jordan asked.

"Well, yes, but it takes time. More so even

than blood, and the donor must take a lot of medications that are extremely exhausting, then their immune system is depleted on top of that. It's not a simple process." Carl kept pacing.

"But people do it, and they survive," Jordan said.

Carl frowned. "I suppose."

"And people do sign up to be donors," Jordan continued.

"For people with cancer."

"For people who are going to die if they don't get the transfusion," Jordan argued.

Carl shook his head again. "It's not that simple—"

"Then explain it to me."

Carl paced back and forth several times before apparently realizing that it was that simple when it came down to it, once the hacking was solved. "Okay, let's say I manage to accept this. Where would we do it?"

It was Jordan's turn to shake his head.

Carl went on. "This takes a number of physicians and nurses, though it's nothing as complicated as a liver transplant. Still, there will be tests, procedures, all that, and what if they test for the cancer while I'm under and realize I don't have it, but I have something else they've never seen and they decide they want to look into it?"

Jordan closed his eyes and tilted his head toward the ceiling for a moment, then opened his eyes and looked at Carl. "I still think we can manage it. Luke had control of nearly twenty people in the driveway when he took care of Diana."

Carl felt his heart jump. It all depended on how the mind control worked. He tried to remember how much of his own thought had remained when Luke employed what he'd called the "prestige." He paced back and forth, thinking. He'd certainly remembered that he was Carl, so he hadn't been taken over completely. He'd felt alarmed, so he obviously still had his own emotional awareness.

"Aren't you the one who doesn't trust Luke?" Carl stopped pacing and looked at him.

Jordan paced the small section of the floor Carl wasn't already pacing. "I don't, but I'm not going to watch you die without a fight. We have to do something!"

Carl stood for a moment, watching Jordan pacing back and forth. He wasn't sure he'd ever seen Jordan pace. "Maybe so, but I think we should gather more information, see what other options might exist before we do something we might regret." He watched Jordan continue to pace. "Jordan…"

Jordan stopped and looked up at Carl but didn't speak.

"You were very clear that you refused to have anything in the contract that said you'd protect me, but you protected me when Luke was here, and now you're willing to go to extremes to ensure that I live. What are you doing?"

"It's not a job, it's a choice, dammit! I'm not gonna let you die on my watch, not if I can help it. I can't let you die! But it's a choice. I watch your back because I choose to, not because I have to. And if you really piss me off, I can choose not to."

Carl couldn't think of anything to say.

Jordan mumbled, "I'm… I need to clear my head so we can maybe… think about some alternatives, like you said." He headed toward the door. "I'm going to thaw some more… chicken?"

Carl just nodded, and watched Jordan walk through the doorway, listening to his feet hit the stairs as he went down to the basement where there was a larger pantry. He walked into the hall and found himself pacing again. The rhythm of his own feet made contact with the floor in a one-two pattern, creating a rocking sensation in his body as his weight transferred back and forth, from one foot to the other, and it became a meditation of sorts, as always.

Jordan was, by nature, extreme in nearly everything he did. Extreme discipline, extreme privation, extremes of emotion, extreme privacy, so extreme loyalty shouldn't be so remarkable. Was it loyalty? Was he just taking his job seriously? Did he protect everyone? Would he protect a complete stranger? Yes, he was almost positive Jordan would protect a complete stranger.

He barely remembered when he first met Jordan, when they were freshmen, because Jordan was not at all remarkable then, really. He was swarthy with a dark complexion; olive skin and black hair and brows, and clearly poor by the way he dressed, but so were many other kids at their high school, and many were darker. But as Jordan bulked up over the years he became a staunch defender of the weak, with no tolerance for bullying. Carl had often seen him with a black eye or bruises barely visible at the edges of his T-shirts. He'd been fighting, but not for himself; no one was foolish enough to take him on after he had developed a thick layer of muscles. But every time he came upon a bully attacking a smaller kid, Jordan leaped in and crushed the bully. Luke was right; Jordan was, by nature, a defender.

*   *   *

The following morning, Jordan stood close as Carl answered a knock at the door and Luke stepped in.

"Thanks for coming over," Carl said.

Luke looked at Jordan, who was standing in the hallway, as he stepped into the parlor. "There are things I will not say over a phone. I had several long talks with Mr. Tesla about freely communicating over a medium that is accessible by anyone, and he had far more faith in humanity than I have. He admitted that surveillance could be performed, though, and I have been wary ever since." Luke sat down on the sofa. "As usual, I don't have much time, but again, this seems important. Talk to me."

Carl shook his head. "Nikola Tesla?"

Luke crossed his ankles as he looked around at the ornate wall casings and oil paintings. "Of course. 2800 years of life affords one the option of meeting many people. He was doing some astounding things that were so far ahead of what others seemed capable of I had to find out if he was a hybrid, or perhaps an alien." His eyes locked onto a silver Grecian statuette of a water nymph that sat on the end table next to him.

"Have you had conversations with every famous person that existed over the last two millennia?" Carl asked with astonishment.

Luke picked up the statuette and appraised it as he answered. "No, just the ones who were important to me. And a few I bumped into while talking to those people." He put the nymph down and looked up at Carl.

Jordan shook his head as he sat down in the wingback chair and scowled at Luke. "I think you're full of shit, and we can't verify either way. I think there's a different explanation for this apparent mind control crap you pulled."

Luke gave him a thoughtful look. "Yes, you would. I think it really irritates you that I was the one in control as soon as I arrived. You have done a lot to maintain perfect control over everything in your life. Then I walk in, and not only can you not control me, I actually control you, which really annoys you." Luke was grinning, now.

Jordan scoffed. "Anyone would find you offensive."

Luke laughed quietly. "No, just those who pit themselves against me. I wish you would stop that."

"Not gonna happen!"

Luke leaned toward Jordan, staring at him intensely. "What if I taught you how to do what I do, and you developed powers that equaled my own?"

"That's just bullshit," Jordan said, with less force.

"We could make it your bullshit," Luke answered with amusement. "Bullshit makes good earth, a rich growth medium."

Carl's head had been turning back and forth between Luke and Jordan as if he were watching a tennis match. "I thought you were saying we need to make this quick?"

Luke glanced at Carl. "I did. I am working on it. I told you this is important to me."

"This isn't what I called you about," Carl replied with exasperation.

Luke appeared to be surprised. "Oh, I am sorry, this is what I came here for. Well, quickly then, what is your problem?"

"I think I can cure myself with a bone marrow transplant, but I'd need your help."

Luke stood up and moved slowly to crouch in front of Carl, staring into his eyes with fascination. Jordan stood up quickly and Carl motioned him to stay back.

"How would that work?" Luke asked curiously.

Carl answered, "That list you gave me; I reviewed the names and none of these werewolf people on the list have blood type O-positive, as does 38 percent of the population. It looks like blood type is the common denominator for people that don't survive." Carl started ticking off the next three sentences on his fingers. "That would be just about one in three that don't make it. The transfusion I got from Jordan made me healthy, temporarily. And you mentioned that those who don't make it can extend their lives by receiving blood."

"Consuming blood is what I said," Luke corrected him with distaste, but he still looked fascinated.

"Well, apparently receiving blood works as well," Carl responded. "At least when it's O-negative, like Jordan."

Luke turned a warm, curious gaze toward Jordan. "Okay, go on."

"If I get a bone marrow transplant from someone with O-negative blood, it can change my blood type," Carl answered.

Luke stood up and walked in a slow circle around the room as he thought about it. "Hmmm. And if this works for you, we will also be able to fix the accidents that otherwise fail to survive, or become blood-sucking vermin. That would be a good thing. It also might appease our masters."

Jordan's jaw dropped. "You just execute these people who did nothing wrong but get bitten by an irresponsible freak? How do you live with yourself?"

"Wait, what masters?" Carl tried to say, but Luke was talking over him, sounding a bit frustrated.

"First of all, it is mercy," Luke said forcefully, "because living like Carl has been living is too much suffering, and he is only in the early stages; it gets worse, and quickly. Becoming a vampire is even more horrific, and for more than just the diseased ones. But more importantly it is the law, and if we do not abide by the law we will ALL be executed. That is what happened to nearly all the other hybrid races. We are down to lupanthrus, whom you call werewolves, and piscanthrus, whom you know better as mermaids, and just a handful of other hybrid species. The bovanthrus – or minotaur, as you most likely know them – and so many others, they have all been exterminated. We will be as well if we do not obey the laws we were given. Fortunately, wolves are an obedient species so it has been easier for us than the others, who had a harder time doing as they were told. We were also one of the last species created and we were given more of the beneficial traits of the aliens who created us."

"And the... uh... fish people? They're obedient

as well?" Of all the things Luke had just said, Carl couldn't imagine why this is what Jordan wanted to hear about.

Luke laughed. "Hardly, but they live at the base of the ocean now, so they have fewer opportunities for a lapse in obedience."

Carl thought for a moment, trying to ignore the information that wasn't relevant to his problem. He latched on to what he'd heard that he needed. "So you can go into someone's mind and erase their memories?"

"One of my many jobs, yes," Luke answered, looking at Jordan.

"And we've witnessed your ability to control a person's mind well enough to incapacitate the person," Carl said.

"Yes," Luke said again, his eyes still measuring Jordan's response.

Luke's disinterest in Carl was unnerving, but he needed answers. "Can you make people do things, while they are still acting autonomously, using their knowledge and skills?"

"Yes, though such a task is not simple, especially when there is more than one person to control. Why?" Luke finally turned toward Carl.

Carl frowned in concentration as he continued pacing. "I'm convinced that I need the transplant. I know you were able to handle Jordan and me both at the same time, but we were both still in possession of our thoughts. Can you take control of a surgical team at a surgical center, and get me a bone marrow transplant by doing so?"

Luke sat quietly for a moment. "Well, there is more than one way to do that with the type of skills I have, but it would probably involve a larger number of people than you have considered."

Carl lifted a hand and raised fingers one by one; "There's the surgeon and a couple of assisting nurses—"

"And the records, which requires identification and control of people with access to those records," Luke interrupted impatiently. "This used to be so much easier, before the computer era. You humans have gotten way too far ahead of yourselves in the last fifty years. Deos, I am so sick of this endless job."

Jordan piped in quickly, "You mean you can handle all the computer end of this?"

Luke glanced at Jordan. "It can be done, with some effort. And with some risk."

Needing more detail, Carl asked, "What risk, exactly?"

Luke replied, "The mental contact works both ways; my own thoughts are exposed to others when I do it, and that is a lot of very privileged information. But worse than that, every time I go into a mind I can only easily access surface level thoughts, and even then there is a chance I will not exit cleanly, that will scramble a brain. At a minimum there is some amnesia. In some cases, complete irreversible dementia. So I avoid it unless I know the being is going to die anyway, or it is of critical importance. If I harm a human, I'd better have a reason that the overlords would consider sufficient."

Carl stopped pacing, wondering which question to ask first; his current need trumped his curiosity. "Dementia? And this could happen to any, or even all of the surgical team?"

"Yes. So it is only done if it meets more important objectives. Which might apply to this situation. It could save countless lives that are currently ended because they are non-viable." Luke replied somberly, looking down at the carpet as he thought it through.

"So this isn't just about me?" Carl asked.

Luke's eyebrows lifted as he looked up at Carl. "Not at all. If it were just about you, you would be dead--"

"What is fucking wrong with you?" Jordan swore.

Luke sighed, "Very little, unfortunately. Except that I am really fucking tired, and I really wish I could just fucking retire. But back to the question at hand. Have you ruled out all other possible solutions?" Luke turned to Carl.

Carl paced. "We haven't had a lot of time to really brainstorm."

"Then let us do some brainstorming now and come to a conclusion," Luke said. "If we are going to do it, sooner is better than later."

CHAPTER 31 – MAKING PLANS

Jordan made a pot of coffee, with a bit of cinnamon and ginger, a dash of pepper, and some fresh turmeric, at Luke's adamant insistence. He claimed it boosted mental clarity and Carl supported the claim, so Jordan did what he was asked. He sure as hell didn't like this new plan, but he couldn't think of any other way to keep Carl alive, and he didn't want to see him die, so he decided to bide his time, keeping a close eye on Luke.

Luke just didn't seem to have any moral compunctions about "executing" people, or any decent self-editing on the subject, even when he was talking to the subject of his suspended execution. He just let what he was thinking come right out of his mouth, not caring whether the person he had said he was going to kill heard it or not. Jordan was half-sure he was simply a psychopath with hypnotic tricks, but he couldn't seem to rule out the distinct possibility that the guy could, and would, handle this transplant

Carl needed. He hated having nothing but bad options, but that's where he was. Again.

He brought the coffee and three mugs into the parlor, where Carl and Luke were busy with dry-erase markers on the windows. Carl had pulled all the drapes aside so the windows were fully exposed and they could use them for brainstorming.

"What do you think?" Carl asked over his shoulder, his hand still in the air, ready to write something onto the window.

Jordan looked at what was written. Carl had "Mind-Control Surgical Team" below which was a straight line down, where he'd written "Luke's connections." There were bullets points marked with dashes under his name, including one that was marked with the words "many moving parts." Jordan had to move sideways to see the last point clearly when he came back in. He put the pot and mugs down on the coffee table, then saw the plus before "complete control over information and process." So those weren't dashes on the other side, they were minus signs. Pros and cons.

"I thought we were brainstorming ways other than a transplant."

"Yeah, well, we can't think of anything. Can you?"

Jordan poured himself some coffee and looked at the window. Then through it. The cedar and fir trees were a deep green. There was a hemlock tree that Jordan always noticed on the far side of the clearing. The tip flopped over as all Hemlock trees did at the top. Hemlock was a notorious poison, and he tended to notice all the ways to die, wherever he went. It was the last thing he wanted to focus on right now. Ways to live. How many ways to live could he come up with?

It's in Carl's blood. It's his blood type. The only possible solution was to change the blood type. That, or go down the path of vampiredom, which sounded horrific even if Luke would allow it, and clearly he would not. Luke certainly had the power to enforce this rule. Jordan shook his head in frustration. "Give me time, dammit! This is all too fast—"

"Not fast enough, in my opinion," Luke answered quietly. "You two have no idea how much patience I am showing you. You have no idea the pressures I am under, the timeline we are on, the immediacy of the need to get this done and move on to other imperatives. The fact that you have a possible solution and that it could save more than just Carl's life is the only reason for my patience. The number of lives that could be saved is huge. But make no mistake, my patience is running out." Luke looked fiercely into Jordan's eyes. "I am doing this for you, Jordan. If you will do this, you will need to get up to speed quickly, and making decisions like this is one of the most critical elements of the job—"

"I'm not taking your fucking job!" Jordan cursed, and Luke leaned back in surprise.

"Fuqua! I am not accustomed to being challenged!" Luke answered, stepping forward.

Jordan leaned in and shouted, "I'm not accustomed to people who can't get it through their thick skull that I said no!"

Luke sat stunned for a moment, then laughed with delight. "The gods themselves must be laughing at me now. I finally have what I have been looking for hundreds of years, right under my nose, and it refuses to do what I ask because it is exactly what I am looking for!" Luke's expression changed to a fierce glare. "I am way too old for this, I am too tired, and I have too much to do. I have forgotten how to work with others with all the solitary work I have had to do, and I have got to find my way out of this labyrinth I have built around myself, but I keep going down the wrong path." Luke shook his head, then looked up and shook his fist at the ceiling. "I hope you are enjoying this! I am certainly not."

Carl and Jordan looked at each other. Jordan shook his head. Surely Carl saw the insanity now.

Apparently not, Jordan thought, as Carl spoke. "So that's it, then. The only option is the transplant. You can take care of the computer hacking as well as mind hacking."

"Not the computer hacking, my current assistant will do that," Luke answered, wearily. "Even if I understood computers, there is no way

I would have time to do both, and I seriously do not have time to clean up any of the details that might escape after the fact. It seems there are always details that escape. The data breach will snowball, and every moment I take cleaning it up there is more mess to clean up. It can take years to get ahead of it, if at all. Consider the Roswell incident. And if I miss a single thing, some government agency will release documents, or someone will hack them, then I have a ton more work to do."

"Can your assistant do it?" Carl asked, setting his curiosity about Roswell aside.

Luke shook his head. "He needs more practice and experience to learn proper judgment. I suppose this would be good practice."

Carl took the mug of coffee Jordan had finally poured for him. Luke poured his own since Jordan clearly wasn't going to.

Jordan took a sip from his mug, then looked down at it. That was actually pretty good. Weird, but not bad. When he looked up, Luke was staring at him. "You've got an assistant, that's great," Jordan said. "That means you don't need me." He suddenly felt anxious as he realized Luke seemed to be planning him into these machinations, and he didn't like it. He didn't want his mind taken over again, but he didn't know how to stop Luke if Luke decided to do it. He was utterly powerless to stop it.

Jordan looked back down into his mug. He

didn't want to look at either of them. Luke was a murderer, insane, controlling, everything Jordan had always fought against. And Carl had been drawn into his spell, just as Jordan's mom had been drawn into his dad's spell. Jordan felt a rising fear. It was a foolish and criminal idea to doctor medical files and control the minds of a group of people. He wanted none of it, but he couldn't see any other answer.

"We'll do it ourselves," he said, finally, and looked up at Luke. "We don't need you."

Carl answered. "You're wrong. We do need him. We can't do this alone."

"Then you don't need me." Jordan slammed his mug on the table and spun to leave. The house had become far too confining.

*   *   *

Several hours later, Jordan took a deep breath and set his nerves aside as best he could, then hiked back down to the house, grabbed the silver handle of the front door, pulled it open, and walked inside.

Luke was still sitting in the middle of the sofa, thumbing through something on his cell phone. He looked up at Jordan, who would have preferred the man already be gone. "What did you decide, Carl?" Jordan asked.

Carl set his mug on the table. "I'll give Luke copies of the records that will need to be entered into my file. He'll get them to his assistant who will call me and put me in touch with the data team he puts together while I find a suitable donor, then he and I will see that the donation request is accepted by a suitable center. When it's time, Luke will be present to assure the appropriate mental state of the staff and coordinate any further records alterations, and we'll take it from there."

"You don't need me then," Jordan said with relief.

"Oh, we most certainly need you," Luke said.

Jordan felt his lip curl as he sized up the man sprawled across the smooth brown leather of the sofa. "What for?"

Luke slowly sat up. "To make sure nothing interrupts us as we perform the process."

Jordan leaned against the doorway. "That's not in my job description," he said finally.

Luke seemed to almost be smiling. "That is your choice? You want Carl to die?"

Jordan looked at Carl. His face was just the slightest bit fuller than it had been a few days ago, but it was still bony, compared to the healthy, younger Carl he had gone to school with. He wondered if Carl's body would ever fully recover from this. No, he didn't want Carl to die, but he wasn't going to work for Luke.

"What if I don't? I'm not taking orders from you."

"You cannot refuse this," Luke said with exasperation. "We will need someone watching the doors for possible interruptions while Carl is receiving the transplant and Dwayne and I are controlling the people and the circumstances. And someone must take charge. Excuse me if I think it is the one who knows how all of this will be done!"

"Well, we don't have to call them orders, or say who's giving them," Carl interrupted. "These are simple roles. Luke does the mind work, Jordan makes sure no one interferes, and I get new bone marrow."

Jordan turned to Carl. "How long will this donation take?"

Carl looked uncomfortable. "Well, that's going to vary a bit..."

Jordan's eyebrows rose.

"The first time—" Carl answered.

"There's more than one procedure?" Jordan cut in.

"Stop!" Luke's voice pounded in both of their heads, seemed to fill a cavernous space in another dimension. Then, still in their heads but at a more tolerable volume, "Enough of this! It must happen. We must do it. We have no choice but to work together. After this is taken care of, we will reassess to see if it worked. I say we have a truce until then; we all work with each other on faith. I will not kill anyone, Jordan will not walk away, and Carl will not die. Agreed?"

Jordan was furious, but he assessed each of the statements, in turn, and had to admit that he couldn't disagree with a single one, regardless of how much he wanted to. "And then you leave us alone?"

Luke responded, his voice back to an entirely normal level. "And then we talk about you, and you will have a choice to make."

Jordan looked at Luke. "And you'll let me choose? You won't force me or manipulate me?"

Luke answered tiredly, "You will have to have free will at that time. I will not force you, and I will not force your mind. The choice must be yours or there is no point."

"That's hardly reassuring when I know you can make me remember or forget whatever you want without any ability to stop you."

Luke's penetrating stare made Jordan uncomfortable. "If I had as much control over you as you claim, there is no way I would have seen a gun on you when you walked away earlier."

Jordan felt queasy. Hed lost his temper and forgotten to hide the gun from Luke when he left the room. And the wording of Luke's response seemed to fall short, though the answer seemed clear enough. The man could be lying, of course, so it hardly mattered. Luke was clearly impatient, and his seemingly omnipotent powers were very disorienting when he chose to use them. And he could apparently use them whenever he wanted. It seemed, though, that he did want to see Carl live. A temporary truce was worth a try. He addressed Carl, purposely avoiding Luke's stare. "Okay. This isn't something I'll walk away from. You've been taking my blood for months, if this works it'll be the last time. Once you're in the clear we can resume the argument over the rest of the crap I disagree with."

"Then it is agreed. I need to get back to the rest of my work." Luke stood up swiftly and left through the front door. Jordan and Carl watched him through the windows as he jogged into the woods and was gone.

CHAPTER 32 –
FINAL DETAILS

Over the next few weeks Carl worked with Luke's assistant, Dwayne, to connect with other people who became instrumental in getting electronic information sorted, changed, and downloaded, so he could get the transplant. He went to the local medical clinic, and once or twice all the way into Seattle, to receive tests and analyses that were then hacked just enough to make it look like he needed a bone marrow transplant.

Carl was standing in front of his computer in the lab when the donor match data came up. There were several matches, most of them O-positive blood type, which wouldn't work. Of the O-negative blood types, one was on the other side of the world, which wouldn't work well. He had the match data on one screen and beside it the hacked information of personal details on each match donor. He cross-referenced each before making a decision, but what caught his attention was one of the names in the match file. The location was listed as Baring, Washington.

When he used the ID number to cross reference the donor file, his own address came up. It had to be Jordan. He stared at the record. If he could use Jordan, that would simplify much of the process. But how were the two of them a match! The best matches tended to be people of the same race.

*   *   *

"Why are you on the bone marrow transplant donor list?" Carl asked Jordan.

Jordan stared at Carl without answering for what seemed like an eternity, then turned away. "That's personal."

"And you updated the records to reflect your current location," Carl pressed, wanting to get to the bottom of Jordan's reluctance.

"That's confidential, Carl. It shouldn't matter whether my records show where I live, it isn't supposed to show who I am. Who the hell are these geeks that hacked my personal file so easily?" Jordan shot back, angrily, pounding a piece of meat he'd removed from the upright freezer in the pantry.

"That's not important."

"The hell it's not!" Jordan whipped around. "If one person can do it, so can the next, and suddenly I'm as easy to find as... as roadkill on a mountain highway!"

"Who would be trying to find you by checking transplant donor records?"

"Anyone who knew my mom's health issues.

Her health has been shot ever since the accident. That's why I'm on the donor list." He called it an accident, though Carl knew better. He felt like his entire life was going off the rails.

"So you were tested in case your mom needed a transplant and you might be the best match?"

"And wouldn't you know, I end up the perfect match for a man who can afford to buy an entire corpse!" Carl flinched as Jordan's steel meat mallet went right through the frozen loin and hit the granite countertop so hard Carl thought he'd better check for cracks. Jordan cursed.

Carl forged ahead. "Not perfect, but surprisingly good considering we look like very different nationalities." Carl was holding his elbows, ankles crossed as he leaned against the refrigerator.

Jordan flipped the loin over and kept pounding it. "It's fucked up. I can't be a match. Especially not if nationality is an issue. You're a friggin' Aryan, and my family is a bunch of Italians and Arabs. Your gene pool wouldn't be caught dead anywhere near mine." Jordan cursed the meat, dropped the mallet and grabbed the loin with both hands. He whipped it over his shoulder, then slammed it down on the counter so hard he felt the vibration through his feet. Carl stared at the counter as Jordan left the meat where it sat for a moment, turned on the faucet to wash his hands, then poured himself a glass of water. Finally, he turned around and looked at

Carl. "Are you really sure I'm a match?" He asked, finally quiet.

Carl considered lying for a moment since this wasn't going well. But Jordan was a surprisingly good match, and using Jordan as a donor could put far more control back in their hands. He unfolded his arms and shoved his hands in the pockets of his jeans. "Data doesn't lie, Jordan."

Jordan snorted. "Yours does."

"The only reason my data lies is because we planned it that way," Carl snapped. "No one else has any reason to doctor these records."

"That you know of," Jordan shot back.

Carl simply stood, in silence, until Jordan finally looked down at his feet. "Okay, I got it. I'm your perfect match."

"Well, no, like I said there are a couple of better matches, but if we use you and Luke can get his hands on complicit physicians we might be able to do this here in the lab and avoid a lot of questions. Or at least have one person we don't have to involve in the deceit." Carl hated pushing Jordan on the matter, but he was extremely uncomfortable with the amount of deceit involved with the procedure. That didn't make it easier. Jordan was clearly having a very hard time accepting that his body might hold what Carl's body needed, and the best answer was that Jordan go through the marrow donation process so that his bone marrow went into Carl's bloodstream. "Jordan, I'm going to give you some time to think about this. There's no law that says you have to do this, you can say yes, you can say no."

Jordan started pacing back and forth, staring at the clean, white vinyl floor. "No..." Jordan's voice was strained. "Look, it's not that I don't... Carl, if something happens to me, what will happen to my family?"

"Family?" Carl said, shocked. "Are you talking about that girl in California?"

"God, no," Jordan scowled. "I'm talking about my mom, my sister."

"I'm not following you," Carl said, slowly.

"I mean... she can't work, Carl!" Jordan said emphatically. "Disability benefits don't cut it. Not even if she didn't need special medicine all the time, and she does. Just getting to the store is more than she can do most days. I've been paying for a nurse to come in and take care of her." Jordan started chewing a nail, still pacing.

"No wonder you didn't have any clothes. You mean you were taking care of me in exchange for someone taking care of your mother?"

"And setting money aside for any emergencies that might come up, and meat on the table every so often. My little sister has been growing like a weed."

Carl's voice was quiet, slightly agonized. "Jordan, you never told me."

Jordan threw his hands in the air, frustrated. "Now you see why I can't do it? If I'm gone, what would happen to them?"

Carl spoke slowly. "Well, donating marrow is a very safe procedure, but I can also take care of that... "

Jordan had stopped pacing, now he looked up. "What do you mean, 'Take care of that?'"

"I've been paying you off interest in my main investment account. A portion the interest bleeds into a separate account, and I write you a check every month from the second account. It helps me keep the funds clear so I always have access regardless of any purchases my broker makes. I can put the proper amount in a trust fund in your name, with qualifiers, like 'as long as you are working for me until death or severe injury' or some such, and you can write it into your will that the account will continue in your mother's name if something should happen to you. But—"

"You would do that?" Jordan asked incredulously.

"Yes, but—" Carl tried to interrupt him.

"That's great! I could stop worrying. That would be perfect!" Jordan exclaimed.

"Jordan!" Carl shouted to get his attention. He spoke in a normal voice then. "I don't want you to do this for money."

Jordan looked at Carl, stunned. "Money? You think I'd do it for money? Are you kidding? I'd go back to my old job and my old closet before I sold my body, or any part of it. It's not the money, it's knowing my family is secure. My family is my final obligation; once they're taken care of I can't walk away as you die knowing I could have done something, even if it kills me. With my family secure, I'm free to live or die." He paused for a moment, hands on his hips, staring at Carl. "God, Carl, you... your bones... they're still sticking out. How long do we have? If we do this, how is it going to work? How much time does it take to set this thing up?"

Carl shrugged. "The sooner we get started, the sooner it's done. If we know the donor we just need supplies and staff. Have you ever acted?"

"What did you think I was doing when you came to tell me my true calling?" Jordan quipped.

Carl smiled wryly and nodded. "Luke agrees that the subterfuge will go over best if we bring people here. Some will be lupans who are in on it, others he'll trick into seeing the lab as a clinic. We'll have to prepare the lab, which will have to be turned into a sterile recovery room. So, you're going to act the part of a delivery man, and I'm going to place an order through Mednet for all the equipment we'll need. You pick it up and bring it here, then we'll get it set up. There's no way they'd be willing to deliver it to a home, that would raise flags."

"You can't really mean to do it here. We don't have the expertise or equipment to save your life if something goes wrong."

"I thought about it Jordan: it takes several months to recover from a bone marrow graft, and they want me within an hour of the transplant center, which would mean an apartment in Seattle. What happens when I turn into a wolf?"

Jordan opened his mouth, then shut it, and suddenly swung around to pound his fist against a wall, driving a solid dent into it. He remained standing there, with his back turned to Carl, his fist not moving from where the blow had landed. Slowly his shoulders lowered, and he turned toward Carl again. "Fine. But if this is our only choice, I want a doctor here, in the lab with you, and a nurse at a bare minimum, on-site at all times, one way or another. If we have to scuttle you out into the trees three nights a month under her nose... damn, Carl, if you're out gallivanting in wolf hide and your immune system is shot, this is not gonna work!"

"One thing at a time, like you said. We don't know exactly how the virus is going to interact with the graft. Maybe it'll do that rapid-heal, like after the bullet, we don't know. We just need to be prepared for all possibilities." Carl's eyes suddenly had a far-off look and he started pacing. "We really don't know what's going to happen. It could be just like any transplant, or it could be way worse, but it could be way better. I hadn't thought of that. This isn't like any other transplant ever performed." Carl whipped around "Jordan, this is groundbreaking research! This is the kind of thing that makes a doctor's career—" Carl was almost laughing with delight, his eyes bright and wide open. "My God, I wish I could be the one doing the procedure. And this poor doctor will have no idea the miracle he's involved in —"

"Stop it, Carl!" Jordan's voiced grated through a nearly clenched jaw.

Carl stopped and looked at Jordan in surprise. "What?"

"You're about to be a fucking guinea pig! You could die!"

Carl's shoulders slumped in realization. "Oh yeah. That kinda sucks, doesn't it?

"Yeah it does, you fucking moron." Jordan pivoted and trudged out the door.

CHAPTER 33 –
THE ULTIMATE
DECEIT

Several weeks later Luke stood by the door to the lab. He had flown in from Brazil that morning. He nodded at Dwayne, who was standing a few feet away from a home infusion nurse; Dwayne was concentrating on making her believe the house was a medical clinic and Jordan was a perfect match. That Jordan was even a partial match seemed odd. Carl said the best matches were people with the same regional heritage. He looked like a completely different genotype than Carl, more Mediterranean and much less Anglo-Saxon. Of course, Carl's genetic matching had changed drastically since he acquired the wolven DNA, but it couldn't be that.

Something about Jordan still bothered him, and he passed next to the IV post to ponder for a moment. Carl wasn't merely human any more, but it was more than wolf that had been added to his body. There was a small amount of alien DNA as well, since the original gene-splicing research the aliens performed was to determine how the Anunnaki genes reacted to being spliced with other species. It was the alien chromosomes that endowed werewolves with the psychic abilities that Luke had learned to control so well. Luke and Carl would likely have been a better match than Jordan and Carl, since Jordan had neither the wolf nor alien genes. Of course, Luke avoided giving blood and had advised his people against it as well. Carl was at a disadvantage in this testing, being half human himself. The donors should all be entirely human.

Luke felt like he could almost remember who Jordan reminded him of; another lupan or an alien, he thought. One or the other. Clearly not lupan. Alien? Jordan was raised human, but so were aliens; they swapped their babies with those in human cribs so they didn't have to be bothered with raising them. Could Jordan be one of these changelings? Could the alien DNA be so strong that even a small amount of it in Carl be enough to draw the data to Jordan as a match? That could explain Jordan's ability to overcome Luke's powers. The powers came from the aliens; his ability to use it, with all his years of practice, would still be inferior to an alien's instinctive use of the same powers.

He wasn't sure it mattered, really. Luke needed Jordan on Luke's side of the equation, and he had no intention of taking "no" as an answer, no matter what Jordan thought. But what could he do if Jordan resisted? Jordan had no idea how powerful he really was. Luke needed to keep him that way until Luke had won his loyalty somehow.

Luke turned his thoughts to the immediate issue and looked at Carl where he lay on the gurney. Carl's skin hung loosely over his now skeletal frame. Yesterday he had shown Luke and Dwayne the instrument readings as they were expected to look, fortunately because he looked exhausted right now.

Luke was pleased to see that the machines showed readings he knew weren't correct. It was Dwayne's job, in addition to handling the nurse, to see that anyone reading the machines would see the illusion of a normal transplant. Luke had drilled Dwayne on the images last night until the boy was able to visualize them clearly and transmit that vision to others so well that he had even fooled Luke. It was another notch toward Dwayne's redemption; everything was going according to plan. His biggest concern was the possibility of rejection. If Carl's body rejected the transplant, they were far from the hospital, and it would be his job to keep Carl's body functioning while Jordan drove them there, in a last ditch effort to salvage the cure. It took more time than Luke had, but if this worked, the ancient battle between werewolves and vampires could end.

Dwayne would be on his own if anything

went wrong, and Luke kept watching him for any signs of fatigue. It would be a huge mess to clean up if it didn't all fall into place, in which case Luke was tempted to just scramble the nurse's mind and walk away rather than do the exhausting work of mental erasure and replacement. If he did so, and was found out by the aliens, it wouldn't go well for him.

But so far all was going well. He was counting on the remarkable rate of healing that lupans possessed, but Carl's condition wasn't good, and the virus could see the transplant as an injury to heal. Either he became fully lupan and his body assimilated the new bone marrow, making it part of a well-functioning system, or his body rejected the cure and they were back to dealing with him as he transformed, instead, into a vampire, which Luke would never allow. Failure would be a death sentence for Carl. And a death sentence for Carl would make Jordan harder to win over.

Carl was watching the IV drip. This would go on for hours. Luke had been shocked when he saw Carl's body convulse as the marrow depleting drugs entered his system in the previous procedure, but Carl had told him to expect it. Receiving the marrow was a much gentler process.

Luke silently went out to the little room with the barred door where Jordan was recovering from the marrow draw, receiving what his own body needed from his own drip.

"How's Carl doing?" Jordan mumbled.

"Everything is going smooth, he is alert and seems to be feeling fine," Luke answered. "How are you feeling?"

"I just hope I don't have to do this again. Those damn needles were huge."

Luke grinned. Jordan clearly hated needles, and the fact that he'd lain down and taken the insult to his body with relative stoicism was a perfect example of his willingness to set aside his fears in countless ways to protect, defend, and sacrifice himself for others. It was glorious. Now it was time to ensure that Jordan couldn't back away from the plans Luke had for him, and this was delicate. He also had to remain aware of Carl's progress while he handled Jordan, but this was his best chance to overcome any objection Jordan might have about becoming part of the culture. And once Jordan was part of it, he would see the sense of being at the top of it. That he was about to go against his own principles and deny someone their free will irked him, but he couldn't pass up this opportunity to have an heir to his own power. Ther seemed to be no other way.

"Is there codeine in your drip?" Luke asked.

"No, dammit. They used to do that when the marrow came out of the hip bones, but the way they do it now they just give me drugs that make me feel like shit." Jordan watched the bag carefully, studiously avoiding looking at the line where it went into his arm.

That wasn't going to work. Jordan needed to be looking away from the bag. Distraction, as usual, would be the first step.

"Do you want Dwayne to bring the refrigerator and stove down so that you have a kitchen here as well as the bed, so you do not have to go up and down the stairs as much?" Luke inquired.

"NO!" Jordan almost shouted, then lowered his voice, looking straight at Luke. "Tell him to stay out of my kitchen, dammit."

Luke smiled as he mentally left a trace of his own image where he had stood when Jordan had reacted so adamantly. He slowed Jordan's mind down so it seemed that the next two minutes occurred in a single instant. He drew the vial of Carl's blood from his pocket, along with the syringe, pulled the cap from the syringe, then quickly withdrew as much blood from the vial as he could. He inserted the syringe into the little tube that came out the side of the main line and pressed the plunger down, watching as the blood turned the liquid in the clear tubing pink, then red. He maintained a very strong image of himself standing in front of Jordan's bed, and the tubing with clear liquid, no Luke anywhere near it, in case the nurse looked in on them. Everything would look normal, no matter how intent her gaze was.

Jordan's mind was strong enough to resist this praestige, but he had to suspect something was up to try, and once Luke invoked Jordan's intense need to control his environment, Jordan's mind was too full of outrage to even consider that something else was going on. It was a technique also used in any sport or magic trick; feint, then do the damage. In time he would teach Jordan ways to avoid falling prey to such tactics, but for now he simply used Jordan's inexperience to achieve his own ends.

He withdrew the syringe, clipped the cap back on, and put it and the vial back in his pocket, to dispose of later. The fewer clues there were about something strange happening, the less likely anyone would recall an anomaly, and it would be easier for Luke to get away clean. He considered tucking Jordan's IV line under the sheet so that he didn't have to maintain the illusion that the fluid was clear, but he knew that Jordan would look much closer at it if something changed unexpectedly, so he simply maintained the illusion. It took very little of his attention to do so. He'd have to remain nearby to keep it up until Carl's blood had fully entered Jordan's veins. He knew there would be no clotting; the virus seemed to prevent that. He shook his head in wonder. The loss of one in three strays had weighed on his heart ever since he first learned of it. If this worked, he would celebrate in ways mere mortals couldn't even imagine. He knew where there were bottles of wine that had been in storage for hundreds of years. Even Dwayne had partially redeemed himself, working hard to master the skills he needed to assure the transplant went smoothly.

"I am sorry, I just thought it might be easier for you. You know better than I do how you want your space set up." Luke dropped right back into the discussion as if there'd never been a pause, which, for Jordan, there hadn't. This was an essential part of the praestige as well; all the real elements needed to match the suggested elements so that the entire illusion was seamless. Luke had been doing this for so long he hardly had to think about it. "I need to get back to Carl. I just wanted to make sure you were okay as well," Luke said, and touched the metal of the IV post to lock the image into the metal so it would continue to be transmitted, then exited. He silently re-entered Carl's room and took his place by the door again. He wasn't invisible, as Dwayne was, but he was unnoticeable. It was a simpler illusion, and simple was good. His life was complicated enough, so he took every opportunity for simplicity that he could find.

"How's Jordan?" Carl asked.

Luke's mind snapped back to the current moment. The problem with unnoticeable was that anyone who expected him to be there would notice him. He rid the irritation from his voice as he replied, "Jordan is doing well. He is complaining about needles, though."

Carl laughed, and Luke grinned with him.

Laughter was a good tool when using a praestige. A laughing mind was an unsuspecting mind. But he had no need to fool Carl. The truth would suffice for him. Of course, he didn't know that Luke had just ensured that Jordan just went from Homo sapiens to Homo lupanthrus. Truth was relative.

Carl was nodding off. The transplant was an exhausting process. Luke watched as Carl slipped into a gentle sleep. From what Carl had said, if it worked as any other bone marrow transplant did, it could be months before Carl was safely on the other side and they all knew whether it had worked. Luke sincerely hoped the powerful healing abilities of lupans sped up the recovery; he wasn't sure they had that much time. The alien overlords were already slightly overdue. With the dismantling of the obelisks throughout the world, Luke wasn't sure he would receive any transmissions the aliens sent ahead of their arrival, so he had no way of knowing when they would arrive. He'd tried to ensure the new obelisk built as a monument in the U.S. capital was set up to operate as a transmitter and receiver, but it hadn't been tested. There'd been a number of setbacks during its construction, there was no way to know if it would work.

He watched the IV fluid drip into the chamber above Carl's chest as it slowly seeped into Carl's blood. It was like the sand in an hourglass, every drop like the tick of a clock. Time was running out. He had things to do. But right now the most important thing was in this room, and the next one over. If he could show the overlords that he had found a way to save the lives of lupans that were currently executed because they weren't viable, he believed he could buy them some time, and with that time he might be able to save them all.

CHAPTER 34
– LOSING IT

Three and a half weeks later, Jordan placed a plate with a thick slab of prime rib on the raised desk in front of Carl as Carl stared at his computer screen in the lab while pacing on the treadmill set under the standing desk. Carl grabbed the fork and knife he offered and dug into it, chewing rapidly. "God, but I hope this hunger dies down before long. I feel like I hardly have time to get anything done before I'm ravenous again."

"It's doing you good. You've gained twenty pounds already. How are you feeling today? Any change?"

Carl shook his head quickly as he chewed another bite, then swallowed and answered. "I feel great, aside from this pain in the ass appetite."

Jordan grinned. "Don't knock it, you're putting muscle on. The treadmill and pulleys are really helping."

Carl looked at the treadmill and the pulleys above it, attached to a second set of pulleys and weights behind him. "Yeah, that was brilliant. I can work out right here while I'm reviewing the research. Speaking of which," He cut off another bite from the steak, then handed the fork and knife to Jordan as he chewed, using the mouse to highlight a range of data on the screen and convert it to a graph. Jordan chopped the steak into several large bites, stuck the fork into one, and handed it to Carl as he looked over Carl's shoulder. Carl ate the steak and dropped the fork on the plate, still looking at the screen. It showed his weight gain gradually increasing, starting the day after the procedure.

Jordan nodded. "It all looks good. You're gaining the weight you need, it's going back on as muscle mass, but what about your blood type? How long before you know if it really worked?"

Carl's eyebrows rose. "Let's go ahead and check. It's far too early, from the studies I've read, but I'm no ordinary patient." He took another bite of steak before going to the sink to wash his hands, then he pulled a packet out of a drawer next to the sink and tore it open. He started placing items from the packet on the counter with one hand while holding a finger under the running water. He turned to Jordan and opened his mouth for another bite of steak.

"Seriously?" Jordan said.

"I'm hungry, dammit," Carl replied, and opened his mouth again. Jordan grabbed another piece of steak on the fork and held it out toward

Carl, who grabbed it and chewed, as he continued to perform the steps on the little instruction sheet, placing a drop of water on the card, then breaking the lancet open, spiking his wet finger and dropping blood in the circles on the card.

Jordan watched him, bemused, as Carl moved the card back and forth, tilting it one direction, then another, then finally setting it down.

"Is that it?" Jordan asked. "What does it say?"

Carl cut another piece of meat and popped it in his mouth, answering around it as he chewed, "Don't know until it dries. Why are you so anxious? I'm gaining weight, I'm feeling good, and it's too early to know about the blood type. Why have you got a death grip on your arms?"

Jordan's hands had such a tight grip on his arms he realized he was probably bruising himself. "I just want to know, that's all," he said, lamely. He'd been feeling strange all day. Sounds seemed louder, and he could swear he smelled Carl's sweat over the smell of the steak, and the scent of the blood Carl had just dripped onto the card was intense, along with the chemicals from the test strips. "Maybe I'm coming down with something."

Carl walked over quickly. "Jordan, you're really pale – I mean, for you. You're still quite a few shades darker than most. Are you sure you're okay?"

Jordan shook Carl's hand away. "I'm fine. Leave me alone. I need to get back upstairs, I left the stove on," Jordan lied as he walked out the door and launched himself up the stairs. He didn't want to talk about his growing suspicions. Maybe it was just recovery from the marrow donation drugs, but he'd been fine for several weeks, and just now he was feeling very strange. The acuteness of his senses, particularly smell and hearing, bothered him the most. Those were the same things Carl had said grew more intense after he'd become a werewolf. Had there been a mistake? Had Jordan somehow become infected with Carl's blood during the procedure? He'd watched the nurse very carefully and insisted she put on fresh gloves every time she walked in the room. If he'd been infected it couldn't have been her. And Carl had strictly been a patient. What about Dwayne... or Luke?

Then it hit him. Luke had said he'd let Jordan choose freely whether or not to work with Luke, but he hadn't promised he wouldn't tilt the scales. The man could wipe memories, control people's minds. It would have been child's play for such a man to infect Jordan with the curse, leaving no one the wiser. Jordan would have little choice between suffering the curse blindly and learning to master the skills Luke wanted him to learn. He walked into the kitchen and started scrubbing the frying pan he'd left in the sink. Of course Luke would do it. The more he thought about it, the more he realized that Luke must have always meant for Jordan to become a werewolf. He couldn't learn how to do what Luke did otherwise, could he? Or could he? Jordan scrubbed the caramelized, encrusted juices from the skillet, cursing silently. Of course. It was what Luke intended all along. The man might not even care whether Carl survived. What the hell was this obsession about? What made Jordan so special that no one else in the world, in 2800 years, could do the job Luke wanted him to do?

Jordan turned the faucet on and rinsed the soap off the skillet, then rinsed his hands. He pulled whole grain bread from the cupboard, slicing the small chunk of meat he'd set aside into thin pieces and piling them high. He reached into the refrigerator to grab the sliced tomatoes and lettuce leaves he had stacked there earlier while the steak had fried. He placed them carefully on the meat that was stacked on the bread, pulled out mustard to squeeze on top, then tossed another slice of bread on top, then looked at the window as he took a bite of the sandwich. There was the hemlock tree across the yard, tip bent down toward the earth. He took another bite and looked around at the other trees, rising tall against the backdrop of the granite cliff face, and thought as he chewed. Yes, it played perfectly into Luke's hand. While he didn't know why the man was obsessed with him, it was obvious he was. Tonight was the first of the three nights of the full moon that held sway over Carl's form now, and Jordan felt like his body was about to betray him. He put the sandwich down. The prime rib was fabulous, but he just couldn't bring himself to eat it. Luke had motive, means, and opportunity, and Jordan had played right into it. Or was he just psyching himself out?

He went to the back door, grabbed his coat and a carrot, and headed to the stable to check on Daisy. Would she still tolerate him? Hell, how was he going to bring Carl down from the heights if they were both naked and lost? Daisy whinnied, not expecting to see him again at this hour. He'd just brought her in from the pasture and put her away for the night. The routine was steady, she probably wondered what was up. He held the carrot out for her and stroked her nose as she lipped it off his hand, just as steady as she'd been when he brought her in. He was being paranoid. Why should he expect anything to change since he last saw her?

He lifted the curry comb off its hook by the door to her stall and stepped in to start grooming her. She nosed his coat, checking for more treats, and he pushed her away with a grin. "Stop it, girl. There's nothing there. Go back to your hay." She'd already finished the small bag of oats he'd given her, knowing she'd be hard at work tomorrow morning climbing the peaks as he rode to find Carl. He stopped for a moment. Or would he? She huffed at him and he went back to his task. He'd started grooming her; he might as well brush her all the way down and check her hooves while he was at it, as long as he was here. Clearly she still liked him. That meant there was nothing wrong with him, didn't it? He continued brushing her coat, moving from the neck to her back, and along the barrel. He brushed with one hand, checking her over with the other, leaning into her and lifting one foot at a time, scraping each hoof out with the hook and checking for stones that might be lodged there. He moved to her other side as she chewed the hay from the tub and continued to work on her.

Was it paranoia, or was it a really strong smelling batch of hay? And he could swear the stable needed to be mucked out again, by the smell of it, but the straw looked as clean as it had when he put it down an hour ago. He could smell the pine of the stud walls, the cedar of the shakes, and the cotton in the halter. A strong aroma of leather and oil was emanating from the tack, and the bright tang of the steel assaulted his nose, along with the sweet scent of oats leftover in the canvas nosebag. It was a cacophony of smells, and it was driving him insane.

CHAPTER 35 – WINNING IT

Luke stepped up to the huge mahogany doors of the Sanders mansion, marveling at the brilliantly decorative silver inlay that seemed as if it were designed to be part of the ornate carvings. He knew quite well the silver had been laid into it more recently, married to it as if it had been part of the design all along. Jordan was nothing if not thorough, and clearly had an artistic eye, along with extreme discipline for his athletic endeavors and a sharp mind for rational thought, though it was often overtaken by his anxieties. It was time for Jordan's first transformation, if the blood he'd been given had taken, and there was no reason it shouldn't have. Luke looked forward to being here for it. The weight of the world hung in balance. It was also time to check on Carl, and these were things he had no intention of discussing over regular phone lines in any case.

Carl came to the door. "Luke! I thought I felt your presence."

Luke was surprised. "You can feel me?"

Carl smiled, "As a matter of fact, yes. Is that a normal lupan ability?"

Luke felt a warm thrill suffuse his entire body. "It is, and I didn't expect it so soon after your cure. How do you feel?"

Jordan came running from the barn. "It IS you!" Carl turned with consternation toward Jordan as he came to a halt at the base of the steps. "What happened to me during the transfusion?"

"Veni?" Luke answered, taken by surprise.

"I feel like I've got a million tiny fish speeding through my veins. It's been growing steadily all day. Did something happen that I should know about?"

Luke felt a sadness as he caught a glimpse of what seemed a rare moment of vulnerability in Jordan. He took a moment to be sure he was fully focused on his words. A misstep here could be disastrous. "What are you concerned about happening? And how did you know I was here?"

"I felt something tickle my mind, and there was an image of you. There was a direction, I followed it, and it led me to you."

Luke nodded in understanding. The lupan early warning system, and he was already responding to it before his first transformation. It almost never preceded the first change, but there had been a few cases of early transference over the years. "That sounds like intuitive awareness. There are many ways people can develop such a thing; becoming lupan is one of them, but I would not expect it so early even if you were infected somehow. Perhaps you are just acutely attuned to Carl, who noticed me?"

"Hell!" Jordan spat. "Did you do this to me?"

Luke frowned. "Why would you think I did anything?"

Jordan held up one finger after another as he answered. "Motive, means, opportunity. Did you put something in my blood?"

Luke held up his hands. "If there was an accident of some sort—"

"With everything else that went flawlessly? As careful as you, Carl, and Dwayne were? As professionally trained as the nurse was? I don't think this can be blamed on any accident. If you did something to me, Luke, so help me God, I will fucking kill you!"

Luke took a moment to think, and to put Jordan off-balance so he could manipulate the situation. He turned to Carl. "First things first. How are you recovering?"

"Good news, actually. The transplant already appears to be effective and in record time. I dismissed the nurse yesterday and Dwayne texted me this morning that his mindwipe was successful. It's a shame we can't report this to any medical journals." Carl stood up straighter and smiled. "I seem to have achieved full acceptance of the graft, and my blood type has completely switched to O-negative already, I just tested it. I've been gaining weight. I definitely feel stronger."

Luke grinned at Carl's exuberance. He had most certainly gained weight since Luke had seen him last. He watched Jordan from the corner of his eye. There was a sense of relief from Jordan. "That is amazing," Luke said. "Lupans are known for quick healing, but I was afraid your illness would take primacy and your healing would be delayed, or worse. If this works, there will be many lives saved." He then turned to Jordan, "But it sounds like we have another issue to attend to. Some lupans report the feeling of vibration throughout their body when they have contracted the curse, and your awareness of yours could be a description of the same thing. Also, you sensed my presence when you were outside. The possibility of infection concerns me. We normally watch to see if you transform and then watch to see if the virus has taken correctly. If Carl is right, that the issue has always been blood type, then the latter will be unnecessary. If your blood type works for Carl, it will work for you. Which leaves us with the possibility that you are evolving to a new form."

"Evolving?" Jordan said, with venom. "You mean *devolving*."

Luke stared, displeased, at Jordan. "Let us simply consider that something might have gone wrong, and you might be changing to Homo lupanthrus. If you consider that devolution, that is your choice. But if it is true, then you and

Carl will both need a pack to be adopted by. There are many things you must learn, including all we know of the lupan hunters and how to avoid them so you do not find another one under your roof by accident," Luke admonished them. "I need you both to perfect this cure, and I'm looking for the right pack to place you in. I want you to stay here for now. I will get you stationed with the pack later." Luke let that settle with Jordan, which it wouldn't, of course. Jordan wouldn't want a pack; Jordan would be drawn to the option of learning directly from Luke, where he would receive the highest level training available.

Luke turned to Carl. "Tonight will be a transformation. I would like to be here and make sure it goes well for you, Carl." He looked at Jordan. "And perhaps you as well, Jordan, if what you say is true." Of course it was, Luke had made sure of that. But it was imperative that Jordan didn't know Luke's hand in it, at least until he was already roped into the role Luke intended for him.

"How will you watch us if you'll be transforming as well?" Carl asked.

"With experience," Luke answered, "you can develop the ability to change form at will, though the cycle is normally governed by the moon's phase. That will be a later lesson, after you have learned the basic survival skills. The pack I am placing you in does not have the most experienced teachers, but you will learn." Luke saw Jordan lean in as he spoke, naturally. Control is what Jordan sought, and right now he felt he had none. Luke could start reeling him in now, before he'd even confirmed that Jordan was infected.

"Jordan, if you are right about this, tonight will be troubling for you. I will watch over both of you. If you both transform, your connection as humans will make you packmates as wolves. I will travel with you tonight and keep you safe, and bring you back here in the morning, as someone should have been doing all along for Carl. I am beyond furious with them for abandoning you." He turned to Carl, not having to feign his anger at all, but knowing this would also work to bring Jordan around, as his protective nature and thirst for justice. "I have dealt with them for their transgression. For now, let us get the two of you through this transition." Jordan looked alarmed, and Luke realized he'd spoken as if he knew that it would be both of them. That was sloppy. Luke was too tired. It had been so long since he'd had any respite. He ignored his exhaustion, though, and portrayed confidence. For now, he had to view Jordan as foe, and show no weakness. Clearly Jordan didn't want to say anything, perhaps hoping he'd misheard, walking on eggshells, wanting no confirmation.

Luke turned to Carl and they discussed all the indicators of proper transformation, which would be new for Carl if the bone marrow had worked, and all three of them took comfort from one good sign after another. Carl grasped the silver door handle firmly and felt nothing. Good – silver should only be harmful if it reached the blood. They went to the paddock, where the horse was chewing on hay, and Daisy startled slightly at Carl's presence, then whuffed at him curiously, trying to reconcile the presence of the Carl scent with the absence of the disease scent. She remained wary, as prey animals often do, but she wasn't frightened out of her skull, as she had been when he'd come close before. But the microscope was the best witness to Carl's apparently full recovery; not a single broken cell. Even the healthy yellow cells were thick in his blood, as they should be on the cusp of a transformation. Lupans had realized their blood looked different under a microscope during these hours; in healthy lupans, the yellow cells emerged only around the time of the transformation and remained hidden the rest of the time.

Luke had quickly verified that the feral pack had followed up on Carl's recent visit to the hospital since he'd last seen Carl. They had done well enough with that, and their cover-up regarding Diana's "disappearance," that he would let them live, for now, though he'd had to execute Gus, the alpha. The rest of the pack, though, were back on track; none of them had tried to speak in his defense at the hearing.

That night they all sat at the picnic table in the backyard after the sun went down. Carl, naked, had put the patio heater on a timer so that it would turn off shortly after sunset. They wouldn't need the heat once they all had fur coats to wear. Luke had told him he wouldn't need his neck pack this time, Luke would bring them back to the house before they shifted back to human form. He was more careful to sound as if he didn't know whether Jordan would change, and he didn't suggest Jordan remove his clothes. Luke sensed there were no humans in easy viewing distance, and in the future Carl would have to be sure he transformed in a less visible location, but for now his job was to reassure, not admonish.

Jordan ended up being the first to shudder, Carl nearly as quick. Jordan looked with panic at Luke, who watched with joy as Jordan's shape began to shift. He had turned to Luke for help – for who else could help him with this?

"Luke, is this it?" Jordan wailed, "How do I stop—"

Jordan dropped to the ground, fighting the shuddering transformation with a force of will that was astounding. For a moment, the transformation almost reversed, then his jaws began to protrude and his legs pulled in toward his body. Jordan howled in agony. The initial transformation was always very uncomfortable as the body endured its first reconfiguration, stretched to its limits. Jordan's entire frame went taut as if being tortured on a rack. The skin of his face almost shone as it stretched outward, becoming paler as the cells tightened with the strain of containing the lengthening jawline. His nose seemed almost like a telescoping ski slope, then the shiny skin disappeared under soft black fur, his ears became upward moving triangles and his head flattened. The fur grew out beyond his own short, black hair, which simultaneously sucked back into his body, as it should. Luke turned his attention quickly to Carl. Jordan was progressing as expected, but Carl's transformation was the critical one. He could see that Carl's hair was pulling into his skin as Jordan's had. Brilliant! This was how a transformation should occur. He looked at the fingernails, which also seemed to melt inward before claws shot out of the shortening fingers. Yes; Carl was transforming correctly. In the sick, the hair and nails fell out rather than being reabsorbed by the body. In moments it was all over, and Luke pulled the clothing off Jordan now that he didn't need it for the rest of the night. The two wolves, one grey and one black (which was phenomenally muscular) looked expectantly at him. They recognized his dominance immediately, as any good wolf would; worldwide alpha gave Luke a fatherly aura. It also helped that they recognized his familiarity, just as they recognized each other. This would be so much better for them, having each other, instead of the way Carl had been so alone. On Jordan's part, that was simply a relief, after the fierce trial of wills he'd given Luke up to this point. Beyond that, there was little of the human they'd been to remain in their thoughts.

They would learn later how to hold onto the human consciousness while in wolf form, and the wolf when they were in human form, as well as how to transform at will, but tonight was the night of Jordan's birth, and Luke was exuberant. There would be time later to pass the final verdict on Carl's cure, but tonight was a good night. Luke shifted into wolf form and led them into the forest. Tonight they would hunt, and celebrate with fresh venison. He could smell the rich scent of a doe not far away, and they were off, following him without question for once.

CHAPTER 36 – WHAT THE FUTURE MAY HOLD

After hunting and gorging, Lukewulf watched with joy as Carlwulf and Jordanwulf cracked bones with their powerful wolf-jaws. Carl seemed so strong. The sick ones usually didn't make full wolf transformations, their wolven form even weaker than the human because the transformation had never been fully successful, but Carlwulf seemed as fit as most lupans. Perhaps his workouts had helped him through this part of the ordeal. Luke considered what it might take to extend this cure to other dysmorphic werewolves as he watched over them protectively. Carl had come into his proper form, without reserve. The cure would require monitoring for quite some time, new as it was. Luke had seen other signs of hope go awry, but so far this bone marrow transplant concept had done more for Carl, in just a few weeks, than he'd seen any other attempted cure achieve. It looked like this was it: a true cure. If they perfected this process, he could give them all greater hope for their offspring, and the energy now spent eliminating the failed transformations could be spent tracking down what remained of the vampires who had become adept at escaping justice. If they all survived the coming alien visitation. For which he needed Jordan's strength and dedication.

He focused on the black Jordanwulf, gulping down a huge chunk of meat he had bitten off the bone. Jordan looked up at him, then dropped his eyes and whined. All wolf, right now, no fight in him. With luck, that would stay with him when he returned to human form. Lukewulf opened his jaws and gently pressed his teeth over Jordanwulf's muzzle, then nudged him toward the rest of the meal. Luke had taken his portion already and was on high alert, as always when he was with other Lupans. Rest never came easy for those in power, not if they cared for their people. And these were his people. Jordanwulf resumed feeding, seemed to truly relish his new ability to completely obliterate bone. Jordanwulf loved the newfound power of his jaws. Soon enough, he would relish the power his own mind could have over other beings.

Luke had no idea how long it might take to train him, but with Jordan's drive toward mastery it should take less time than the others he'd educated. He hoped so. He looked up into the sky and saw the slightest paleness in the east. He stood quickly, and the other wolves suddenly stopped, rapt attention on him. He lifted his tail high, and they jumped up, at full attention, though Jordan was just a bit slower as he looked with longing toward the meal he'd just been told to vacate. They needed to be back at the house before they returned to human form. Luke leaped down the slope, and the two manwulfs followed him at a quick lope.

They jumped across ravines and galloped through meadows, twisting around underbrush and diving down slopes and back up hills, running quickly to get back to where they belonged for now. They arrived back at the picnic table just as the sky began to brighten all the way across. They'd made it just in time, as Luke had planned. A good night; now, for morning.

He shifted quickly into his own man form, disguising his features as always with the blond, blue-eyed man so different from his real form. His true form was Italian, with the dark skin, brown eyes and wavy black hair of all his contemporaries of the Latins. Just like the Romans, who didn't exist when he was born. Luke's brother hadn't founded Rome until they were older. That's where they had parted ways, Romulus becoming an urbanite, and Remus fleeing into the hills, where he ran with his newfound mother's pack. Romulus had escaped the trans-formation and turned his back on his brother. Roman mythology, like all other religions, was an attempt to explain the unexplainable, includ-ing werewolves. And, also, like religion, it had gotten things partly right and partly wrong.

Luke, formerly Remus, gave his naked body a semblance of clothes, just as he'd clothed it with Aryan features to disguise himself. It was much easier to maintain this minor praestige than to keep losing clothes every time he transformed. When he was working, he went nearly naked, and these days it seemed he was always working. With a sigh, he turned the patio heater on and sat his seemingly blond and clothed human body on the bench as he watched them both spasm, then shift their forms. Jordan's transformation was smooth this time, he didn't fight it. But he'd been in wolf mode, so that was expected. But Carl; how would Carl do? Luke saw with relief that the wolf fur pulled back into his skin, as it should. Yes – his body was reabsorbing the wolven form, all of it, instead of rejecting it, even in part. Soon it was a naked Carl and a naked Jordan lying on the ground. Luke grabbed Jordan's clothing and tossed it to him. It was cold out and they were shivering. He led them into the house. New cubs always took a few moments to pull through the shift and speak, and they were still amnesiac.

"What the fuck?"

Luke spun around. Jordan had stopped halfway through pulling his sweatshirt on.

"Veni?" Luke answered as he took a moment to absorb the unexpected response. That was fast. Carl was staring at Jordan, still unable to speak, and not entirely present as human consciousness. If he were alone, he'd still have his eyes closed as his body adjusted to the re-transformation, and he'd just now be finding his bearings. It would be another minute or two before he had full control of all his faculties; he was still following Luke like a cub. But not Jordan. Of course not. He should have seen that coming, as obstinate as Jordan could be.

Jordan jerked the shirt down over his body and glared at Luke. "What the fuck just happened? Why am I putting my shirt on?"

The wolf amnesia should have covered that transition. He'd had them responding to him so that they were able to move about much more quickly than normal and he'd expected Jordan to be unaware of the transition. As always with Jordan, though, it seemed he would not be so lucky. At this point there was no option to deny, he'd have to confirm Jordan's transition here and now, rather than inside where it would seem safer. He sighed.

"I am sorry, Jordan; you transformed, just like Carl did. You have become Homo lupanthrus. You are one of us."

Carl stopped in his tracks and slowly turned around to stare at Jordan, his mouth open. "Oh my God, Jordan! I am so sorry!"

"Save it," Jordan hissed at Carl. "You're not the one who should be sorry. What the fuck did you do to me?" he looked murderously at Luke.

Again the warrior, fully defiant. Nothing came easy these days.

"You transformed, Jordan. Something must have happened within the past month that caused you to be infected. I don't know when or where it happened, but it happened, and you are one of us now. You can argue over where and when if you choose, but you can't change the fact that it did happen. You are no longer a mere man, you are now more than that."

The three stood, looking at each other, and Luke watched the slow resignation take place on Jordan's face. Jordan lunged at Luke, and Luke let him come. Tearing at Luke's hair with one hand, Jordan drove a fist into his belly. Luke strengthened his skin with an intentional shape-shift, protecting his organs and fusing his bones against the volley of blows that rained down on him from above as Jordan's weight bore him to the ground.

Luke remembered from long ago how his Judo instructor had told him that one of the most powerful moves was a sacrifice; bring your own self down as you bring your foe down if you must. And Luke was out of other moves. Jordan had just lost the last shred of control that he could bear, and Luke must give him something new until he could face what had just happened. This would be very strange. Luke had not let himself be dominated for... ever? Had he *ever*? Jordan hooked an arm around Luke's neck in a chokehold, and Luke let him.

"Stop, Jordan – stop!" It was Carl, who had regained his senses. Then Jordan's senses came back to him as well; he seemed suddenly aware of himself. He still held his grip on Luke's neck. He couldn't know, of course, that Luke had complete control of the placement of every part of his own body. He had shifted his carotid artery and his jugular vein downward into his muscles so the chokehold wouldn't cut off the oxygen to his brain. He'd also calcified his esophagus so it couldn't be crushed by the tight grip Jordan had on him. But Jordan didn't know that. Jordan thought he was strangling Luke.

Suddenly Luke was free, and Jordan was on his feet. Luke gasped as if he hadn't been able to breathe. That was the sacrificial move: go down and let Jordan believe he'd lost control of himself. The fury he'd felt toward Luke fueled him to action, and this demon, his fear of not being in control, defeated him. Jordan could not bear to feel he wasn't in control. He stomped off, and Luke kept up the appearance for Carl's sake, continuing to gasp, his hand at his neck. Jordan had to fully believe Luke had been in danger, even though he wasn't.

Luke saw Carl's hand come down to him and

he let Carl lift him up as if it were hard for him to stand. Carl seemed strong, which was good. He dusted off what appeared to be his clothes. "Well that was awkward, and quite painful as well. Thank you. Can I get a glass of water? My throat is a bit sore."

Then he looked accusatorily into Carl's eyes. "Have you been careful with all the bloodletting you have been doing?"

There was doubt in Carl's eyes, as he shame-facedly turned to go into the house. Luke heard the distant sound of a hammer striking an anvil out in the barn. Jordan, taking his rage out on in-animate objects. Very productive of him. Jordan was not one to whine or snivel; he got things done.

Luke followed Carl in. Luke was so thirsty. Oddly enough, mental work made him even thirstier than the physical, and he'd just done a lot of both. This is what it meant to be alpha. One way or another he had to get things done, and there was no time for insubordination. If he couldn't overcome it honestly, there was always deceit, and no one was a better deceiver than Luke. His own nickname reflected that truth, prophetic from the moniker he'd given him-self when he met his Julia: Lucianus. Bringer of light, he'd explained to her back then, wanting to light up the life of this beautiful woman he'd just met. He took the glass of water Carl offered him, drained it, and poured himself another.

The name, though, was also associated with the greatest deceiver of all time: Lucifer. Sometimes Luke felt very close to the devil himself. Was he a God, or was he something much worse? Only time would tell. The true masters would soon return, and they would not be happy. Either Luke would deliver his people, becoming their salvation, or he would fall from his lofty perch, like his ethereal namesake, and the rest of them would follow him into death.

With an ancient prayer, Luke again lifted the glass to his lips and drank deep. *May this all turn out well in the end.* The overlords were coming. May the gods save them all, for Luke wasn't sure he could do it alone.

If you enjoyed this book and want to see more like it, please post a review on Amazon to help other readers find it. I hope you enjoy the following preview of my next book, "Kindred Moon."

Read on for an excerpt from:

KINDRED MOON

Book two of the "Moonphase" series,
coming Summer of 2018

Jordan felt the walls as they went down the staircase, checking for hidden seams. Finn opened a section of the wall halfway down the staircase. It opened into a hall-way, and Finn looked back with a grin as he walked into a room. Jordan looked both ways down the hall and saw several doors and three light globes in the ceiling. He made note of the distances between them, then stepped through the door behind Finn. There was a huge TV screen at the far end of the room, beyond a curved line of well-padded, fur covered lounge chairs with cup holders in the arms. The walls were painted an even darker red than the hallway above, and the floor had long, oval rugs of the same kind of thick brown pelt as the chairs were covered with. A harpoon gun hung on the wall.

"What kind of movies do you like?" Finn asked.

"Documentaries," Jordan answered. He preferred action movies, martial arts, but he was curious if there was anything in particular these people studied.

Finn gave him a puzzled look. "I'm not sure we have any documentaries."

Movement to the left caught his eye and he looked over to a chair where a dark, slender, handsome young man stood up and turned around. His skin was swarthy and his black eyebrows thick and low, a shock of black hair dangling in threads over them, so it took Jordan a moment to see that his eyes were entirely black, like those of a horse. He also wore heavy gold chain around his neck and wrists, like Finn, and he was clothed in the same soft black garments Finn wore, as if it were a casual uniform.

"Who's this?" The man said, in a gravelly Scottish brogue.

Jordan felt a brush against his mind and saw the man's eyes widen. He tried to push the feelers that began to grope through his head away, but his mind seemed to slip off that of the other man, who simply walked toward them, asking, in a hoarse voice, "Is this the man Mother's been going on about?"

The feel of the mind in his own,was gritty and hard, like sand on granite. There was a deep blackness to it, yet tiny colored winks of light and metallic streamers appeared and disappeared. It was entirely unlike Luke's mind, or Subedai's; much more nuanced, and very solid.

Jordan shook his head. The strange feel of the man's intrusion was extremely unpleasant, and he wanted to get rid of it, but didn't know how.

Finn glared at the dark man. "LIN!" he said, angrily. "Why aren't you down at the beach?"

The man looked at him, the large black eyes making the gaze seem otherworldly. "We're on restriction, little brother. The beach is off limits until this one gets fitted with the chains."

Finn looked at Jordan. "Oh, that makes sense. He's got a few more hours to roam freely then."

Jordan looked at the stranger. "What's wrong with your eyes?"

Finn laughed and answered for him. "Those aren't eyes, they're just big marbles! He can't see a thing unless he invades someone else's eyes. He's probably in your head now."

Lin gave a contemptuous look at Finn. "I'm well able to see, hear, AND feel, as long as there's eyes near enough by, laddie. And speaking of feeling, who's been loving you lately, you poor bastard? I haven't seen any lasses coming around. Do you think they're onto you? Happy hunting, me boy," he gave Finn a look of sharp disdain.

Finn glared angrily back, then turned to Jordan. "Let's find something else to do. We don't have to hang out with bottom feeders."

Lin chuckled, and it made Finn angrier.

"What chains?" Jordan asked, interrupting their verbal sparring match.

Lin turned those eerie eyes back toward him, but the touch of his mind disappeared entirely, then his jaw dropped. "By the gates of Hell, you have enough muscle to wrestle a bull, don't you? She didn't lie about that!" Lin said, black eyes disturbingly wide.

"Get OUT of my head, Lin!" Finn swore.

Lin ignored him. "It'll take plenty of ore to lay a full chain around that neck." Lin touched the chain around his own neck. "Like this, laddie. We don't wear these by choice, and they're not for looks either, though Mother has appearances to keep. She can track us across any land by these wicked things, though it's far more difficult when we're over water. And once the chains are on, your thoughts are not your own, either. Your life becomes a living hell, nor are you given leave to die. Neck and wrist chains together assure that. More than six hundred years I've been dragged around behind her like a wee doggie, never my own life to live. Finn is just now learning how miserable it is to be the offspring of the queen, and it chafes him. He thinks he can escape her black clutches."

The strange mind was in his own again, flickers of cascading light against the deep darkness of the immensely solid weight, and the tendrils snaked through his thoughts.

"Let's go, Jordan," Finn said, striding toward the door, but Jordan wasn't done. He didn't like the strange feel of the heavy mind in his own, but he was sure there was more to learn from this black-eyed enigma.

"When is this planned?" Jordan asked.

Lin was completely focused on Jordan now. "Later this afternoon. You're on your last hours, laddie. It takes some time to prepare the metal, and there was no point starting until she had you; there's a brief window of time the metal can be worked. But I spoke to Roscoe before I came up, for the daily report. He says they're near done. I'd leave now, if I were you. Not that there's much chance you'll escape." Suddenly he cried out, and collapsed to the floor, writhing on his back and clutching at the chain around his throat. Jordan felt a seething agony of pain himself, but it seemed vastly diminished from what Lin must be feeling; he seemed to be the source. He also heard a voice in his head, saying loudly, *you were told to keep your conversation within bounds. Do you need to visit the pit again?* Lin kept gasping and clawing at his neck. *I will--* suddenly the voice cut out.

"Was that her speaking?" Jordan asked.

Finn looked at him. Then started laughing, with vicious delight. "Oh, brother dear," he said, clasping his hands together. "She's going to RACK you for transmitting her voice! And I'm going to watch. I'll bring popcorn! Look at this, Jordan –" Finn reached over and pulled Lin's shirt up. Jordan caught a glimpse of deep scars, in long lines punctuated by ragged ovals, then Lin knocked Finn's hand away and yanked his shirt down.

Lin's torment seemed to be fading, and he looked up at Jordan. *Brother,* his voice said, in Jordan's mind, as the pain increased again. *Get out if you can, while you can. I wish this fate on no one. There is no doubt you are her son, half human like meself. Your mind is too like mine, part human, part Sh'eyta. She will torture you as she has me. Finn does not know what it's like to be half Sh'eyta. Our mother is a vicious tyrant, and she has tried to get her clutches into you for years. She did the same to me, and that is why I am blind myself. I spend my days on the beach, away from this hell as much as I can. Better for me to invade a seagull's mind than the twisted mess that remains of Finn's. She'll toss you down the oubliette when she is angry with you. Get away now, if you can.* "Go, Finn," he said aloud. "And take the poor captive with you! See if the lasses will come out for you, if you dangle him by the edge of the boat. They'll not come for yourself anymore, but fresh meat could tempt them."

"Mother said--"

"Who cares what Mother said? He has no chains, and she'll be working me over for several hours now, at the very least. There'll be no chance to escape her for weeks, once I'm thrown in the pit. Are you fool enough to do her bidding when you have the choice? You have the Faraday shawl, don't you? Wear it." The television came on, and the volume rose until it was impossible to hear anything over it. *I've given you space, brother. Use it. And if you make it to safety, find a way to set me free and I pledge my remaining days to you. She's near upon us, lad, you must go now. Finn will follow the path I've laid for him.*

Finn motioned to Jordan, and they left the room. "He's an asshole, but he's got a point. Mother listens in everywhere except out on the water. I have a way of hiding the Rigellium over one of us. Good thing you're free of the chains for now."

Jordan focused on Finn as he replayed Lin's voice in his head, sorting through the thick accent and the warning of captivity and torture. Clearly he needed out, and fast. But was the black-eyed man truly related, by a mother who wasn't even from this planet? It seemed as unlikely as werewolves, but he had no basis for judging truth anymore.

Made in the USA
Monee, IL
26 May 2022